HONOR OF THE STAR

A JACK SAGE WESTERN - BOOK 8

DONALD L. ROBERTSON

Edited by
PAULINE NOLET

Illustrated by
DAMONZA.COM

COPYRIGHT

Honor of the Star

Copyright © 2025 Donald L. Robertson
CM Publishing, LLC

Books@DonaldLRobertson.com

ISBN:979-8-9912601-8-3

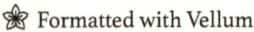 Formatted with Vellum

1

April 30, 1876

Jack Sage blinked at the sudden flash through the windows. Instantly a clap of thunder rolled over Fort Smith, shaking the boarding house and rattling those same windows. He gave his head a shake and spoke to the empty room. "I sure hope we see blue sky soon. Otherwise, there's gonna be some unhappy women tomorrow." *I won't be exactly thrilled myself,* he thought and lifted the paper to continue reading.

His eyes had barely focused on the lead story when the door opened, and the sound of rain instantly went from a low rumble to a roar. It was nearing noon, and Jack surmised one of Grace's dinner customers was early, in an effort to get a head start on the others, though Jack figured there would be plenty of food to go around since few folks would brave the storm today.

The door closed, and the clump and jingle of boots and spurs sounded. Instead of entering the dining room, the boots and spurs turned into the parlor.

Jack continued reading.

A gruff, demanding voice grated across Jack's nerves. "Looking for Jack Sage."

Only minutes before, Jack had stretched out on the divan. He had been helping Pauly, the blacksmith, build new wheels and tires for Jack's three wagons. After scraping the mud from his boots, he had gone to the trouble of removing them before entering the parlor and stretching his lanky body out on the divan. His stocking feet extended over the armrest that faced toward the front door. Earlier today, he had completed testifying in a Judge Bell trial of the men he had brought in from Texarkana and hoped now to catch up on Little Rock's current events, as reported by the paper.

Without lowering the newspaper, his response was equally harsh. "Why?"

"I'm going to kill him." The *him* coincided with the sound of a hammer ratcheting to full cock.

Like most people, Jack figured the sound of a hammer cocking meant no good, and he was the only person, besides the man with the gun, in the room. Jack's left foot dropped from atop the arm of the divan, braced against its side, and shoved. He was propelled from the couch while at the same time drawing and rolling.

When the gunman saw his face, he hesitated and then fired, the blast crashing through the parlor, and a neat hole appeared in the top of the wadded newspaper, only inches to the side of Jack's face. Since he had been a lawman forever, at least it seemed that way to him, he was on a not-so-friendly basis with death— call it a nodding acquaintance. He had enough bullet holes in him to prove it, and he could feel the grim reaper's presence. Jack hoped the collector of souls wasn't there for him, since he was getting married tomorrow.

It was a race for the next shot. Jack's draw was quick, but the stranger's firearm was ready. All he had to do was cock and recover the weapon from the recoil, bringing it down on the falling man, while Jack had to clear leather, cock, aim, and fire his Smith & Wesson while he was falling and, ultimately, striking the floor. He held low, knowing his arm, after being jarred by the floor, would shift his aim upward. He slammed into the floor a moment before he fired. *He's big like me,* Jack thought a second before his gun roared.

The muzzle of the stranger's Colt had begun to center on Jack when his .44-caliber 216-grain chunk of lead plowed into the stranger's upper chest, knocking the big man back and causing his bullet to punch into Mary's comfortable divan.

Jack immediately yanked the hammer to the rear and waited to see what the gunman would do. He didn't want to fire inside the house again if he could prevent it.

The stranger's left hand jerked to cover the wound, but his right still held his weapon. He steadied himself and took two steps forward, managing to get out the words, "You're Jack Sage," hoarser now, but still gruff.

Jack nodded and stood, keeping his weapon on the man. "That's me."

Footsteps came running from the kitchen, and Jack yelled, "I'm fine, but don't come in here. Send Billy out the back to get the doctor." To the stranger, in a conversational tone, he said, "Why don't you drop the gun and sit."

The man looked down at the Colt in his right hand. He stared at it for a moment, as if he was surprised it was still there, raised his eyes to Jack, and began to lift the weapon, but Jack had moved closer. With one step, his long arms were in range of the man's hand. Jack swung with his left hand, chopping down on the stranger's wrist. The Colt clattered to the floor.

Immediately, Jack grabbed him by the shoulders and pulled him to the couch. Blood seeped from the wound while the stranger's gray eyes stared at Jack. His voice was still gruff, but weaker. "I can see the resemblance. I should've shot when I saw your size. There couldn't be two as big as you." He slid down far enough on the couch so he could rest his head on the back, but his eyes stayed on Jack.

"What's your name?"

The man's eyes closed, and the front door banged open, letting in U.S. Marshal Buck Walker, the doctor, and then Billy, all three dripping wet. Doc pushed by Buck and rushed to the stranger's side. He grasped the man's slicker and shirt at the throat, one hand on each side, and yanked. Doc wasn't a big man, but he ripped the two pieces of clothing apart like he was tearing paper.

Gently, he removed the man's hand from the wound and leaned near it, listened for a moment, and shook his head. "This man's been shot through the lung, and he's drowning in his own blood. There's nothing I can do." He looked at Jack. "Who is he?"

Jack, who sat next to the stranger, shook his head. "I haven't the slightest idea." Then softly, almost to himself, he said, "But he looks mighty familiar."

His breathing was no longer steady, but his eyes opened, and he turned to Jack. "You sure look like him."

Jack's forehead wrinkled, and his voice slid into its demanding, no-nonsense tone. "Who, I look like who, and what's your name?"

The stranger gave Jack a knowing smile. "You'll never know until it's too late." He coughed, and blood ran from the corner of his mouth.

Jack looked up at Marshal Walker. "Do you recognize him?"

The marshal shook his head. "Nope, I don't, but he's got a faint accent of some kind. I can't recognize it."

The doctor stared at the wounded man. "He looks like you, Jack."

Grace and Mary had entered the room and stepped close enough to ensure Jack was fine. He could see the tension leave her face when she realized he was alive and unharmed. Then she turned back to the dying man. Surprised, her statement almost leaped from her mouth under its own volition. "Jack, he could be your brother."

The front door banged open again, and Judge Bell, followed by two deputies, burst into the parlor, hatless, wet hair plastered to his head, and eyes wide. His booming voice filled the house. "What the blue blazes is going on here? I heard shots. Is everybody alright?" He saw the dying man on the couch. "Who is he? Who shot him?"

Mary, Jack's future mother-in-law, stepped to Judge Bell's side and slipped her arm in his. "We're all fine, Judge, but we don't know who he is. It seems he came into the parlor and tried to kill Jack. Thank goodness he was unsuccessful."

The judge glared at Jack and demanded, "Why would he try to kill you, especially today? You're getting married tomorrow."

Jack ignored the judge's question and leaned closer to the dying man. The brusque tone was gone, and in its place was the kind, concerned voice he used with the boys. "You don't want to go to your maker with this secret. Tell me why you wanted me dead. You'll feel better for it."

Moments ticked by in silence. The stranger slowly opened his eyes and stared at Jack. "I didn't really want to do it . . . after I saw your face. It was like looking at him." His eyes slowly lost their focus, and he stared past Jack. His face relaxed. He released a long slow breath and was dead.

The room was silent.

Doc leaned over, felt the man's neck, and shook his head. "He's gone. My work's done." He straightened and turned to Buck. "The mystery belongs to you, Marshal. My report is he bled to death due to a bullet wound." He looked around the parlor, "Gentlemen, ladies," and headed for the door.

Marshal Buck Walker let out a long sigh. "I guess it's up to me to get this feller out of here." He turned to the two deputies who had escorted the judge. "You boys take this"—he paused, trying to come up with a word, shrugged, and continued—"here stranger who was dumb enough to try Jack Sage, and haul him over to the undertaker." As the men moved to the dead man, he added, "And keep the blood off Miss Grace and Miss Mary's couch and rug."

"Thank you, Marshal," Mary said, smiling her gratitude.

Buck left with the body and the deputies.

The judge lingered. "Marshal Sage, are you trying to tell me this man came in here to kill you, and you don't have any idea who he is?"

Jack could feel his anger rising. The judge's brusque manner had that effect on him.

Grace whispered in Jack's ear as he stood, "Jack, patience."

Judge Bell was a tall man, but there were few who reached Jack's height of six inches over six feet in his boots. The judge came up to about his chin. "Judge, let's get something straight. I've never seen that fella before. I don't know who he is, why he was after me, or where he came from."

Judge Bell looked up at Jack, his squinting eyes relaxed, and a corner of his mouth lifted. "Jack, you were the most effective marshal I've ever had, and the absolute worst for taking orders. Thanks for testifying today." He patted Mary's hand. "And thank you for inviting me to the wedding of your daughter, though I hate to think what Fort Smith will be like without Ma Nelson's Bed and Eats. We are surely going to miss you and Grace and the boys."

Mary beamed up at the judge. "I don't know what we would have done without you and your help starting this place. Thank you, and don't forget, Matthew Marcel will continue to provide you with good food and lodging."

The judge gave a small bow and turned for the door as a shaft of sunlight cut into their conversation. "Look at that. Maybe you'll be having a fine day for a wedding after all. Good day." He disappeared through the doorway, and Jack grinned at Grace.

"Looks like he could be right. You might have a clear day for your wedding."

She clapped her hands, and her full lips spread in a wide

smile. "Oh, Jack, I have been so worried about all this rain. And don't forget, tomorrow is also Billy's birthday."

Jack laughed, the assault on his life pushed to the back of his mind. "How could anyone forget about that birthday? He manages to mention it at every meal. I can't wait to give him his present."

Mary's frown was followed with her comment. "I don't think you need to be giving that boy a gun at his age. You have relatives back in Virginia. You should send him back there to learn how to be a gentleman, not a ruffian like ..."

Grace's smile disappeared. "Like Jack? Is that what you were about to say, Mama? My goodness, can't you see the need for a boy his age to be able to defend himself, especially with us going to the frontier?" Grace unlimbered her left index finger, shaking it at her mother. "Have you so soon forgotten. If it weren't for Jack, we might have lost our boys, and Elijah might never have been saved." Her chest heaved, and she exhaled with gusto. "I can't believe you would say such things."

Jack did what any smart man would do. He stayed quiet. He knew Mary Nelson liked him. They had talked on several occasions, and he had learned quite a bit about Grace's mother. The woman had grown to adulthood in the home of a Pittsburgh Presbyterian minister. Her father had believed that discussion was always the solution to any problem, and he had drilled it into his favorite loving and devoted daughter.

Unfortunately for her, as far as her father was concerned, she had fallen in love with an adventurer who took her west, into the land of the Indians, the lawless, and sudden death. Though she had loved her husband, she had held onto her father's beliefs, and sometimes they slipped out.

He took no offense to what she had said. Jack knew Mary loved him. She didn't love his violent ways, but he was well aware she saw him as a challenge, and since she was going with them, she would have ample opportunity to change him and influence the boys. He grinned to himself, thinking, *She's got her work cut out for her.*

He squeezed his soon-to-be wife's arm. Her head turned, and those emerald green eyes flashed at him. "You know I'm right, Jack."

Jack grew serious. "You're right about the need for the boys to know how and be willing to shoot when necessary, but you aren't right to think that Mary doesn't like me." He gazed at Mary. "I'm right, aren't I?"

Mary stepped forward and placed her hand on his arm. "Oh, Jack, I couldn't ask for a better man to marry my Grace and look after our boys. I think you are perfect for my headstrong daughter." She smiled at Grace. "But sometimes, I wish the boys had the opportunity to grow up as refined gentlemen."

Jack smiled. "Mary, refined and gentleman don't always go together. I've known some very refined men who would slit their fellow man's throat for two bits. Though I'd prefer not, we'll be running into those kinds. I want our boys to be able to recognize and deal with them."

Mary's eyes dropped, and a touch of sadness drifted across the older but still lovely face. "I do too, Jack. I just hate for them to have to face such a dark world at their age."

Jack thought of Billy getting his rifle and couldn't help but laugh. "I somehow don't think he'll be seeing it as a dark world when he gets his gifts tomorrow."

She smiled up at her future son-in-law. "No, I doubt he will."

Several people entered the boarding house and looked questioningly into the parlor before turning toward the dining room. Grace stretched and gave Jack a kiss on the cheek. "I'm happy you weren't hurt, but with the weather clearing, we may have more people for dinner than was expected. I'd better get to the kitchen to help Matthew."

Mary took off ahead of her. "I'll help, too. No telling how many folks may show up, especially after the shooting. Jack, when the boys get here, would you have them help you move the couch to the storeroom? We've got to get it cleaned and repair that ugly hole in the cushion."

Grace disappeared after her mother, and Jack gave the couch another look, bent, and fingered the bullet hole in the cushion. It was a small hole, easily repaired. *Funny,* Jack thought, *how something that makes such an insignificant hole in a couch cushion could end life so brutally.* Jack put the thought out of his mind, straightened, and strode to the front door.

It was the last day of April. Everything was blooming, and, after the rain, everything was steaming. A mosquito buzzed around his head. He waved the irritating little insect away and moved down the boardwalk to one of the rockers, where he took a seat. Surveying the town, he realized it wouldn't be long before this chapter would be closed for all of them, and they would be headed west, back to Texas.

Of all the places his travels had taken him, he liked Texas best. Oh, the mountains were nice in the summertime, and even the late spring and early fall, but after that, it was just plain cold. *And,* he thought, *these bones are getting too old to put up with cold weather. If I could choose my weather, I'd head south to Mexico along the beaches of the Yucatan, but I don't think the girls would go for it. Cherry Creek will have to do. I have friends there, and plenty of land is available for ranching.* He paused for a moment. *At least there was five years ago.*

He was pulled out of his reverie by youthful yells.

"Pa."

Elijah had wanted to start calling Jack pa before the wedding, and it seemed to also please Billy. Jack happily went along with it, since Mary and Grace agreed.

The boys were racing, as best they could in the thick mud, toward him and waving. He was constantly amazed at how fast they were growing. Billy would be thirteen tomorrow, and he was developing wide shoulders with thickening biceps. *It's that wood chopping,* Jack thought. *More proof that hard work never hurt a young fella.* He laughed to himself. *It never hurt an old fella either, except for a few more aches.*

Elijah was also growing, not as fast as Billy since he was younger, but a person could see the changes.

The boys stomped on the steps up to the boardwalk and began scraping thick mud from their boots.

Billy looked up. "Tomorrow's the big day, Pa." One corner of his mouth lifted in a mischievous grin. "You getting nervous?"

Jack frowned. "Why should I be nervous? Do you know something you haven't told me?"

Billy's grin widened. "Maybe."

Jack laughed. "Come on in, boys. I need you to help me move the couch to the storeroom. It needs a little work."

Elijah's eyes narrowed. "Does it have anything to do with the shooting we heard? What happened? Was anyone hurt?"

Jack shook his head. "Give me a hand, and I'll tell you all about it."

With a hand on each boy's shoulder, the three trooped into the parlor.

2

Jack stood towering over the Presbyterian minister as the organ screeched out its dreadful sound. *I forgot to tell her I can't stand music, especially piano music. But I don't think it comes anywhere close to the way I feel about this screeching, grunting assault on my ears. I swear my ears are going to die before it quits.*

But when he thought he could take the torture no longer, Grace stepped into the aisle on the arm of Judge Bell. She had always been beautiful, but today she looked like an angel. The collar of her pale green gown pulled snugly around her long neck. Her long black hair was gathered on top of her head, exposing her dainty ears. She filled the gown perfectly, and as she moved, the gown swayed with each step, giving the illusion she was floating along the aisle of the church. Her lips were full and red, slightly stretched into a tantalizing smile. One he would never forget.

But it was her eyes he felt he might drown in. They looked like two perfect priceless emeralds, gazing at him with all the promises available to man.

She and the judge stopped. The judge took her lovely long-fingered hand and placed it in Jack's massive rough and battered paw. The minister began to drone. All Jack knew were her eyes gazing up at him with a promise he had hoped for through all these years of roaming and fighting. And then, for an instant, he saw another pair of eyes, promising like those of Grace, but dark and exotic.

Yasmina, and she's smiling. His breath caught, and she disappeared, replaced with Grace's joyful gaze. The minister said, "I now pronounce you man and wife. You may kiss the bride."

Grace smiled up at him. He grasped her arms, and she came to him. Her head tilted, and her soft lips lifted to him. He lowered his head to hers, and their lips touched. For a moment, the world went away. The fights, the killings, and hangings disappeared in her embrace.

Clapping filled the chapel while a raucous cheer went up from some of the more rowdy guests. Jack raised his head from Grace's smiling face and gazed out across the pews of the church. A large group of deputy marshals stood together at the back, and they were creating most of the noise. His eyes drifted across the spectators, and he was shocked to recognize several friends he hadn't seen in years. Bronco Fenn and Montana Huff, his partners in their Texas ranch, were near the front, with grins so wide it looked like their faces would break. Hank Marsden, his partner in the goldmine near Silver City, New Mexico, was sitting next to them. Texas Ranger Major Gordon Wilson was there from Fredericksburg, and Dr. David Pratt with his wife, Martha, also from Silver City, sat next to Grace's mother, Mary. *How in the blue blazes did Mary even find out about those folks?* he asked himself.

Jack's forehead had wrinkled, and his eyelids were pulled down into a frown while he tried to figure out how Mary Nelson had been able to contact all those people and persuade them to travel so far. He spotted one face in the crowd, from Virginia, he knew the man, but he also knew they were more acquaintance than friend. What was he doing here? He was the most puzzling of all.

In their turn to face the crowd, Grace had looped her arm in his. With her dainty fingers resting along his wrist, she pinched the daylights out of him. His frown deepened as he looked down into her green eyes. The face that held those eyes was frowning back at him.

"Jack, stop your frowning. This is supposed to be a happy day."

To another burst of loud cheers and applause, he swept her into his arms, lifting her off the floor, and kissed her again. She threw her arms around his neck and, returning the kiss, squeezed him tight, but only for a moment, then she slapped him on his shoulder and pulled her head back.

"Put me down, Jack Sage. This is a wedding, not a barn dance."

At her slap on his shoulder, a larger round of applause, laughter, and yelling shook the church's windows.

Jack grinned at his new bride. "Yes, ma'am, anything you say, Mrs. Sage."

The comment brought a smile to her lovely face. Watching her, Jack thought, *How could I be such a lucky man?*

Grace interrupted his thought by pulling on his arm and guiding him down the aisle. As they walked between the packed pews, the women oohed and aahed at Grace, telling her how lovely she was and what a wonderful wedding it had been, while their husbands either tried to shake Jack's hand or pounded him on the back, making comments, some of which garnered glares from their wives.

Stepping through the front door, Jack was shocked. Lieutenant Westfield McMillian, who had been with him when he found Elijah and the remains of the boy's family and friends, had his cavalry troop lined up outside the church. They were on each side of the path that led from the church to the decorated, frilly carriage that was parked, waiting for them with Pauly as the driver. The cavalrymen had drawn their sabers. The sabers were lifted across the walkway, forming an arch for Grace and Jack to walk under. He glanced at the grinning Lieutenant McMillian and shook his head. The grin widened.

Jack looked down at Grace. She was absolutely glowing. Her eyes brimmed with tears when she looked up, and her lips spread in a happy smile. She crooked her finger, and he leaned his head down. "Mama thought of everything."

Yes, he thought, *she truly did.* He nodded to the lieutenant—who immediately ordered, "Invert sabers"—and slowly walked Grace under the shining blades. As soon as Jack handed Grace into the carriage, Lieutenant McMillian called, "Return sabers," and the troopers snapped their weapons down and into their scabbards. Pauly clucked to the two-horse team, and they stepped out. Jack turned and nodded his thanks to Lieutenant McMillian.

Pauly leaned back, speaking out of the side of his mouth. "Congratulations, folks. That was a mighty nice wedding. Y'all were funny, too. Grace, you slapping this big galoot just about brought the house down. I swear them rafters were shaking."

Grace leaned closer to Jack. "If he hadn't been frowning at the whole congregation, I wouldn't have slapped him, but, my goodness, did you see that frown?"

Pauly laughed again. "I sure did. It looked like he was trying to figure out an escape route."

"See." She poked Jack in the ribs hard enough to make the big man jump. "Everyone saw it. We'll never live it down."

Concerned, Jack turned to look at his bride. She was smiling, and her green eyes were twinkling. He felt relief flood over him. "I saw friends who had traveled far, and I was trying to figure out why and how."

"Oh, Jack. Those people love you. Mama sent tickets by telegraph, either for the stage or train to get them here, and she notified them very early, when we first mentioned we were getting married. When you extended the date for the wedding, it actually helped out."

Jack was still mystified. "I find it hard to understand how so many of them could break away from their ranches and businesses. It's a long haul from New Mexico and Texas. And speaking of long hauls, what's old Darby Griffin from Norfolk, Virginia, doing here? Why would your mother contact him?"

She gave him a puzzled look as Pauly pulled the carriage against the steps leading into Ma's Bed and Eats. Putting off further questions, Jack climbed down and, placing his hands around Grace's slim waist, swung her to the boardwalk. There was a crowd waiting, and the people began cheering. Grace's cheeks became a bit pinker. She waved to the crowd and hurried through the open door held by the new proprietor, Matthew Marcel.

"Thanks, Pauly," Jack called, stepping through the door behind Grace. He swung it closed and turned, but before he could say or do anything, Marcel spoke up.

"Grace, I must remind you to hurry. Change your clothes before the mob of people arrives from the church."

She gazed up at Jack. "Yes, thank you, Matthew. Do you have all the waitstaff ready?"

Grasping her arms, he turned her and began pushing her toward her room. "Yes, now don't worry. Go. Change." He turned to Jack. "Marshal Jack, you must also hurry. I don't think you want to travel in that suit. The train leaves in four hours, and you shall be talking to so many people, you won't have time later."

Jack watched Grace's slim figure hurry along the hallway and disappear around the corner. "Yeah, thanks, Matthew." He headed for his room. Reaching it, he stepped inside and closed the door. His new light gray Stetson lay on the bed next to his suitcase and saddlebags. Picking it up, his big hands curled the sides of the brim and placed it on his head. With one hand on the front brim and the other on the back, he leveled it until it was positioned just the way he liked it. Once that was accomplished, he changed clothes.

For the wedding, the reverend had tried to persuade him to leave his Smith & Wessons in his room, but he wouldn't even consider the suggestion. When the sky pilot had called Mary over to reinforce his argument, Jack became more insistent, referencing the incident that had happened the day before. Finally, they had given in, and to his future mother-in-law's horror, he had worn them in the church during the wedding. Now, after changing clothes, he swung them back around his waist and fastened the buckle in the same worn and widened hole it had been in for the past four years. He removed his hat, stared at it for a moment, and placed it on the bed again, next to the saddlebags and suitcase. He'd be doing enough ducking without the hat.

Jack turned and examined himself in the dresser's mirror. The face that stared out at him wasn't the face of six years ago. It carried more scars and more wrinkles. Not something that he ever noticed, but now that he was about to see his bride, her mother and their guests, he took a moment.

At the corners of his eyes, new wrinkles had gathered. The gray orbs still looked surprisingly clear and lively, but the surrounding skin had changed, thanks to the sun, wind, and time. The four punctures, where the spur rowel had hit him and rolled, looked like freckles, only darker and larger. Where the heel of the boot had torn his forehead, he had a jagged scar, like a shaft of lightning, which ran from his hairline to his right eyebrow. He laughed at the face staring at him. "You never got a wound on your body from fighting in all those wars, but look at you now." Jack glanced at his hat one more time. He could hear folks arriving. An assortment of voices came from the dining room and parlor. *I guess I'd better go face the music,* he thought. *I don't want Grace to have to do it by herself.*

Jack opened the door, bowed his six-foot six-inch frame,

thanks to the extra two inches of boot heels, passed through it, closed the door, and headed toward the noise.

Billy and Elijah raced down the hallway toward him. Billy yelled out first. "Pa, Ma said to hurry up. Did you know there's a Texas Ranger major out there, and he says he knows you?"

Not to be outdone, Elijah shouted, "Yeah, and Lieutenant McMillian is here, too, with some of his men. There's a bunch of folks out there. There's three people from Silver City, New Mexico. Did they name it that because you can pick up silver in the streets?"

Jack knelt and put a hand on the shoulder of each of the boys. "Slow down. Yes, I know your Texas Ranger, and it'll be good to see Lieutenant McMillian, and no, you can't pick up silver in the streets. Now why don't you two see if you can be a help to Matthew." Jack watched the grins fall, and countered immediately, "Just for a bit, so he doesn't get snowed under, and then I want you both out there so I can introduce you to my friends." The grins jumped back on the young faces, and the excitement returned.

Billy grabbed Elijah's arm. "Come on, Lij, let's hurry so we can have some fun."

The two of them raced to the kitchen, and Jack rose, following them. "Anything I can do to help, Matthew?"

"No, Marshal, you go ahead and enjoy yourself. Everything will be just fine. I'll need the boys only for a few minutes, and then they'll be joining you."

Jack waved and stepped into the dining room, which was alive with people. The crowd flowed into the parlor and out onto the boardwalk. He looked around for his bride and spotted her with her mother, both surrounded by a mass of people. She saw him and waved. He gave her an acknowledging wave just as a big hand slapped him on the back.

"Boy, I swear you've growed more, but it don't matter how tall or big you got, that pretty little filly's done roped and hogtied you."

Jack would never forget the familiar voice of his good friend and partner Bronco Fenn. He turned to see the man, older and grayer, maybe a little stooped, but still a man he wouldn't want to tangle with, and his other partner and good friend Montana Huff. He took the hand of each and gave them a warm and friendly shake. "I can't believe you two would leave our ranch just to see an old reprobate like me get hitched."

They both grinned, and Montana, not looking a day older than when they had ridden their separate ways in Texas, said, "It's good to see you, boy. I'd say you latched onto a fine woman. Congratulations."

"Monty, it's good to see you, too. Both of you fellas are looking mighty good."

Bronco spoke up. "Well, we ain't taken up rockin' chairs yet. But sometimes, after one of those cattle drives to Kansas, I'm thinkin' these old bones might be ready to try one out."

Jack gave his friends a knowing nod. "Yeah, I remember how hard the drive we did together turned out to be. How's the ranch doing?"

Monty stepped a little closer so that he could lower his voice and still be heard. "Jack, boy, we've made four drives since you left, and more money than two old cowhands deserve."

"I figured you were doing pretty good to wire me that stack of change. That was an unheard of amount."

Bronco eased closer. "Boy, that weren't nothin'. We could sell the ranch right now, walk away, and live high on the hog in New York City for the rest of our lives."

"Bronco's right, Jack, and you've got more coming, but we figured you might be moving to the ranch, and you could take over."

Jack saw Grace motion him over. "Fellas, my bride is signaling to me. Let's talk later."

Bronco grinned. "You'd best snap to, boy. You're on a leash now." Looking around the crowded room, he grew serious. "It looks like you're gonna be tied up for the rest of the day, and we know about your honeymoon. Don't worry about us. We've planned on stayin' until you two get back. We can talk then."

Monty nodded his agreement.

Jack looked around the crowded room. "Good, lot of folks I need to talk to and not much time to do it. I'll see you when we get back. Enjoy yourselves."

They both grinned back at him. "We aim to," Monty said. "Now you get going and do your duty."

Jack started toward Grace, who saw him approaching and smiled before turning back to two women who had her cornered. She had barely looked away when a hand grasped his arm.

"It's been a while, partner."

Jack wheeled to stare into the smiling face of Hank Marsden, the man who had taught him about prospecting and joined him in his gold mining venture near Silver City, New Mexico. Alongside him was Dr. David Pratt and his wife, Martha. A wide smile leaped to his lips. "It's a wonder to see you, Hank." He shook his friend's hand and addressed the Pratts. "Doc, Martha, I can't believe you traveled all this way. That stage must've been murder."

Both Doc Pratt and Martha laughed. Jack remembered the tinkling laugh from when he was healing. He might have died if it hadn't been for them.

Martha spoke up. "I must say, it was longer and dustier than I remembered a stage could be, but I am thrilled we came." She pulled Jack down and planted a soft kiss on his cheek. "We are so happy for you. I was just speaking with your bride, and she is a wonderful person."

"Yep," Jack said, "she is that and more. I'm a mighty lucky man, in more ways than one. I'm lucky you folks were in Silver

City. If you hadn't been, I wouldn't have made it. You saved my life, and I'm more grateful than you'll ever know."

The doctor chuckled. "I think we have an idea of your gratitude, Jack. We'll never be able to thank you enough for making us part owners in your mine. That was totally unnecessary but greatly appreciated. When Mary wrote us of your impending wedding and Hank indicated he was going, we had to come. I'd say congratulations are in order. It looks like you've got yourself a fine woman."

"I sure do, Doc. I've always been a lucky galoot, but I think I outdid myself with Grace, and I'm glad I was able to make a difference in your lives. You sure did in mine. Thanks for making that long trip. You gave me a chance to tell you one more time how much I appreciate your efforts and kindness."

Jack would have continued, but Hank said, "Jack, Grace told me your schedule, and we'll be leaving on the morning stage. I need a few minutes with you."

Jack looked over at Grace, who was watching him with a touch of impatience. He held up a finger and mouthed, *Sorry*. Her eyes widened, then she saw whom he was speaking with, nodded, and mouthed, *Hurry*.

Doc Pratt smiled. "Go ahead. Hank has already told us he has some business he needs to discuss with you, and we know you don't have much time. It was good seeing you again. I hope you have a safe and wonderful life."

Martha took his hand. "Thank you, Jack Sage. You've changed our lives."

Jack bowed and gave her a swift kiss on the cheek and grasped Hank's arm. "Come on, but we need to make this quick."

3

A fter stepping into his room, Jack closed the door behind him. Hank pulled a multipage document from the inside pocket of his frock coat.

"I figured you would want to change the beneficiaries of your portion of our goldmine, should something happen to you. Do you have your copy handy?"

Jack stepped to his saddlebags, opened one side, and pulled out a letter-sized leather case. He untied the leather ties, searched through the papers for a moment, and pulled out the contract. "Yep, right here."

"Good." Hank stepped to the dresser and unfolded his papers, flipping to the correct page. "The Pratts are thrilled with their five percent. You had your twenty-five percent going to them, but I'm guessing you'd prefer it to go to your family if something happens to you."

"Yep."

Hank drew a neat line through the Pratts' names and glanced at Jack. "Grace's full name?"

"Grace Kathryn Sage."

He filled in her name and initialed it, slid it over to Jack, who did the same. When both documents were completed, each man picked up his copy. Jack returned his to the leather envelope, and Hank slipped his into his coat pocket.

While Jack slid the envelope back into his saddlebags, Hank said, "We could have done this out there, but I wanted to talk to you." His face broke into a wide grin. "Jack, we are rich as Croesus."

Jack's forehead wrinkled. "What do you mean, Hank? The vein isn't playing out?"

"Not only is it not playing out, we've hit a wider vein, and it just keeps going and going. Our mine has the potential for us to pull over a hundred thousand ounces out of it."

Jack let out a long whistle. "That sounds like a lot of gold."

Hank shook his head. "I forget you're not well versed on mining. Gold right now is almost twenty dollars an ounce. That means, roughly, if the gold stopped at a hundred thousand ounces, your twenty-five percent will pay you five hundred thousand dollars. Jack, you'll never have to draw a gun again or lift a hand if you don't want to. We are rich, my friend, rich. You want to take your family back to Virginia and live a comfortable life? You can do it. Shoot, if you want to move them to Paris, you can do that, too. You can live anywhere you want to."

Jack was stunned, trying to get his head around Hank's figures. "I never thought those nuggets in the creek would amount to that kind of money, Hank." He shook his head. "I can't even imagine it."

"I know. I haven't gotten much sleep since we struck the second vein. At some point, we're gonna have to hire someone to run the mine, because I'm itching to spend some of my part, and there's not much to spend it on around town." Hank's grin faded. "Along with this good news, I have a question to ask. Would you be willing to come out to Silver City for a while to spell me? Perhaps you could do it before you folks settle down. I'd be willing to up your share to thirty-five percent. That's not bad,

Jack. The way this thing is going, with the additional ten percent, that might mean as much as a million for you."

"That's mighty generous of you, but I'll have to talk to Grace before I made any decision."

Hank nodded. "I figured. Why don't you talk to her over this trip to Little Rock? I'll be gone, but you can shoot me a wire with your decision. I really need help, and I'd prefer not to bring in someone we don't know."

Jack grinned and extended his hand. "We'll figure out something. Thanks for the good news."

"Oh, with all this, I forgot. I've transferred another fifty thousand into your account."

Jack opened the door and, placing his hand on his friend's back, ushered him toward the hallway. "You are full of surprises. Thanks, I already feel like I've got more money than I'll ever spend. Now I've got to get back to Grace." Reaching the dining room, and before they split, Jack said, "I'll let you know as soon as we decide. Thanks for coming out, and have a safe trip." He headed toward Grace.

He could see her smiling. Billy, Elijah, and her mother, Mary, were at her side, and he recognized Texas Ranger Major Gordon Wilson and the Schmidts, along with their daughter Marlene, who had been ten when she was kidnapped four years earlier. She was tall for her fourteen years, with wide-set eyes. Those eyes had been focused on Grace, but they caught Jack approaching. She broke away and ran through the crowd. Reaching him, she jumped into his arms and pressed her face to his chest.

"Oh, Ranger Sage, it's so good to see you."

He held her close, remembering the kidnapped little girl, and said a silent prayer of thanks. She'd come so close to being gone forever. "It's wonderful to see you, Marlene. I can't believe how much you've grown." He gave her a last squeeze and lowered her to the floor.

She shoved her little hand into his and led him back to the

group. Nearing her parents, Grace, and the others, Marlene gave him a little frown. "I thought you were going to wait for me."

Grace smiled, though her eyebrows rose.

"You know I told you there would be somebody for you more suitable to your age."

She grinned. "I know, and you *have* gotten older."

Mrs. Schmidt spoke. "Marlene, that's not a nice thing to say to the man who saved you."

Marlene grinned. "I'm just teasing, Mama. After what we went through, I think I have the right."

Jack grinned at the girl. "So, have you found someone more suitable yet?"

At Jack's question, the girl's eyes grew wide, and her fair complexion turned rosy red.

Her father said, "She's sweet on the boy from the farm next to ours."

Marlene swung toward her father, and her hands snapped to her hips. "Papa, I am not."

Mrs. Schmidt had grasped her husband's arm and squeezed.

Changing the subject, he turned to Jack, extended his hand, and said, "Congratulations, Ranger . . . or Marshal Sage. I wish you two a great life."

Jack took his hand, shook it, and asked, "How's the rest of the family?"

"Doing fine."

Mrs. Schmidt placed her hand on theirs. "Yes, we all are, thanks to you. You saved our Marlene and our family. Thank you so much."

"Well, ma'am, I did nothing more than what anyone else would. I'm glad it all worked out."

Their shake broke, and Ranger Wilson extended his hand. Jack took it.

"Marshal Sage, I just want to let you know there's a captaincy waiting for you. I hear you're planning on returning to Texas. You could be a great help. This time you'll get paid."

Jack glanced at Grace, who was smiling through pursed lips. "Major, it's no longer just up to me."

Wilson glanced at Grace and smiled. "We could sure use him, ma'am."

"Yes, Major Wilson, as I was telling you earlier, my hope is that Jack's days of wearing a badge are over."

The ranger nodded. "Yes, ma'am, I can understand that hope, but Texas could use your man."

Grace, her tone hardening, replied, "I too have plans for my husband, Major Wilson, and they don't include the Texas Rangers."

Jack gave his head a single shake for emphasis and tossed the ranger a grin. "I guess you got your answer, Major."

"Yes, and very clear."

Jack hadn't missed Judge Ronald Bell standing nearby, eyeing him. As usual, waiting wasn't the judge's best quality. When he caught Jack's eye, he jerked his head to motion him over. The judge was an imposing man. Not as tall as Jack, but over six feet and broad shouldered. His hawklike face seemed always to give the impression he was ready to pounce. Now, his thick eyebrows were drawn together, and his forehead wrinkled as he stared at Jack.

Judge Bell's federal court was responsible for the Indian Territory, which sat between the northern border of Texas and the southern border of Kansas. The territory covered seventy thousand square miles, and its eastern border butted against Arkansas. Law was enforced by the thirty U.S. Marshals the judge employed to bring lawbreakers and miscreants to his court. He was known more for justice than mercy, keeping the hangman busy. Today, a day of happiness for Jack and Grace, appeared to not have interfered with the judge's prime goal—justice.

Grace, who like her mother, loved the judge for his help and kindness to them, also knew Judge Bell and her new husband did not get along well. Though Jack had worked with the judge, he would never admit to having worked for him, because, in Jack's view, he worked directly for the president. Judge Bell held an opposite opinion. In almost every meeting, the two men struck sparks. In fact, at one of their meetings, the judge had stepped close to the line, insinuating Jack was lying. In response, Jack had sprung to his feet, towering over Bell, and informed him if any other man accused him of such a thing, he would kill him. Bell, one of his few times, had apologized, but all of their meetings were tense. When she followed Jack's gaze across the room, she was just in time to see the judge jerk his head. She smiled at the judge and placed her hand on Jack's thick forearm. With the noise of countless conversations going on throughout the rooms, it was necessary for Jack to tilt his head close to his new bride's mouth.

Her smile grew more radiant when he looked at her. "Jack, stay calm. Remember, this is a wonderful day. Don't let the judge dampen our joy."

He patted her hand, his pursed lips relaxing into a smile, and winked at her. "I'll be as sweet as your peach pie, honey." Straightening, he addressed his friends. "I'm really glad to see you folks, especially you, Marlene, but it looks like I'm being summoned."

"Judge Ronald Bell," Ranger Wilson said. "We'd like to have him in Texas. Killers don't get off in his court because they know somebody."

"You're right there. If you folks will excuse me." Jack turned and headed toward Bell.

Reaching him, Bell thrust out his hand. "Congratulations, Jack, I'm sure you and Grace will have a wonderful life, though I wish you wouldn't take them away from Fort Smith. I don't know what we're going to do without Ma's Bed and Eats."

"Thanks, I think, and Matthew will keep the tradition going, though I'm sure the name will change. What's on your mind that's so urgent?"

Immediately the judge's eyebrows slammed together, and the wrinkles across his forehead leaped back into place. "You need to postpone your trip."

Jack's voice turned cold. "Which one do you want to mess with, the honeymoon or the move?"

Buck Walker, standing next to Bell, jumped in. "Jack, we really need your help. A gang, we have no idea of how many or who, ambushed and hanged two of our deputy marshals."

Jack couldn't believe it. "They did what?"

"They hanged two of our deputies, then tied their bodies across their horses. An army patrol found them and brought them to Fort Smith."

Jack could feel his anger rise as he thought of the two innocent deputies.

The judge moved closer, one of his habits of intimidation he used not only on criminals but with anyone he wanted to win a point, knowing most people would take a step back.

Jack's gray eyes appeared to harden, jaws tightened, and he stepped forward, putting the two men almost nose to nose.

Judge Bell cleared his throat and took a step back. "They just came into town, and there was a note pinned to the back of Everett Mason. It said, we'll hang every marshal who comes west of Fort Smith." A small red point appeared next to each of the judge's eyes.

Jack had learned this was the judge's tell. The judge's anger was like a pot of boiling water. When those two little red points appeared, he was about to boil over, and it never bode well for a defendant.

"I will not have my marshals threatened by the likes of this bunch. I want them in my court, and we will see how many marshals they'll hang then."

Jack gave a sharp nod, for he was nearly as mad as the judge, and for a change it wasn't at him. He looked at Buck. "So what are you doing about this? Why do you need me?"

Buck shook his head. "It couldn't have happened at a worse time. All of the deputies are deep in the territory. None of them are scheduled back for over a week, and we need to get someone after them right now."

Jack gave Buck a long look.

Buck didn't respond well to Jack's apparent inference. "Listen, Jack, I can't leave Fort Smith, or I'd be on their trail right now."

The judge interrupted. "I ordered him to stay. He was preparing to leave, but I stopped him. I don't need the man who is running this outfit gallivanting around the countryside."

"You can't be telling me you don't have a single deputy here?"

Buck said, "We have one deputy in town, young Davey Cole, and he's too inexperienced to send out alone. He's good with a gun and willing, but he's not ready." Buck shot Jack a look. "But if he went with an experienced marshal..."

This time Jack shook his head, knowing Buck was giving him the opportunity to step up. He pulled out his watch, checked the time, and slipped it back into his pocket, all the while his mind churned. *What if this gang runs into other unsuspecting marshals? They're out there, and it's possible for me to head out, but Grace is depending on me. Everything is scheduled. We can get away and be alone on our own time.* Jack gazed at his bride. *Is it too much to ask? I can't let others, with no knowledge of their intent, ride into this bunch, but I can't let my wife down.*

Grace turned, and the evening sun filtering through the gauzy curtains lit her eyes. They flashed their emerald green. She turned her head at an angle to the window, but kept her eyes on him. Her brilliant white teeth glimmered in a smile that pulled at his heart. His smile was less engaged, less open. Hers disappeared, and she glanced at the judge, then back to Jack. He could see she had discerned what was happening. Her smile disappeared, and she started toward them.

Impatiently, Judge Bell said, "Well, Jack?"

But Jack ignored him and wrapped an arm around Grace as she stepped near.

Her voice had no life to it, as if she knew he had already made up his mind. "What has he talked you into?"

Bell began, "Now just a minute, Grace—"

Jack had never heard her voice this hard and cold. "Listen to me, *Your Honor*, he has promised me he is done." Her head turned to her new husband, and those lovely eyes searched his.

The chatter in the rooms ceased, and everyone turned to watch the bride and her groom and the judge.

Grace's voice lost its edge. A resigned tone filled her words. "And I see you have won him over. Whether you said it or not, you appealed to his compassion or his honor. That's why I married him, for both of those qualities. I fear yours will not be the only time he's taken from me, until the last time." She turned and buried her face in Jack's chest.

His arms encircled her, and he glared at Bell and Buck, but he knew he couldn't turn them down. It wasn't in him. His mind was filled with thoughts of unsuspecting men riding into this new threat in the territory, and he was the one who had the skills to take care of the problem. It was what he did, and he and his poor Grace had believed his promise, though Jack realized now he would never be able to turn down protecting the innocent. It had never been, nor was it now, in him to walk away.

The judge, knowing he had won, simply said, "See me in the office before you leave," and, with Marshal Buck Walker following, left the building.

Jack could feel Grace's body shake with her sobs. Guests, wanting to leave the newlyweds to their privacy, quietly slipped from the party. When everyone had left, only the boys, Mary, Matthew, and his waitstaff remained. After moving the furniture back into place, Matthew herded his employees into the kitchen, where cleanup work began. Mary took the boys to their room and stayed with them.

When everyone was gone, Grace looked up at Jack. "I'm sorry I was so terrible. I was just surprised."

Jack led her to the loveseat. The faint rose scent of her enveloped him, filling his heart and squeezing it tight with the knowledge he might lose her, but knowing he couldn't lie to her about who he was. After she sat, he lowered himself beside her and took her hands. "Grace, I'm the one who should be apologizing. I don't know how you knew, but, in my heart, I had accepted Bell's proposal when you looked over."

Silence filled the parlor, but the sadness in her lovely green eyes spoke volumes. He took a deep breath and began.

"Let me tell you a story, and I'll keep it short. Five or six years ago, I had taken off the badge. That was when I met Monty and Bronco, and we went into the ranching business together. Coming back from Kansas after our first cattle drive, we were passing through the territory, and we came upon thieves robbing returning cattlemen, much like us. We caught or killed all of the bandits. After that bloody encounter, Monty said something to me. He said that I was born to help the downtrodden, and my way of doing it was the law. I recognized it then, and I recognize it now. Unfortunately, for a while I forgot. I think I allowed myself to be blinded by the promise of you, and I'm sorry I did this to you."

A curl of her thick black hair had fallen out of place and hung over a dainty ear. With his massive hand, he lifted the raven hair and slipped it gently behind her ear, and in moving his hand away, he paused, caressing her soft cheek. Her eyes filled again, and a single tear traveled over the rise of her cheek. With his thumb, he wiped it away, his heart breaking. He had never wanted to hurt this woman, and now he had, deeply.

She grasped his hand, turned it, and pressed her lips to his palm. Silence filled the room.

Finally she looked up. "I should have known, Jack. In fact, maybe I did, somewhere deep inside me, but I kept it smothered. I wanted you for myself, and I didn't want to worry about you being brought home across Smokey's back." She gazed directly into his eyes. "I still don't want to." She took a deep breath, letting it out in a long sigh. "When do you leave?"

"Today, after I get supplies together and stop by the judge's office. I don't know how long I'll be gone. What will you do?"

"We'll stay here. We can help Matthew, and when we sold the boarding house to him, he said we could stay as long as we need, and with all the money you've given us, we'll be fine. I shall have time to think about us. Jack, I honestly don't know if I can be married to a lawman. I've lost one husband to violence. I don't want to lose another."

Jack nodded. "If you find it would be too hard for you, the judge will annul the marriage. We've done nothing to complicate an annulment."

This time it was Grace who nodded. "I know. I love you, Jack."

"I love you, too."

"But I just don't know if I can live your life."

"I know."

She leaned toward him, and he took her gently in his arms. Minutes ticked by before they pulled apart.

"You need to tell the boys goodbye."

He kissed her softly on her cheek and stood. "Goodbye, Grace."

She was still holding his hand. She squeezed and released it. "Goodbye, my love. Be safe."

4

—————

"Ireckon I don't give a wet cow pie how old I am." Facing Jack, Bronco's chin was thrust out, and his hands were clamped at his hips. "It don't affect my aim, and I can outride you any day of the week." He kicked a horse apple hard enough to send it skyward into the street.

Jack hung the last pack on Stonewall's packsaddle. He was riding Pepper and leading Thunder. Smokey needed to rest and put more muscle on before he took off on another long trip, and Jack had no idea how long he would be gone. After ensuring the pack was solid on Stonewall, he turned to his friend. "Bronco, I know you mean well, but you aren't a lawman, you're a cattleman."

Bronco raised a finger and shook it in Jack's face. "You look here, you young whippersnapper. I've fought Comanche, Kiowa, Apache, rustlers, and outlaws. I know more about trackin' than you'll learn in a lifetime. You don't want to take me because I've got a few years on me, and that's enough to fry my bacon in your sight. I ain't appreciating that one bit."

Once Jack had declined their help, Monty had said nothing,

but Bronco was making up for him. He had been going nonstop since before they had left Pauly's stables.

Jack tried one last time. "Look, Bronco, I appreciate you and Monty wanting to help, but I'm the marshal. I'm the one with the authority, and you can't come. You two need to get back to the ranch and keep it running right. You don't know what's going on down there."

Monty pitched in. "He's right, Bronco. You've had your say, and it hasn't changed anything. Let's get back home and make sure we still have a ranch."

"I don't like this, not one bit. Jack, you're gonna need help."

"I've got help. Davey Cole will be with me."

Bronco spit a long brown stream into the street. "Humph. That young feller's a babe in the woods. You'll be babysitting when you should be watching for killers."

At the mention of the deputy's youth, Jack thought, *You may be more right than you know. I haven't met the kid yet, but I sure hope Bronco's off target on this one.* "That's unfair, Bronco. The kid's a good shot. All young Cole needs is a little experience under his belt, and he'll be fine."

"Did I hear my name?" A young man wearing a deputy marshal's badge stepped out of the mercantile. This being the first time Jack had met him, he looked him over. In his boots, the fella stood a couple of inches over six feet. Wide shoulders supported a thick neck and large head. Bushy black hair pushed out from under his gray hat. His eyes were such a dark brown they looked black. The only real distraction was the few strands of black hair on his upper lip. It was comical, and laughter was nothing a marshal needed when he was facing a tough hombre or two.

He didn't get that neck and those shoulders sitting around playing marbles, Jack thought. *If he'll get rid of that puny mustache, he'll actually look the part.* He stepped onto the boardwalk and thrust his hand out to the younger man. "Jack Sage."

The young fella took it and grinned at Jack. "I know who you are, Marshal Sage. I've seen you around a lot. I saw you take Clagg the first time. He should've counted himself lucky and left well enough alone."

Jack liked what he saw except for that danged mustache. The black eyes were honest and calm, and this fella could probably handle himself in a fight. If he couldn't, Jack had a few tricks he could teach him. "Howdy. You ready?"

"Yes, sir, my horses and mule are loaded and ready in the corral behind the marshal's office."

"Good. I need to check in with the judge, and we'll be on our way." He turned back to Monty and Bronco. "I'm obliged to you two coming all the way up here. Sorry things went the way they did, but I'll see you when I or we head down to Texas."

Monty stepped forward. "I'm mighty sorry, son. I'm hoping things will work out so you can have a full and happy life. If anyone deserves it, you do."

Bronco stepped up. "I'm still mad at you, but I hope your girl comes to her senses and realizes it's better to have someone who loves her, even for a short time, than to have no one atall. Keep your eyes peeled, and we'll see you in Texas."

The two ranchers touched their brims to Davy Cole and stepped out for Pauly's stable.

"Friends of yours, Marshal?"

Jack watched them go. "Good friends. What do you like to be called?"

"Well, sir, I figure if I'm gonna be taken seriously, I'd better drop the Davy handle. How about Dave or David or Cole." One corner of his mouth lifted in a grin. "Use what you like. My ma does, especially when she's upset."

"So you want to be taken seriously, Dave?"

"Yes, sir, I surely do."

"Then get rid of that poor excuse for a mustache. Go get your animals, and meet me in front of the courthouse."

Dave's hand reached for his lip, and his fingers ran across the few hairs. "Shave my mustache?"

"You heard me. That thing makes you look like a schoolkid. You get in a gunfight, you won't have to shoot your opponent, he'll laugh himself to death. Get rid of it." Jack swung onto Pepper, cutting the conversation short. Leading Thunder and Stonewall, he headed for the courthouse.

Folks nodded as he passed, and he could hear the whispered conversations begin once they thought themselves clear. *People sure like to gossip,* he thought. *It's going to be tough on Grace for a while.* At the thought of Grace, he felt a deep loss. *Will she leave me before we actually get started? But that might be the best thing for her and the boys, because she's right. I could end up dead on this hunt. It could happen anytime.*

He pulled up at the courthouse, swung down, and tied his animals to the hitching rail. "I won't be long, boys." After climbing the stairs to the doors of the courthouse, he entered and climbed the wide stairway to the second floor. As his head rose above the second-floor level, he was surprised to see Buck, the U.S. Marshal over the territory, sitting at Bell's secretary's desk. Jack stopped in front of the desk and stared down at Buck.

Buck glared up at him. "What?"

"You here to take a letter?"

"Very funny. The judge needed help with scheduling. That's what I'm doing."

"What about the new secretary? He sick?"

"His rear's in a saddle. I told you every deputy we have is out chasing crooks or killers."

"There's not another soul around?"

"Yeah, there is, and you got him. That's it, no more, and the second verse to that little ditty is the judge says we ain't hiring any more."

"Speaking of the man, is he available?"

From inside his office, Judge Bell called, "Get in here, Jack, and stop jawing with the hired help."

Jack grinned at Buck, who was shaking his head and had already picked up a pen.

He stepped to the door and pushed it open. Bell was rising from his chair. The judge hurried around his desk and grasped Jack's hand. "I am really sorry about the blowup, Jack. If I had known how Gracie would act—"

"You'd have done the same thing, Judge, and you know it."

The eyebrows rushed together again. Bell returned to his desk and sat, waving Jack to the couch.

For a moment his eyebrows remained together and brow wrinkled, but at last the eyebrows traveled back to their normal position, and his brow smoothed as much as it could. "You're right, Jack. I am a mission-minded man. I usually don't think of another's feelings until after the event. Sometimes I feel bad for what happened, sometimes I don't. I guess that makes me human. However, when I tell you I am sorry for your and Gracie's difficulties, I am being sincere. The two of you are some of my favorite people."

Inwardly, Jack laughed at the last sentence, thinking, *I know Grace is one of your favorite people, but I'm not so sure about me.* He removed his hat and wiped his hand around the sweatband. "Thanks, Judge. I have to warn you. You might be getting a visit from Grace."

The judge cocked his head, and the eyebrows moved a bit toward each other. "Really, about what?"

"Annulment. She was expecting me to give up being a lawman, and I thought I could."

"I could have told you that, Jack. You are a different breed of man. Enforcing the law, and the violence that goes along with it, doesn't bother you. The average man, it does. I'm not saying killing and hurting your fellow man is something you enjoy. What I'm saying to you is it's something you will do to protect others, and though you regret a death, you don't dwell on it. Yes, you are the breed of man this country needs, whether it's here or Texas or wherever you may be. It's in your blood. You live to help and protect the little guy and to enforce the law."

"You're right, Judge. I recognized that fact thanks to Montana Huff, one of the ranchers from Texas who came to the wedding. You may have met him."

The judge nodded. "Yes, the quieter of the two, and I would say the more dangerous."

"You'd be right on both counts. After a little incident, he pointed out that trait and said about the same thing as you." Jack paused, staring out the window, then turned back to the judge. "I forgot it when I met Grace."

"Yes, a woman like Grace can do that to any man. If she does show up here, you are alright with having the marriage annulled?"

Jack looked down at his hands gripping his hat. They were big hands, built for fighting and drawing guns. Not for the tender touch a wife needs. "Yes, Judge. As much as I don't like it, if this is what she needs, I am agreeable to the annulment."

The judge heaved a long sigh, shifted his position in his chair, clasped his hands, and placed them on the desk. "Well, Jack, I will take care of it if the need arises. Now, you must be on your way, and I have something to say to you."

Jack recognized the change. Judge Bell was back in his official role.

"If you can, I need you to bring these men, no matter how many, back to this courthouse. They have threatened the lives of every marshal who works for me, and they need to stand trial here and, if found guilty, hang by the neck until dead." Papers jumped when the judge emphasized the last statement by slamming his hand on his desk. He pointed out the window to the street below. "There will be a gallows set up right there for the purpose of meting out justice. I will not have my marshals threatened. Do you hear me, Jack? Bring them back." He paused for a moment. Jack watched the man calm himself. "Bring them back if you can. Don't get yourself shot trying to do the impossible, but if you can."

Jack nodded. "I'll do my best, Judge. I can't make any promises, but it might ease your mind to know that I believe those men who hanged our two marshals should expect the same death. I have no personal need to shoot them."

The judge stood, and Jack began to stand, but Bell waved him back to the couch. "There is someone who needs to see you before you leave. The dustup this morning interfered with his plans, and he came to me. You can have my office."

Jack was mystified. He waited while Bell stepped from his office into the alcove. He could hear the steps between offices. Voices made it back to him, and he recognized old Mr. Miller's voice. He had wondered what he was doing here when he saw him this morning. Mr. Layton T. Miller was his uncle's personal and business attorney. The man had handled Uncle Teddy's affairs for as far back as Jack could remember. In fact, Jack had dealt with him when he had been asked to run the company for a couple of years. He stood.

Miller walked into the room, bringing the heavy smell of stale pipe tobacco with him, his hand extended, and a faint smile drifted across his face. "Hello, Jack. It is good to see you." The smile disappeared from his face. "I'm sorry for the difficulty you had with your new wife. I do hope everything will work out well for the two of you."

The judge spoke up. "I'll leave you two. I'll be down the street for a cup of coffee and a piece of pie. Just send Buck when you're done." Exiting, the judge pulled the door closed.

Jack pointed to the chair across from him. "Mr. Miller, what brings you out here? Is the business in trouble?"

The lawyer shook his white head. "Oh, no, Jack. Since you

came back and helped, it has been doing quite well, but we do have a problem. Your family has died."

"What? My aunts, Uncle Blain, and Jeff?"

"Yes, you were the sole heir."

Jack was totally puzzled. His aunts and uncles had children, but all but one had either died of diseases or the war, but his cousin Jeffrey had been in good health when Jack returned west, and it had been less than two years since he had left. "What did he die of?"

"A .54-caliber ball, I'm afraid. He was in a duel and was killed, struck right through the heart."

Jack shook his head in consternation. "I don't understand. Jeff wasn't a fighter. He would never duel with anyone."

"Someone tried to kill you yesterday?"

Was it only yesterday? Jack thought. *With everything that has happened, I totally forgot about it.* "Yes, he just walked in and started shooting."

"Did he say anything?"

Jack considered the question while examining his hat. It was new. He had bought it for the wedding and honeymoon. He thumped the gray felt brim of the Stetson and looked at Miller. "Not much. He walked into the parlor and called for Jack Sage. I had just come in and was stretched out on the couch, reading the paper. It hid my face from him. I reacted when I heard the hammer of his sixgun pull back, among other things. I moved the paper. In that instant, he saw my face. If he had fired right then, he might have hit me, but he hesitated a split second. That was all I needed. He missed. I didn't. When he was dying, he said I looked like someone else, and that made him hesitate."

Jack's lips pursed, and his forehead wrinkled, creasing the center of his lightning-bolt scar. "What's really funny is several people said he resembled me enough to be my brother."

Miller had leaned forward in his chair as Jack spoke. "Your uncle Teddy always said you led an exciting and dangerous life.

I'm glad to see you also lead a blessed one. Derek Slater met his maker instead of you. I stopped by the undertaker and examined the body. I am positive about his identity"

Jack's features remained calm and didn't change, but he was shocked that Miller, from Norfolk, Virginia, would know the gunman who attempted to kill him here in Fort Smith. "Where do you know him from, and do you know why he looks like me?"

"I shall answer both of those questions. First, I wouldn't say I know him, but I have met him, his brothers, and his late mother. That is why I am here. One of them killed Jeffrey."

Jack's puzzlement deepened, but he remained silent, knowing lawyer Layton T. Miller would give him all of the details in his own time.

"I gave you a copy of your father's will when you were last in Norfolk."

It wasn't a question, but Jack could see the man was awaiting his acknowledgment. "Yes, I have it with me. It's downstairs in my saddlebags."

Miller gave a satisfied nod. "Good. Then you remember everything was left to you, including his portion of the shipping business."

Jack nodded.

"Your uncle Theodore had a similar document, as did your other aunts and uncle, all of whom have died in the past year, several in questionable circumstances, but I will explain those later. As I said before, you *were* the sole survivor, but no longer. Approximately a year ago, a very attractive woman, older but still attractive, appeared at my doorstep with her four sons, two of which were twins. You killed one yesterday. He was your half brother."

Jack was aghast at the thought. *I killed my half brother? How? Who is he? But he gave me no chance. He would've killed me.*

Miller, watching Jack, reached across the space and patted him on the knee like he would a boy in his Sunday school class.

"Don't let it eat at you, my boy. He was, of a surety, set on taking your life. You have his twin to thank for that." He pulled a photograph from his briefcase and handed it to Jack. It was of a blonde woman with her husband and four sons. The oldest two appeared to be in their late teenage years. The oldest was the tallest, but he did not have the wide-shouldered build of his siblings. He was slim with almost no shoulders and hips, and his face looked just like Jack's. He looked up at Miller, his eyebrows raised in question.

"You are looking at the Slater family twenty years ago. Mr. Slater was a comfortable, wealthy businessman from England, who expanded his shipping business to Bermuda. There he met and married the woman you see, and she became Mrs. Slater. He adopted her two children, and they had two more boys. It is a story you would think would be a happy-ever-after tale."

Jack attempted to hand the photograph back to Miller, but he waved his hands. "You keep it. I have more. Learn the faces, and that single act may save your life."

5

Jack was getting tired of hearing Miller's tale. He had questions and was tired of waiting. "How do I have two half brothers?"

Miller's lips pursed, his trademark expression when interrupted. "I'll get to it. Just be patient."

"Look, Mr. Miller, I don't have time for a long, detailed story. I am about to leave town in search of men who hanged two U.S. Marshals, so tell me how I have two half brothers and finish this up, quick."

Miller's lips pursed even tighter, and his fat little wrinkled cheeks reddened. "Very well. Your father, before he was married to your mother, was quite the sailor. He covered most of the world. He sailed to every exotic port known to man and was a handsome young devil. I knew him—"

Jack stood. "If you're not going to tell me what I need to know, I'm arresting you and putting you in jail. You can wait there until I return, because I'm leaving right now."

"You can't do that, young man. I am—"

"Watch me." Jack walked to the door, opened it, and leaned

out. "Buck, would you take Mr. Miller to jail and hold him as a material witness in the shooting at Ma Nelson's Bed and Eats?"

Jack stepped back, and Buck entered Judge Bell's office. Without a word, he grabbed the old man by the arm and lifted him out of his chair.

"Alright, Jack," Miller cried, slapping at Buck's hand. "I will make it short, though you need the additional information I have. I cannot believe you would resort to throwing an old friend of your family in jail. You are just as short-fused as you were as a boy. I remember when you were a little tyke at church and broke your cousin's nose in front of both sets of parents."

At the comment Buck started Miller for the door. "Stop hitting my hand. When we get to the jail, you can tell me that story about Jack. It sounds interesting." He winked at Jack. "We'll have plenty of time. I'm suspectin' he'll be gone for quite a while."

Jack returned to his place on the divan. "Turn him loose, Buck. Maybe he can get to the point this time, but don't go way. He'll get no second chance."

Buck released the old man's arm, waved, left the office, and began pulling the door closed behind him.

Jack saw Judge Bell coming up the stairs and called, "Judge, why don't you come on in here. I think you should hear this. You can be a witness to this crazy story."

Miller watched the judge enter. He nodded. "No offense to you, Your Honor, but, Jack, this is about your family and your father's indiscretion. I would think you would want to keep it private."

Jack shook his head. "Judge Bell and I have few secrets. Feel free to be candid—and short. Now have a seat and get this over with."

The judge walked in, nodded to Buck as he departed, closed the door, and returned to his chair. He sat without a word and waited.

Making his way back to the chair, the old lawyer was almost

beside himself. "I have never been treated so badly by law enforcement in my life."

"Get on with the story. I don't have time to waste."

After pulling his waistcoat down and smoothing it out, Miller began. "Before meeting your mother, your father had a liaison in Bermuda. From that"—he looked around the room as if he could find the word he was looking for on the wall—"uniting, your half brothers were conceived, but your father knew nothing about them. He sailed out the next day, and they never saw one another again. Evidently life was hard for her, and she traded on her beauty to survive and provide for her two boys until she met and married Carlilse Slater."

"So what's going on now? Why are they trying to kill me?"

Miller held up his hand to hold Jack off. "Yes, yes, just wait. I am getting there." When Jack started to respond, the lawyer quickly replied, "I will make it quick and informative. Please wait."

Jack nodded his assent.

"Evidently she had a nice life on Bermuda, and everything clicked along quite well until Mr. Slater had an accident. While fishing with the boys, he fell off the boat and drowned. I'm sure Mrs. Slater expected to be well taken care of, as wealthy as she considered her late husband."

Jack folded his arms across his chest and stared at Miller.

"Alright, Jack, give me a moment. It is difficult for me to decide which points are important for you to know and which aren't." He thought, took a deep breath, and began again. "Carlisle Slater was a gambler, and that would be Mrs. Slater's undoing. Shortly after his death, the authorities arrived at her residence with a court order evicting her and confiscating most of their property. The court left enough for them to have a very modest stipend, but their lavish lifestyle was finished. I don't know when she thought of your father, but she decided to bring her boys to the states and search for him. I'm conflicted as to whether she was asking only what was due her or planning to apply a little blackmail. She showed up at my office shortly after you had returned to the west."

Jack pulled out his watch, checked it, and gazed pointedly at Miller.

The old man squirmed in his chair and began speaking faster. "I was aghast at this attractive woman and four big bruisers entering my office. Immediately I saw the resemblance of the twins to your father, and to you. Since she and her brood were strangers, I expected the worst. She wanted a part of your father's estate. I believe the woman was sincere in not desiring to disenfranchise you, but she believed she and her two sons deserved a portion of your father's estate, and under Virginia law, she was destined to get it. She had no documentation, but all she had to do was show up in court with those two boys, along with you or your picture, and there would be no doubt."

Jack stood. His patience with Miller was slimmer than a worn thread. This was a good story, and any other time, he wouldn't mind relaxing in the parlor, listening to this lawyer ramble on, but he had killers to bring to justice.

"Wait, Jack. I'm almost done, I swear. You need to hear this."

He slowly lowered himself back to the couch.

Miller searched the walls for a second. "Yes, well, where was I? Oh, yes. She stated her case. I, of course, said she had no case, knowing she would easily win, and showed her the door. She actually pleaded with me, but I suggested she return to Bermuda. There was nothing here for her or her boys."

A thought raced through Jack's mind. *Miller has always been a single-minded ruthless old guy. I guess that's why Pa hired him. I would've split the estate with them. They have the law on their side.*

"So she stood, along with her boys and the tall twin. He is skinny as a rail but as tall as you and intimidating. He turned his hard gray eyes on me, just like you are now, and told me to expect a contact from their lawyer. He also said they were also expecting to get a part of the business. That was the first contact I had with him. I didn't like him then, and I like him less now."

Miller leaned back and heaved a long sigh. "That's it, Jack, other than to say they won their case in court. Each of the twins received a quarter of your estate, including the business. They have an attorney, but Devin, that's the tall one's name, is now running the business since the deaths of your family members. His mother died from consumption during this upheaval, along with all of your relatives. Of course, you met his brother, Derek, momentarily. So until yesterday, you had two partners in your business, now only one. They will also have a claim on your holdings, even those separate from the shipping business, should you die. Do you see now why you had to hear this? Your life is in danger. If you have anything else of value, were I you, I would strive to keep it secret or protect it legally."

Jack directed his gaze to Bell. "Can you believe this story? I don't think I could make one up this crazy."

One corner of the judge's mouth barely lifted, giving him a sinister appearance. "It even includes evil twins, or did until you took care of one of them yesterday." His head turned, and he focused on lawyer Miller. "Can he be trusted?"

Jack nodded. "With my life. I've known him since I was a boy. He was my father's attorney before me."

The judge nodded at Jack's answer and continued, "As melodramatic as this story sounds, it is equally deadly. You must be ready. I believe Mr. Miller is right in his assessment. They will be coming after you. When they get wind of your ownership of a highly profitable gold mine, they will be even more motivated. Be careful, Jack." He laughed. "Listen to me telling you to be careful, even as you go after a gang of killers. Just stay on your guard."

Jack stood. "I've got to be on my way. Mr. Miller, you said you had a number of those pictures. Could I have another?"

Miller retrieved an additional picture from his briefcase along with a thick sheaf of papers.

Jack took the picture, looked at it for a second, and handed it to the judge. "This is a picture of the Slater family. You might let Buck know to be on the lookout for them. The tall one killed my uncle in a duel, and my remaining relatives have died over this past year."

The judge studied the picture. "Aren't duels illegal in Virginia?"

Miller spoke up. "Yes, Your Honor, they are, but they still happen."

Jack asked, "What are the names of the other two? In fact"—he handed his picture back to Miller—"would you write their names across each?"

The judge dipped his pen and handed it to the lawyer. Miller finished quickly. Jack had always admired the man's precise and legible writing. After allowing it to dry, he handed it back to Jack. "In order of age, you have Devin and Derek, the sons of your dad, and Dustin and Dante, the sons of Slater. Be careful, Jack, they are all devious and dangerous." He paused, realizing what he had said. "Sorry, it just came out like that."

Jack shrugged it off. "You feel certain they killed my family?"

Miller gave a slow but positive head nod. "I can't prove it, but from the evidence I've gathered, and the witnesses I've spoken to, they have been too close to each incident to not have been involved. And we know for certain that dueling is illegal in Virginia. I have witnesses of Blain's murder. He never had a chance."

"Alright, Mr. Miller, I have to be on my way. Thank you for making the trip out. With the knowledge you have of these killers, I think you should also be alert. They might try for you next."

Miller pulled a Pocket Colt from his briefcase. "I'm ready if they try, and they won't be the first."

Jack turned to the judge. "Anything else, Judge? Cole probably thinks I've been waylaid."

Judge Bell stood, picked up a stack of papers with his left hand, and extended his right. "Here's a few John Doe warrants. Hopefully you'll need them. Good luck to you, and stay safe."

Jack took the stack of warrants and shook the judge's hand. "Thanks, that's my plan."

Miller had dipped the judge's pen, and now handed it to Jack. "You need to sign this new agreement."

Jack took the pen and whipped his signature across the pages. When he was finished, he received a copy from the lawyer. He took it and headed for the door. Stepping outside, he looked for Buck, but the marshal was gone. He shrugged and headed down the stairs, taking three at a time. Dave Cole was waiting in front of the courthouse with the horses.

"Thought I might as well move my animals over here with yours. You ready?"

"Yep. I need to secure these papers, and we'll be on our way."

Moments later, he was swinging into the saddle and processing everything that Miller had told him. *I'm glad they're after me,* he thought. *It means I don't have to chase them.* He was about to cluck Pepper on his way when he felt a hand on his knee. He glanced down to see Mary Nelson, Grace's mother. Glancing at Dave, he said, "Why don't you start out, and I'll catch up in a few minutes."

Jack received a nod of acknowledgment, and the thick-necked young deputy marshal moved out.

Jack couldn't help but see Mary's eyes were red and swollen.

She leaned her weight on Jack's knee. "I'm so sorry. I should have seen that coming. Grace was heartbroken when she received word of her husband's death. It took her a long time to recover. In fact, she hadn't considered another man until you came along. She has discussed your occupation with me several times. It makes her very apprehensive. She is a basket of nerves every time you leave."

Jack patted her hand. "Mary, don't worry. I knew I couldn't

walk away from this business. I just forgot for a while. I understand if Grace needs to separate herself from me. She has to do what is good for her."

Mary looked up at the man who would have been her son-in-law. Tears welled up in her already red eyes. "Oh Jack, I think I love you nearly as much as Grace does. I would have loved you dearly as a son."

He leaned down and kissed her on the cheek. "You're a special woman, Mary. You did a fine job raising Grace, and you're really good with Billy and Elijah. They both love you."

She sniffed and wiped at the tears. "They are heartbroken."

Jack couldn't stand the thought of losing the boys. Both had clung to him desperately when he had said goodbye. Elijah had wanted to go with him, but he couldn't think about them right now. He had a job to do, and if he was going to do it, he needed to leave, and right now. "Yes. I've got to go, Mary."

She stepped back. "I'm so sorry, Jack. Go with God."

"You too."

He bumped Pepper and, with his heart heavy, rode west out of Fort Smith.

His mind was racing, trying to cover all that had happened over the last two days. He had been shot at, killed a man, gotten married, taken another job from Bell, had his marriage break up, and found out his family in Virginia were murdered, and the killers were after him. A low rueful laugh escaped his lips. "Pepper, no one can say we lead a boring life, can they?"

Thunder whinnied for an answer, and Jack searched ahead through the trees, spotting Dave with someone else.

Making a couple of turns and twists through the sugarberry, willow, and dogwood, the trail brought him to Dave and, surprisingly, Monty and Bronco. This had been a tough day, and his anger was simmering just beneath the surface, waiting for an excuse to explode. At the sight of his friends who had pushed so hard to go with him after the killers, he clouded over like a Texas thunderstorm. "What are you two doing here?"

Bronco, the most volatile of the two, grinned at Jack. "We're headin' to Texas, thought you and your young marshal here would like to ride along with us a ways. We don't mind, since this here is a free road." He paused, still grinning at Jack. "Ain't it?"

Rather than answer Bronco, Jack looked across the horses at the young deputy marshal. "Dave, your lessons might as well start now. There are times to step up and fight your battles knuckles and skulls, and there are other times when you are outgunned, and the smartest move is to make a strategic retreat. This is one of those times the latter choice should be exercised."

Bronco's grin got wider. "Sounds like I taught you just right."

Jack switched his gaze to Monty. "Did he ever teach anyone anything?"

Monty shook his head. "Not much. He usually left it to me."

Bronco cackled, enjoying the attention.

Jack removed his Stetson, wiped the sweatband with his hand, and leveled it back on his head. "Alright, boys. You've got me on this one, and I suspect this was Monty's idea. I can't control where or how fast or slow you ride, but I expect you to follow my lead and do what I say. Otherwise, I'll ride back into Fort Smith and get the army to throw you both into the stockade and keep you there until Dave and I return. Can you abide by that?"

Monty leaned back in his saddle. "Jack, I can speak for both of us. We'll do what you say. You won't have to worry about us."

Jack watched Monty for a moment and turned to Bronco.

"Put your mind at ease where I'm concerned, Marshal. When Monty gives his word for both of us, you can consider it done."

"Good, and you're headed for Texas? If we have to turn off west or north, you'll continue to Texas?"

Monty flexed his back. "You can trust us. You've got our word. So who are you after?"

"You fellas know as much as I do. You were at the wedding

reception. We have two deputy marshals hanged and sent back on their horses. We don't know who did it, or how many, or where they're located. We're going to start looking west of here where the army found their bodies. It hasn't rained, so we should be able to pick up some tracks."

Bronco spit. "Yeah, if them soldier boys ain't ridden all over the sign."

"That's true, but there's only one way to find out. I hate to bring up personal things, but it could affect all of you. There are at least three killers after me."

The only way anyone could tell Monty had heard what Jack said was the wrinkles around the edge of his eyes. They tensed, flattening slightly.

Bronco leaned forward in the saddle, his head thrust forward and his wide chin thrust toward Jack. "They got a death wish, boy?"

Jack couldn't help but grin at Bronco's assumption his pursuers would be killed if they caught up to him. "You must think pretty highly of my gun-handling skills."

"Shoot, no. I think mighty highly of mine. Monty ain't too shabby either. We're here to protect you."

Jack shook his head, knowing better than to be drawn into that conversation. "Anyway, I have property left to me in a will back in Virginia, and it seems I have some long-lost relatives who have, this past year, come to light who have managed to secure a portion of the property. The unfortunate fact is they want it all. Since their arrival, all of my aunts and uncles have died, some suspiciously. The man who tried to kill me yesterday was one of them. Seems he was a half brother."

At the revelation of the dead man being a half brother, Bronco uttered an oath.

Monty shook his head. "Not the kind of family you want to discover."

"No, but they are now after me, and I thought you should

know. This is what they looked like when they were younger." He pulled the picture from his inside vest pocket, unfolded it, and passed the photo around.

Bronco was the last to see it. He let out a long, low whistle while handing the picture back to Jack. "That is a mighty pretty woman. She after you, too?"

"No. She died about a year ago, consumption. Evidently this whole idea belongs to the tall, skinny kid, but they've all gone along with it."

Monty, brows wrinkled, had been thinking since seeing the picture. "Jack, it looks to me the two oldest might be twins."

Bronco nodded. "Yeah, I saw that, too."

"Yes, but only one of them is still alive. I killed the burly one yesterday."

Monty grinned. "Reckon we need to keep an eye out behind us as well as in front."

Jack folded the picture and shoved it back in his pocket. "Reckon so." He bumped Pepper. "Let's ride."

Jack led out, and Monty fell in at his side with Dave and Bronco behind them.

Bronco spit and wiped his mouth. "Tell me, Davey boy, how long you been in this marshal business?"

6

_____

After locating where the cavalry patrol had come upon the dead rangers' horses, it took little time for Bronco to find the tracks of the horses. Jack knew he was fortunate to have Monty and Bronco along with him, though their dwindling physical ability, as they were getting older, concerned him. Bronco wasn't just bragging when he said he was the best tracker in the bunch. Once he cleared the area the cavalry had obliterated, he went to work, and in a short time had located the animals' tracks, which had come from the southwest. The horses had been working their way back to Fort Smith and home, but they weren't in a hurry.

The tracks told the story. The animals meandered in the general direction of Fort Smith, grazing as they traveled, finding water, grazing some more, and continuing unerringly toward the town.

Bronco had led the way for over three hours, deciphering the trail. Daylight was fading when they rode onto a tiny creek. Jack pulled Pepper to a halt and looked around, then glanced at Monty, who nodded.

In a low voice, Jack said, "We'll camp here. We've got water and grass for the horses. It'll be a cold camp tonight so we don't alert any of that bunch. Let's get the horses taken care of before we do anything else. Keep them on lead ropes long enough to feed comfortably, but short enough to catch them up quick if we need to."

The other three nodded and stepped from the saddle. It took only a short time to take care of their tack and rub down the horses. Once they were secure, the four men situated their saddles and blankets in a circle. When they spoke, their voices carried only a short distance.

Monty edged over to Jack. "How do you want to set up the watch tonight?"

"You first, then Bronco, Dave, and me. Make it two-hour shifts."

"Sounds good, but if we sack out early, it could leave you with a long shift in the morning. You alright with that?"

"Early wake-ups never bother me, and when I wake up in the morning, I'm awake. There's no going back to sleep."

"Yep, I was like that."

"Do you want the fourth shift?"

Monty shook his head. "Nope, since we got the ranch, I can roll over and go right back to sleep. Must be my clear conscience."

Bronco stepped up. "Humph. Instead of sheep, you just count all the girls you let get away."

Monty was silent.

It took a moment for Bronco to realize what he had said. He then kicked a prickly pear pad, and the pad stuck to his boot. He started to bend over, stopped, and placed a sun-scorched, wind-dried hand on Jack's shoulder. "Son, I'm right sorry for that remark. You know me, shoot off my mouth before I think. I sure meant nothing by it."

Jack shoved his hat back and looked down at his penitent

friend. "Bronco, you and Monty have stuck by me in the worst situations. I would never think bad of you. Forget about it." He punched the old rancher lightly on the shoulder. "Now, I might get mad if your comment had something to do with my roping ability."

Bronco cheered up. "I forgot just how bad you are."

"I'm not that bad."

"Son, you're deadly with those guns, but never draw a rope in self-defense. You'll be in real trouble."

Jack released a low laugh. "I'll have to remember that."

Bronco walked off talking to himself. "Never draw a rope, heh, heh, heh. That was pretty good."

Monty looked up at his big friend. "You know he meant nothing by it."

Jack let a small grin lift the corners of his mouth. "Monty, I know Bronco. He'd never say anything to hurt a friend. He just trips sometimes between brain and mouth. I'm fine."

Jack could see the concern in Monty's eyes. "Thanks, now let's get this camp finished and hit the sack."

THEY BURNED a day of slow trailing, following the two horses' tracks. On the morning of the third day, Bronco signaled a stop. He swung off his horse and waved Jack forward. After dismounting, The lawman eased forward to Bronco's position and spoke softly. "What's up?"

"We're about to ride into a clearing. I recognize this place. There's a big ole oak in the middle of it, and these tracks look like they're taking us right there. I suspect that was where the deed was done. I'd recommend all of us moving up to the edge, and so no tracks get stomped on, I'll ease out there and look around. What do you think, Marshal?"

"You say the clearing is right up ahead."

"Yessiree, that's exactly what I'm saying."

"Good, I like your idea, but I'm making one change."

Bronco's forehead wrinkled with a frown. "What's the change?"

"I go into the clearing instead of you. If they have anyone waiting to shoot us, I want him shooting at a lawman, not a civilian."

Bronco's crusty voice took on a whine. "Now listen here, Jack, boy, if you get shot, this whole outfit of ranchers and lawmen gets turned around and pointed back to Fort Smith. If I get shot, you just fix me up, and we keep going. That's simple."

Jack gave his friend the look that had frozen killers in their tracks. "Bronco, you never quit, do you?"

Bronco's face broke out in a wide grin. "Boy, the day I quit is the day you can wrap me in linen and drop me in a deep hole."

"Go tell Monty and Dave what we're doing. I'll take over here. We might as well close up. You three cover me when I ride in. Stay hidden. I don't want him to suspect anything. If he takes a shot at me, I'll come out of the saddle like I'm hit hard. Maybe it'll sucker him up. Don't you fall for it. I want him alive."

Bronco gave a sharp nod. "Your fall may not be fake if that feller is a good shot."

"Don't borrow trouble. Let's go."

Bronco started to say something else, thought better of it, and swung into the saddle. Doing so elicited an involuntary groan. It was stifled as soon as it left his mouth, but Jack heard it. "Need a hand?"

Bronco jerked his horse around. "No, dang you. I don't need no hand, and I never asked for one."

Jack watched his friend ride away. He chuckled. Usually Bronco was the one needling everyone in range of his mouth, but he had just received one for himself, and he obviously didn't take it as well as he dished it out. His relaxed slouch was gone, and he sat stiff and erect in the saddle. Watching his friend ride away, the grin disappeared as he chastised himself. *That wasn't called for,* he thought. *He's the jokester, not you. He's getting older, and there'll come a time when he'll have to give up gallivanting around, and I'm sure it's on his mind. Knowing Bronco, he'll fight it every inch of the way.* He waited as his friend explained to the others, and they eased their horses forward, at the same time pulling their rifles from the scabbards. He waved, stepped into the saddle, and started Thunder toward the clearing.

Reaching the edge, he stopped Thunder. Only the horse's big gray head extended beyond the trees. He searched the edge of the clearing for anything, a glint, a movement, the smooth side of a horse, or any difference in the wall of trees and brush.

A tall bush thrust above the others almost directly across from where they were entering the clearing. Jack thought he caught movement next to it, but after watching for several minutes, he could make out nothing. He was about to move Thunder forward when a blue jay dove to light in the bush. The bird had slowed and was about to grasp a bush when it leaped skyward and released a raucous screech. It flew almost straight up, turned, and disappeared into the trees. *Yep,* Jack thought, *that's where you are. Of course, there could be more than one.*

Jack clucked softly, and Thunder pushed through the brush and into the clearing. He kept the big oak's trunk between him and the bush, only allowing a narrow edge of vision past the thick trunk. Riding slowly forward, his head gradually rotated, examining every possible hiding place among brush and trees, but he saw nothing else.

Finally, as he was nearing the trunk, a voice yelled, "Take him, Wylie. I ain't got a shot."

Jack forced himself to wait a fraction of a second, then hurled himself from Thunder, and, at the same time, threw his arms wide, releasing his rifle and allowing it to fly end over end through the air. Instantly, a rifle fired. Jack had no idea where the blast came from or how close it was. His two hundred pounds slammed into the ground, and he let himself bounce and his limbs flail. Before they stopped, his right hand found, under his unbuttoned vest flap, the .44-caliber Smith & Wesson he had shoved behind his waistband.

It was all he could do to keep from gasping for air. The collision with the ground had slammed the wind from his lungs, and they screamed for air. *Slowly,* he told himself, *small breaths, don't let them see your chest moving.* He felt like he was dying for a deep breath, but gradually managed to suck in small breaths, enough to calm his maddening demand for air.

"Whoopee! Wylie, you drilled that no-good lawman right through his breadbasket. That's what I call mighty good shooting."

Jack had fallen where the big oak's trunk completely blocked the bush the blue jay had spooked from. He knew there was a guy there, but right now, he was more worried about this Wylie, who had taken the shot. His mind was going over possibilities while, with eyes slitted, he tried to pick up any movement. *This reminds me of being on the couch the other day. I'm getting a lot of shooting practice from the horizontal position.* He waited.

"Did you see the way he come out of that saddle, Gordo? Why, I ain't never seen a body hit so hard."

There was no answer from Gordo.

The grass crunched behind him. He had no chance. There was no way he could turn his body and fire from this position before Wylie the bushwhacker had put a piece of lead into him. His mind went to Grace and her comment about him being brought home over a saddle. *This might be the day, but it won't be for lack of trying,* he thought. *I'll let Wylie get a little closer, and if one of the boys hasn't fired, I'll go for it.*

"Gordo, I asked you if you seen the way that lawman come

flying out of the saddle. Why, he threw his rifle so hard it stuck in the ground like an arrow. We're gonna have to do a pile of cleaning to make that shooter work again. I think I ought to get it, don't you?"

Silence continued to greet Wylie. His voice sounded less confident. "Gordo, are you funning me?"

Bronco's voice drifted softly across the clearing, a touch of humor in it. "No, old son, I'd say my partner has Gordo all roped and hogtied. Now, if you don't want me to blow a hole in you big enough to drive a herd of cattle through, you might ease down on that hammer and lay that Winchester on the ground."

Jack didn't want to move until he knew he could do so without getting shot. He lay listening.

Wylie's voice was shaky. "Mister, who might you be?"

Bronco, still speaking softly, replied, "I might be the feller who's holding this ten-gauge scattergun aimed at the center of your belly, Wylie. That's who I might be. Are you gonna lay that rifle down and then drop that hand-tooled holster, or am I going to have to blow backbone, blood, and guts all over that fine rig?"

Jack could hear movement. Then he heard a holster hit the ground.

"Alright, Jack," Bronco called, "if you didn't break your neck leaping off your horse, you can get up now."

Jack sat up and turned around to see Wylie. The bushwhacker's eyes were wide and his mouth open, staring at him. He brushed the imbedded grass from his legs and stood, drawing his Smith at the same time.

Wylie finally spoke. "You ain't dead?"

Jack shook his head, and Bronco and Dave walked out from the edge of the trees. "No, Wylie, I'm not. I do want to thank you for not shooting a second earlier, though. You made everything work out perfectly."

Bronco laughed as he pointed at Wylie's gunbelt and rifle. Dave stepped forward and retrieved them. "I'm telling you, Jack, that there was acting of the first order. You ought to be on stage in New York City. Yessiree, you were fine entertainment."

Jack could feel his body stiffening. Over the next few days, he would pay for that fall. He holstered his revolver, placed both hands on his hips, and bent backward as far as he could go. Several pops sounded from his spine. He felt better. Straightening, he turned to Bronco. "I'm glad I could entertain you. Maybe I should charge admission."

Bronco couldn't contain himself. He broke out in laughter. Dave had a wide grin on his face.

When Bronco saw it, he said, "I hope you were watching, boy. That there is real marshal work. I hope you learn how to make such a leap."

Dave managed to say, "Yes, sir," through his ear-to-ear grin.

Jack walked to his rifle and pulled it from the ground. It had rotated, end over end, several times before it speared the soft ground and sank to the front of the lever. He pulled it out and watched Gordo ride into the clearing, followed by Monty and his Winchester. "I guess Monty slipped around while I had their attention?"

"He did," Bronco said, "and it don't appear he's gotten too old to corral himself a young buck."

Jack felt the needle from Bronco, but ignored it.

Blood ran down one side of the approaching Gordo's face.

"Hold up there," Monty said to the outlaw. Gordo pulled his horse to a stop. Monty leaned forward, rested one hand on his saddle horn, and his rifle across that hand, the muzzle on Gordo. "Looks like everything worked out well, this time. Jack, I've never seen such a fool thing in my life. You could have broken your neck."

Jack nodded. "I'll have to admit, it wasn't the finest idea I've ever had, but it did work."

Monty wasn't finished with his friend. "If he'd been a split second faster, you would've been lying right there with a hole through you, and that would've fulfilled your sweet wife's prophecy. You've got to stop acting like you're twenty years old." He turned to Dave. "No offense meant, Dave. I'm just making a point."

"No, sir, Mr. Huff, no offense taken. Anyway, I'm not twenty."

Bronco shot a surprised look at Dave. "How old are you, boy?"

Dave grinned. "Nineteen."

Monty shook his head.

Bronco whipped his hat off and beat the dust from his chaps. "Heaven help us."

Jack pulled two sets of handcuffs from his saddlebags. He tossed one set to Dave and took the other. Since he was closest to Wylie, he stepped toward him. The prisoner extended his hands, and Jack shook his head. "Turn around."

The man looked up at Jack. "You're not gonna handcuff us behind our backs, are you? We can't ride like that. How do we control our horses?"

Jack said nothing and buckled the irons on Wylie. Once they were on, he asked, "Where's your horse?" Jack could see Wylie's confidence had grown, and waited.

Wylie grinned. "I don't think I remember."

May had been a difficult month for Jack, what with his half brother's attempt to kill him and then his having to kill his assailant, and Grace's breakdown, plus everything else that had happened. He almost felt like thanking Wylie the bushwhacker. He hit the man with a short right. It landed on the bushwhacker's temple. He made a perfect quarter turn, collapsed to the ground, and lay still.

Gordo's eyes had grown large. He stared at Jack. "You killed him."

"Maybe. Now, where's his horse?"

Gordo couldn't tell Jack fast enough. "See that sweetgum tree sticking above the brush. His horse and gear are right over there."

Jack glared at the bushwhacker. "You'd best not be lying to me, Gordo."

"I ain't lying to you, Marshal. I swear on my mother's grave. The sweetgum, that's where it is."

"There's no one else around?"

"No, Marshal, not a soul. We are all by our lonesome. The rest of the boys headed over to Texas for a spell. Down around Sherman. They figured the two of us could take care of everything until they got back."

Bronco piped up. "They figured wrong, didn't they, Gordo?"

"Yes, sir, they sure did. They surely figured wrong, but we weren't really aimin' to hurt anyone. We was just supposed to put a scare into whomsoever come along. That's all we was supposed to do."

His watery blue eyes switched back and forth between Bronco and Jack.

Jack looked to Dave. "Get Wylie's gear and bring it back here. If he's not awake when you get back, tie him on his horse."

Wylie began moaning.

Jack turned his hard gray eyes on Gordo. The killer squirmed and looked away. "Look at me, Gordo."

Slowly, the man's eyes shifted back to Jack. "Gordo, what's your last name?"

Without hesitation, Gordo spit out, "Smith."

Jack shook his head slowly, looked down, raised his head, and pinned Gordo with a hard but sad gaze. "That's the second lie you've told me today, Gordo. Would you like to join your friend in a little snooze?"

The man's voice was trembling. "No, Marshal, I sure wouldn't. A man hit that hard might never recover from having his brain slammed like that. I swear my name is Sm—"

Jack held his index finger to his lips. "I'm going to give you one more chance, Gordo. If the next words out of your mouth are lies, you are joining Wylie. Do you understand me?"

"I do. Yes, sir. I surely do. My name is Gordon Taylor. There might be paper out on me. You can ask me anything. I'll tell you."

"Good, Gordon Taylor, I appreciate your cooperation." Jack moved to the outlaw's side. "Here's the question. Were you and Wylie ordered to hang any marshals who came along? This is a simple question, Gordo, yes or no."

The outlaw licked his lips. Jack could see the fear in his eyes. His bottom lip was trembling. Jack reached up and grasped the man's vest and dragged him from the saddle.

"Don't hit me, Marshal. Please don't hit me. Yes, we were ordered to hang any marshal who came along. We had to do it, though. Morgan would kill us if we didn't. I'm not kidding. He would. Dead."

"Who's Morgan? What's his first name?"

"Tate, Marshal. It's Tate Morgan. He's a bad one. I saw him kill a farmer just because he didn't like the rows that young feller was plowing. Said they weren't straight."

"Is that his full name?"

"All the name I know, I swear."

Jack looked down at Wylie. "Dave, get him on his feet. He's been faking it for the past ten minutes."

Dave grabbed the man by his upper arm and yanked him to his feet.

"Ow. That hurt." Wylie rubbed the left side of his head where Jack hit him. "You could've killed me."

Jack said nothing. He had the two killers in front of him. When he was sure Wylie was alert, he untied his bandanna and yanked it off. They both focused on Jack's rope-burned neck where he had been hanged by another gang of killers. Their eyes grew large. Jack stepped closer. "Take a good look. Another bunch, just like yours, did to me what you did to our deputy marshals. I was more fortunate than them. Do you think I would have any qualms in stringing you up to this oak just like you did those men, who had wives and children?"

Gordo was the first to answer. "No, Marshal, I don't think you'd mind doing it at all. In fact, you just might get a little pleasure out of it."

Jack smiled. "You finally made an honest statement. Keep it up, because I have several more questions for you fellas. Dave is going to keep track of who has the most honest answers. I may not hang that man."

7

The interrogation didn't last long. The two bushwhackers weren't the type of hardcore bad man as they had described Tate Morgan. They wanted to think of themselves in the same way, but had a long way to slide to qualify. They just weren't that tough, and the threats from Jack were enough to prompt them to spill their guts.

When he had finished, Jack dusted his hands off. With mixed feelings, he had struck neither of the two killers again. "Dave, why don't you load these two on their horses, and we'll head down to Sherman. We're not far, and we can unload these two with the sheriff or town marshal. The wagon from Fort Smith will pick them up, and they'll be out of our hands."

Dave dragged Wylie to his horse and lifted him high enough so the outlaw could get his foot in the stirrup, and then propelled him the rest of the way. Since Wylie had his hands cuffed behind him, he couldn't grasp the reins and had to depend solely on his legs to keep from falling from his horse. He would have failed if Dave hadn't held on to him until he settled in the saddle. He moved to Gordo and did the same thing with him, but Gordo stabilized instantly.

Jack gave Dave a look and received a nod from him. Gordo would stand watching. He might be able to break away without control of the reins. They didn't need the added distraction of having to chase him down.

Jack mounted Thunder. This had been an easy day for the big gray, and there was only a couple of hours of daylight remaining. He'd let Pepper have a full day of rest without having to carry his two hundred pounds plus gear. He glanced back at Stonewall. The mule and Smokey, his grulla he had left to rest and recuperate in Fort Smith, had been his companions since before Laredo, almost seven years, and neither showed any signs of slowing. Jack would usually switch between the horses on hard days, but Stonewall had his load day in and day out. The mule never complained, even in the mountains. He was always ready, as he was this time. He'd give them all cookies tonight, maybe two.

Monty pulled up beside him. "Good thing you caught these two. That'll slim down the odds a mite. According to them, if they were telling the truth, you're still up against six more men, and this Tate Morgan sounds like a real wall-eyed steer."

"Yep. I like slimming them down, and I like not having to haul these turkeys back to Fort Smith. I've never had the opportunity to use this wagon pickup system, since I had no jails to leave them in, but I'm looking forward to it. With the information we've picked up, Dave and I should be able to scoop up Morgan and his gang with no problem."

Monty was quiet, and for a change so was Bronco. All that could be heard was the occasional clop-clop of the horses when they rode onto harder ground. Finally he spoke again. "You know, we can be a big help to you. Four of us could make a real difference catching these killers."

Jack remained quiet. A covey of about twenty bobwhite quail blew up alongside the trail, startling the horses, but only for a second. The little brown bombs' wings whirred for a short distance and then set as they glided toward a large patch of broomweeds. Jack watched them sail toward the thick yellow patch. Finally their wings whirred again to allow them to settle among the weeds. "Pretty birds."

"Yeah, I like sitting on the ranch house porch, listening to them in the morning and evenings, especially when the coveys get broken up and they're trying to get back together before it's time to roost. It's mighty peaceful." Monty turned in the saddle to look at his younger friend. "What are you planning to do when you get this bunch caught and back to Fort Smith?"

Jack shook his head. "I don't know. I've always been a lucky kind of guy, but with Grace, I think I've really messed that up bad. I figure when I get back, the marriage will be annulled, and I'll be on my own again. I really thought I had something this time." He was silent for a minute. "I'm sure going to miss those boys."

Monty waited a respectful time. "Back to my original question. What are your plans after this mission?"

Jack hadn't talked about his dreams with anyone in a long time. Even when talking with Grace, he hadn't completely opened up, but Monty was a good friend. He was a lot like Sully in Cherry Creek, so he began to share his plans.

"I think I'd like to go back to Cherry Creek. Six years ago, there was still plenty of land and cattle. I have good friends there, and I think I could settle down. You know, Monty, like I said earlier, I have always been lucky. I get in tight situations, and I end up coming out on top. Oh, I know that can't last forever. I'm getting older, and I'll be slowing down, maybe I'm slowing already, but if I retire, it doesn't matter."

Monty stared at his younger friend. "You know you already own a ranch. The Flying J is as much yours as it's mine or Bronco's. We only split it the way we did to satisfy you. We'd be real happy if you moseyed on down and joined us. That's what Bronco and I always planned."

Jack shook his head. "That place is yours. You two put your own blood and sweat into it. All I put in was a little money."

Monty glanced ahead and then back at Jack. "Boy, we ain't got a single heir, no family atall. We always planned for you to have the ranch. In fact, we was tickled pink when we heard about you marrying that widow with two boys. There's nothing better for a ranch than havin' boys on it, unless it's girls. If you could make up with that fine woman and convince her this business was behind you, you and her still have time to make a few kids. That old ranch would perk up, like a pasture after a good rain, if we could hear the laughter of boys and girls."

Jack said nothing.

"Either way, Jack. You've got a place ready for you. We didn't drive a herd to Kansas this year because the word's out that Fort Worth is getting a stockyard and train. You know what that means? No more long drives. We can get them animals mostly fattened on our range and then put the finishing touches on them during the drive to Fort Worth. We'll have close to five thousand head ready to move next year. With such a short distance, we can make two drives."

Jack could feel Monty's excitement and sincerity. The three of them were good friends. Any doubts of being welcome disappeared. "That's mighty nice. I don't know about more kids. The years are stacking up on me, but I thank you. You've given me something to think about, but there's still my attraction to the law. You were the one who pointed out that I was cut out for what I'm doing right now, and it's been true. I've never been able to turn down a request for help."

Monty shook his head. "Jack, this is the last I'll say about that. A man can be good at something and still give it up at the right time for the right thing. These folks who keep asking you to chase one more crook can find someone else, like that Davey boy back there. Train him up right, and you'll have a fine lawman.

He's like you, big enough to swat most without ever having to draw a gun."

Monty scanned the trail ahead before continuing, "Any man is replaceable. It'll be like taking your hand out of a bucket of water. When the ripples die down, no one can tell it was ever there. Family's keep you alive in their hearts and minds long after you're dead and gone. Don't forget that. You go back and make that green-eyed beauty believe you believe it, and have a real life at the Flying J ranch. You'll make a couple of old men and two young fellers mighty happy, and you won't regret it."

Jack was silent for quite a while. The two men rode the trail as they'd done before, feeling the bond that can only build from the knowledge and trust the man next to you won't turn and run when the bullets start flying. Finally Jack spoke. "I'll tell you, Monty. It sounds good to me. I had thought of going to Cherry Creek, but I think the boys will find the Flying J a most welcoming place, though they might drive you two crazy."

From behind them, Bronco spoke up. "You come on down to the Flying J. Those boys'll need someone to teach 'em how to rope a steer, and we all know that ain't you."

Jack grinned, shook his head, and kept on riding.

STANDING on the boardwalk in front of the sheriff's office, Jack watched his two friends ride south until they crossed Choctaw Creek and disappeared behind the willows. Watching them ride out of Sherman, he was deep in thought about what he and Monty had discussed on the trail. *Is it really time for me to hang up this badge? I've tried so many times before. In fact, I never really wanted it in the first place, but people have always needed help, maybe now it's time for me to help Grace and Mary and the boys.*

Dave, standing next to him and looking like a shorter version of himself, shoved his hat to the back of his head. "What now, Marshal?"

Jack, jerked from his thoughts, pulled out his pocket watch, popped it open, checked the time, and slipped it back into his pocket. "What say we get the horses, pick up our supplies, and head out? I'm thinking Tate Morgan and his bunch are feeling pretty confident right now."

The two lawmen turned and headed up the boardwalk. Jack's eyes searched both sides of the street as they walked. He had little desire to be ambushed in Sherman, or anywhere else. Ahead, they would be passing the Hole in the Wall saloon. Jack thought, *Aptly named. I may have seen worse, but I sure don't remember when.* Out of habit, Jack checked the leather loops on his holsters, which secured both handguns, to ensure they hadn't accidentally slipped over the Smith & Wessons' hammers. They were clear.

Dave followed his boss's example.

The two lawmen had just stepped back up onto the boardwalk, after crossing the alley, when a younger man rolled backwards through the swinging doors of the saloon. The man, dressed like a farmer, wore a gun high on his right hip. He tumbled across the boardwalk, down the steps, and sprawled in the street. He lay there for a second, shook his head, then staggering slightly, rose to his feet, ripped the beat-up hat from his head, and dusted himself off. Satisfied, he pulled the hat tight on his head and, with head down, started toward the Hole in the Wall's still swinging doors.

Reaching the steps, one of his beat-up boots caught on the bottom step, and he fell, catching himself with both palms against the boardwalk. He looked up just in time to receive the sole of a boot, belonging to a slick-looking gent, in his face.

It was too late for Jack to stop the gambler's kick. All he could do was watch the boot slam into the farmer's head. The blow knocked him back into the street again, to lay sprawled in the dirt, but only for a moment. He lifted his head, shook it, throwing blood from his torn cheek in both directions. The kick hadn't affected his eyes. He saw the gambler and, with blood streaming from his cheek, struggled to his feet. The gambler watched, lip curled in disdain, waiting until the farmer made it to his feet, then his hand shot to his tied-down sixgun on his right hip.

Jack, who was no more than fifteen feet away, said, "I wouldn't do that if I were you, fella."

The gambler spun, eyes wild with anger, to face Jack, his hand hovering over his sixgun. Dave took three steps forward and unleashed his right fist into the man's temple while simultaneously yanking the Colt from its holster. "The marshal told you not to do that."

The gambler was struck with such force he was propelled sideways, off the boardwalk, across the steps, and into the dusty, manure-strewn street where, only moments before, the farmer had lain. Stunned, he stared first at Jack's badge and then at Dave. Regaining his senses, he struggled to his feet and slowly straightened.

The farmer waited patiently while the no-longer-slick-looking gambler rose to his feet. Then, obviously a quick-thinking young fella, he slammed his right fist into the same spot Dave's had struck. It sounded similar to the dull thunk of an axe striking a green tree trunk. This time, the gambler collapsed to the street like a worn-out rope and stayed down.

The young farmer watched a wagon pass, its wheels barely missing the gambler's head. He reached down, grabbed the man by the back of his shirt, and dragged him clear of the heavy wagon and horse traffic, dropping him on the steps to the saloon.

"What the blazes is going on here?"

At the sound of the voice behind him, Dave spun, the sun glinting off his marshal's badge.

Jack, immediately recognizing the man when he stepped out of the saloon, said, "Hello, Korkeran, it's been a while since the Gilded Lily."

Jack wasn't a man who was easily missed, but Korkeran had been concentrating on the farmer, his gambler, and Dave's back. He had no idea Jack Sage was anywhere near. At Jack's question, Korkeran's head jerked around in surprise, wrinkles coursing across his forehead, while dark eyebrows drew together. He examined Jack and his badge. His face immediately relaxed, but as much as he tried to hide his feelings, Jack saw the malignant hate in those green eyes.

Interesting, Jack thought, *it feels just like the day I threw him out of Cherry Creek.*

"If it isn't Jack Sage, and still wearing a badge." A glint of evil humor touched the corners of his pale green eyes. "Is there a lawman convention in town I don't know about?"

Jack didn't smile. "What's going on here, Korkeran?"

For only a moment anger flashed across the man's face but was instantly replaced by his mask. He nodded his head toward the farmer. "That drunk young fella is Levi Carter. He's a trouble-maker I've warned against fighting, but he refuses to listen."

"That's a lie," Carter shouted. "Beck was cheating."

Jack pointed a finger at Carter, never taking his eyes from Korkeran. "What were you playing?"

"Roulette, Marshal. I don't win much, but I like that spinning wheel." Cooper's voice rose. "I know they're cheating me, Marshal, and I ain't the only one."

Memories of the last time he had dealt with Korkeran flooded Jack's mind. *Be careful,* he thought. *This guy is a snake and just as fast.* Before Korkeran could make a move, Jack stepped forward and grabbed his right arm at the wrist. He felt the hideout gun through the sleeve of the silk shirt and twisted, lifting Korkeran's arm high. With his right hand he ripped the loose cuff back, exposing what was strapped underneath.

Jack was aware a crowd was gathering around them. The people were angry, and, at the sight of the hideout gun, an audible gasp rushed from the mob.

He lifted the arm higher so everyone could see the gadget attached to the gambler's arm. "What's this for, Korkeran?"

The pale eyes of the man flared with hate. "Self-defense, Marshal, for when my life's on the line, and you're hurting my arm." His voice was low and cold like winter seeping into an unheated cabin.

Jack released Korkeran's arm. "What about the Colt on your hip? Isn't that enough insurance?"

Korkeran's voice rose so the crowd could hear. "Sometimes no, Marshal Sage. There are times when this is all that stands between me and dirt in my face."

Jack wasn't going to argue the point in front of an early morning crowd. "It's not illegal, but it is a mighty lowdown tool for self-defense. You're not under arrest, but I want to see that roulette wheel. You know how I feel about cheating folks out of their hard-earned income."

Someone in the crowd yelled, "Yeah, I wanta see that wheel, too."

Jack watched Korkeran's face. He could almost see the gambler remembering Jack taking an axe to his equipment and running him out of town. He grasped the owner's bicep and shoved him through the swinging saloon doors while at the same time glancing at Dave.

The deputy had moved to the side and was following Jack, pushing the still woozy Beck ahead. Cooper had moved up alongside Jack.

A man of average height and build pushed past Dave and moved quickly toward Jack. Dave's hand dropped to his revolver when the man called, "Marshal."

Jack paused and looked back as the man stepped forward and extended his hand.

"Morning, Marshal. I'm Tom McAllister, town marshal of Sherman."

Jack took the lawman's hand. "Marshal. As you can see, I'm a little busy. What can I do for you?"

McAllister cleared his throat. "Well, this is kind of an awkward subject, but I owe it to my constituents to bring it up. You see, this is inside the city limits and, therefore, my jurisdiction. The sheriff and I pretty much have an agreement. He looks after the county, and I look after the town."

8

J ack said nothing.

Uneasy, Marshal McAllister continued, "And, well, you're a U.S. Marshal, but you work directly for Judge Bell out of Fort Smith. That means you only cover the Indian Territory, what with you working for Judge Bell and all, since that's the area he's over. However, you're in Texas now, specifically, Sherman, Texas, where I have jurisdiction and you do not." McAllister paused to allow Jack to respond.

The crowd, now silent, had pushed in behind them and was listening attentively.

Jack's hard gray eyes were locked on the much smaller marshal, and he still said nothing.

McAllister cleared his throat and continued, "What I'm saying, Marshal, you can't be in here inspecting equipment because you have no jurisdiction." The man stretched to his full height. "I am telling you to cease and desist."

The corners of Jack's mouth lifted in a humorless smile. "Finally. Marshal McAllister, are you also the city attorney?"

"Why, uh . . . no, I'm not. That would be Mr. . . . ." He stopped when he heard laughter running through the crowd, and his face reddened.

Jack reached into his inside vest pocket and withdrew the letter of authority from the president and handed it to McAllister. The man read it. His eyes widened, and he carefully refolded the letter, returning it to Jack.

"You see, Marshal McAllister, I don't work for Judge Bell, though I see how it could seem so. I work for President Grant, and, as such, I have full authority to enforce the law, both local and national, wherever and whenever I find it necessary. But while we're on this subject, let me clear up one thing for you. Though Judge Bell's marshals are sworn in by him, they are still U.S. Marshals and have the same rights as I have. Now, does that satisfy the jurisdictional requirements you are so concerned about?"

Jack caught McAllister's quick glance to Korkeran. If there was anything he hated worse than cheats, it was crooked lawmen. "Marshal McAllister." His voice was so hard and sudden McAllister jumped.

"Yes . . . yes, Marshal Sage. I understand completely, thank you. Sorry to interfere."

Disgusted, Jack looked at Korkeran and caught him, eyes almost bugging out in his glare at McAllister. Realizing that Jack had turned toward him, his mask fell into place, and though concern could still be read from the faintly wrinkled forehead and tight lips, the false smile returned. "Check anything, Marshal. You'll see I run an honest place."

"Liar," Cooper lashed out. "Check the roulette wheel, Marshal. I know it's rigged."

Korkeran gave Cooper a look that would freeze a rattlesnake, but remained calm and smooth. "Check till you're satisfied, Marshal. You'll just be proving what I've already told you. I run honest games."

Reaching the roulette table, Jack ambled around it, letting his right hand drift along the edge of the table. *Nothing,* he thought. *Korkeran's too confident. If he has a trigger or wire, it's not going to be readily evident. I almost missed the trigger on his roulette wheel in the Gilded Lilly. This one will be ten times more difficult to find.*

The town marshal was feeding off Korkeran's confidence. "I'm afraid you'll be owing Mr. Korkeran an apology when you're through checking, Marshal. He runs an honest game, and I believe you will be finding that out for yourself."

Jack said nothing, concentrating on examining the table. He knelt at a corner and sighted along both edges, then did the same at each of the three remaining corners. All sides were straight, with no protrusions. He rose, picked up the ball, and tossed it in the air several times, catching it each time. The weight felt right. Then he shot the ball around the track. It bounced at several places, which he followed up by checking. Nothing. The ball didn't seem to be a dead ball or weighted.

Finally, he moved behind the table to the croupier's position. He glanced up to see the Hole in the Wall saloon was packed, with citizens pressed against the walls and the bar, but giving him plenty of room to check the table. Jack saw several ladies present, obviously uneasy in the saloon, but grasping the opportunity to see inside, and too curious to leave.

Korkeran stepped boldly to Jack's side. "See, Marshal, just like I told you. Nothing but an honest game here."

Jack ignored the saloon owner and spun the wheel. It was heavy and smooth. Whoever had built the wheel was a crafts-man. His hand holding the ball whipped around, releasing the ball in the opposite direction of the wheel's rotation.

Korkeran, still close to Jack, and obviously feeling confident to the point of being cocky, said, "Not bad. You ever lose your marshal job, look me up. Looks like you'll make a fine croupier."

Jack said nothing, watching the ball.

It raced around the outer edge of the roulette wheel, and Jack searched for anything, a button or something that might appear as a splinter, something that protruded from the edge or around the table. He found nothing. Momentum decreased, the ball drifted slowly from the rim and arced toward the slots, finally bouncing and coming to rest in the black slot number twenty-two. He'd found nothing. The ball fell naturally.

A sigh of disappointment rose from the crowd. Everyone wanted him to be successful, for Korkeran had few friends.

Korkeran couldn't resist. "I told you, Marshal. I run honest games in the Hole in the Wall. You should trust me."

"Nothing would make me happier, Korkeran, than to find you've gone straight, but I don't see that happening." He spun the wheel again while at the same time launching the ball. His mind drifted as the ball circled. *Maybe I'm wrong about this man. Maybe he has gone straight, and this fella Cooper is just a sore loser.*

Jack's leg was bothering him. It had been hurting since their second day out from Fort Smith. He didn't look forward to the upcoming ride. In fact, the thought of hanging up his badge brought a smile to his lips. *I'll have to get four rockers for the ranch, and Grace can join the three of us on the porch. We'll watch the younger fellas work, and talk about our pains.* He chuckled at the thought, realizing he'd forgotten Grace's mother, Mary. He'd have to make it five.

Continuing his search for something, anything, he caught Korkeran's quizzical look and chuckled to himself again. It was good for Korkeran to worry. A shooting pain moved from his thigh to his foot. The ball dropped, and this time, it landed on red twenty-five.

Exasperated, Jack thought, *Everything looks to be on the up and up.* He took his weight off his bum leg and braced it against the leg of the roulette table.

It moved.

At least he thought it moved. He shifted his leg away from the table's leg and gently eased it back. He felt it. It definitely moved. Not much. in fact, if he had just bumped it, he would have never noticed, but by applying the pressure from his leg, he could feel the movement. There was no audible click, just a short movement of the leg.

Jack grasped the edge of the table and lifted. The roulette table was heavy, but his thick shoulders and biceps easily lifted it from the floor far enough to see the print of the leg in the sawdust. It was oval, not round. The leg movement had kept the sawdust pushed out of its path. He lowered the table and watched the leg touch down at one edge of the oval. *I should have seen the space in the sawdust on one side of the leg,* he thought. *It's a dead giveaway for movement.*

He picked up the ball, spun the big wheel again, and sent the ball racing along in the opposite direction. After a full round, he pressed against the table leg. The ball shot off the rim and slammed into the cups, bouncing until it came to rest on red ten. He picked up the ball, repeating the process, except this time he let it pass the red ten before he bumped the leg. The ball acted exactly the same way, coming to a stop on black seventeen.

The crowd had been silently watching Jack's efforts. Those who were gamblers had seen the ball leap unnaturally from the rim at too high a speed. They were watching Jack with rapt attention. He glanced at Korkeran, who had edged toward the back door, then at Dave, thought better of it, and turned to the Hole in the Wall owner, who was no longer trying to hide his hate for Jack. "Hold up, Korkeran. Forget what I said in Cherry Creek. All I'm going to do is destroy this table and take you to jail. There's no need for guns. We've got too many innocent people in here, someone will get shot, then you could end up at the end of a noose."

Roman Korkeran still allowed the public to see only his mask. His eyes were the tells. They flashed with anger. It was difficult to tell what color they were because they were pulled so tightly into slits. "Sage, I don't know how you found that leg. I had that table made especially for someone like you. It's been examined by professionals who were unable to find the key, and then you come along. This is the second time you've ruined me. There won't be a third."

Dave called, "Marshal, I've got him covered. If he goes for a gun, he's a goner."

Jack shook his head. "Don't shoot, Dave. There's too many folks in here. Holster your weapon."

Korkeran smiled at the deputy. "That's right, Dave, holster your weapon. Your marshal doesn't want any innocent people hurt, do you, Marshal?"

Jack could feel the calm taking over that always showed up in a gunfight or battle. He had always been blessed with this calm, a peace. "Listen to me, Korkeran. You don't want to make any wrong moves here. You heard what I said, you're going to probably spend a few days in jail. After you settle your debts to folks like Mr. Cooper, you'll probably be on your way, so just relax."

Korkeran thought for a moment before he spoke. "Like I told you, Sage, this is the second time you've ruined me, this time right after I got started again. It took me a long time to make enough money to buy this place, and then you come along. Why, I even went along with what you wanted in Arkansas and didn't shoot up the horse trader's place, and this is what I get for my efforts. Well, I want something for it this time. I want you to meet me in the street. I want satisfaction. You owe me that. I'll even take off this hideout rig. Just you and me."

Jack's mind raced with thoughts. *If we shoot it out in here, people will definitely get hurt, probably some killed, and when he recognized me in Arkansas, he didn't pursue it. I do owe him.* "Think about it, Roman. You don't want to go up against me. I'll kill you."

Korkeran was shaking his head. "No, Marshal, you won't. You're getting old. Age slows the hands and eyes. I've got the edge now. I'm younger than you. Why, I'm in my prime. This will be our last meeting. I'll see to it."

Jack smiled. It always unnerved his opponent, but Jack felt

like smiling. What Korkeran had said was funny. Yes, he was older, and most people did slow as they aged, but he had gotten faster. He couldn't explain it, but the speed was there.

He shook his head. "Korkeran, I'll grant you your wish, but you are making the biggest and last mistake of your life. I've gotten faster. I can't explain it, but I have. You'll be dead before your Colt clears the holster. Now's the time to be smart. Take your medicine and move on. You can even clean up your life. Find a good woman."

Korkeran's laugh was more like a bark, then he said, "Like you? Forget it." He pulled up his sleeve and unstrapped the hideout gun, laying it on the table next to him.

The crowd immediately started thinning. They couldn't get outside fast enough. A few were headed home, away from the upcoming bloodshed and possible killing, but most wanted a vantage point from which to watch the gunfight.

Jack watched the people pushing their way out the door, then yelled to the bartender, "You have a sledge or axe?"

The man behind the bar looked at Korkeran.

"Give it to him. He won't stop until the roulette wheel is destroyed." He glared at Jack. "Or do you want to wait until after the gunfight?"

Jack shook his head. "No sense in waiting. If I don't do it, the sheriff will after he gets the reports from the citizens."

The bartender opened a door, was gone for a short time, and emerged from the room with an axe. Shaking his head, he brought the axe to Jack and handed it to him. All the while Dave watched the man's every move, his hand resting lightly on his revolver. When Jack took the axe, Dave relaxed, but the bartender stood in front of the roulette table, shaking his head. "It's a real shame to destroy it. A finer piece of equipment you'll never find."

"You're right," Jack said, "but it's built to steal, and needs to be stopped." With one smooth action, he swung the axe high over his head and brought it down, burying the blade in the table's edge. It drove through the table like it was paper, splitting the side and down into the leg supporting that side of the table.

It collapsed.

Next, Jack went to work on the wheel. In no time, all the roulette wheel and table were good for was firewood.

Korkeran stood to the side, his Colt holstered, and watched with sad eyes. "That's the second expensive roulette table I've seen destroyed, and they were both done by you, but this one will be your last."

Jack grinned at the saloon owner. "Roman, you are so wrong, and that error is going to cost you the most valuable thing you own." He turned to the bartender. "I'm not through. After this is over, I'll be back and finish with the rest of the tables." Turning back to Korkeran, Jack said, "If there's any papers or anything you need from your safe, you'd best get them now. Though it won't be much use to you. You'll be dead in a few minutes. Are you sure you prefer this to going to jail? Like I said, you'll probably be out in a few days."

Korkeran shook his head, his eyes gleaming like he had a fever.

Jack motioned to the swinging door. "Go ahead."

Dave had moved to his side. "Marshal, are you sure you want to do this? He's got a point, you are older than he is, and you sure don't have anything to prove, plus you've got a wife and sons waiting for you in Fort Smith. I can take him and Beck to jail right now, no question."

"Dave, I owe him this chance. Don't ask why, I just do. Get Beck to jail and then get back up here, just in case Korkeran has friends around."

"Don't forget those people who tried to kill you in Fort Smith."

Jack nodded. "Them, too. Don't dawdle."

Dave grabbed Beck by the arm, dragged him through the

swinging doors, turned down the boardwalk, and almost ran him toward the sheriff's office.

When Jack pushed through the doors, Korkeran was waiting in the street. Traffic had ceased on Sherman's main street, and the boardwalks were full of spectators. *Crazy people,* Jack thought. *They're Texans. They know better than to expose themselves like this. Some civilians are liable to get shot before this thing is over.* He stopped on the boardwalk and pulled each of his Smith & Wesson .44-caliber revolvers from their holsters, pressed their latches, and broke them open, checking their loads. Satisfied, he slipped them back into their holsters and checked they were loose.

He strode to the edge of the boardwalk and raised his voice almost to a shout. "Folks, I'd suggest you clear out. Most of you know what could happen. There's a good possibility of stray bullets, and they could find one of you. Were I in your boots, I'd hoof it as far away from here as possible."

Before he finished, the majority of spectators had already begun to move, but a few still remained. He shook his head, thinking, *You just can't help stupid.*

Korkeran lifted his voice. "Sage, are you getting cold feet? Get on out here and take your medicine like a man."

Jack thought of Grace. Was she still his wife, or had she called on the judge? The thought of her annulling the marriage sent the first twinge of fear. Surprised, he thought, *I don't want to live without her.* His eyes shifted to the gunfighter. *He's the picture of confidence. Just like me, he knows he's the fastest.*

Jack stepped into the street. It was shaping up to be a typical Texas summer day—hot. There was an unusual stillness along main street. No wagons or horses moved, but those were the only things still. A horse neighed from the stable while the sounds of a large herd, moving toward Kansas, could be heard just west of Sherman. There was the constant lowing of longhorn cattle, their six-foot horns rattling against those of nearby companions. The yell of cowhands keeping the cattle pointed north drifted across the prairie. Nearby dogs barked, and a lone fluorescent green hummingbird zipped among red flowers hanging in a large wooden planter in front of the barbershop.

Korkeran stood facing Jack thirty feet away. Sweat slowly coursed down his cheeks and from his thick sideburns. He watched Jack as he stepped into the street. "You took your own sweet time."

Jack removed his gloves and tucked them over his gunbelt. "Gonna be a hot one today. You sure you want to go through with this? If you stop and think, it doesn't really make any sense. We can call it quits right now."

Korkeran moved his hand to wipe sweat from his forehead. He slung it into the dirt and then wiped his hand on his trousers. "It's time to stop talking, Sage. It was nice knowing you," and he drew.

9

For the first time, Korkeran surprised him. He had expected the man to talk because he was a talker. But he had stopped talking and started drawing. Since Jack was surprised, Korkeran was the first to reach his revolver, and Jack could see the pleasure the gunfighter was enjoying for his accomplishment.

Jack was disappointed in himself. Usually he was well ahead in a gunfight. He could read people like open books, normally. He hadn't this time, and Korkeran was ahead of him, but Jack wasn't flustered, he was calm. His cool demeanor was one of the things that helped him win gunfights. Since he was a little kid, he had always felt this calm come over him. It was like he was outside his body watching the action.

This time, he could see himself late, but not slow. His having been surprised by his opponent had given the man a temporary edge, but that was changing. He felt and saw himself touch the butt of his Smith & Wesson, his hand closing around it and lifting. Both of them were moving in slow motion, and Korkeran was still ahead. *But not for long*, he thought.

He found himself wondering what Korkeran would think

when he figured out he was slower than Jack. Not by much, because of the surprise, but enough. The gunfighter still had the satisfied expression on his face he had had when he realized he'd caught Jack by surprise.

I bet you're a good gambler, Jack thought, *always catching your opponents by surprise, but that's going to work against you today. If we had drawn at the same time, I would have had time to place my shot so that I might have only wounded you, but now, I have to depend on instinct, and I know where the bullet is going. It's going where I practiced putting it so many thousand times.*

He saw Korkeran's satisfied smile change, and his opponent's eyes widened as Jack brought the muzzle of his revolver to bear and fired. Korkeran's handgun had not leveled when the Smith & Wesson's .44-caliber slug plowed into him. Korkeran fired reflexively and pulled the hammer to the rear, bringing in line with the barrel and hammer an unfired chamber, but he didn't raise the barrel.

He can't, Jack thought. *He's still on his feet, but he's dying.* Jack felt both an elation for not being the one dying and a sadness watching the death of Korkeran. He started moving toward the man, his weapon still leveled and ready.

Korkeran's grip loosened, and his Colt made a half turn around his trigger finger before dropping from his hand into the dust of the street. He stared at Jack, surprise his only expression. Jack reached him, picked up the Colt, shoved it behind his belt, and grasped the gambler by his shoulders. He slowly kneeled and brought the man down with him.

"I . . . thought I had . . . you."

"Don't talk. It won't be long."

The man's head dropped back on Jack's arm for a few moments, then he turned it enough to where he could look into Jack's eyes. "You're right." He broke out into a series of weak coughs, and blood sprayed from his lips.

Jack yanked his bandanna from around his neck, and the

crowd gasped. Korkeran saw the rope scar around his neck. "You've had . . . some trouble since Cherry . . . Creek."

He wiped the blood from around the man's mouth, and one corner of his lifted in a lopsided grin. "You could say that."

Korkeran's pale green eyes were staring at Jack when they changed from bright and alive to dull and lifeless. His final breath was a quiet sigh. Jack held his head up for a few seconds longer, then wiped the blood from around his mouth one last time, slipped his arm under his legs, and lifted the gunfighter. He stood, walked to the Hole in the Wall, and pushed through the swinging doors. The bartender came in behind him. "Where's his office?"

"Follow me." He hurried to another door at the opposite end of the bar, pushed it open, and stepped aside, allowing Jack to enter.

Seeing the couch, Jack laid the dead man on it, stretched him out, and straightened his legs. He looked down on Korkeran. "He should have listened to me. I was trying to help him."

The bartender nodded. "I heard you, Marshal. You tried several times, but he wouldn't listen. I think it was the roulette wheel. He loved that wheel. It was so smooth."

Jack turned to the bartender. "You have any other rigged tables in the house?"

"No, sir, that was the only one, I swear."

Jack nodded. "Then you can put the axe up. I won't be needing it." He glanced back at Korkeran. "For a bad man, he had a good streak. He saved a family from a fight a while back. I was there."

The bartender stared at Korkeran's body. "Yes, sir, Marshal. I reckon even the baddest ain't all bad, and the goodest ain't all good."

Jack nodded. Dave was standing inside the swinging doors of the Hole in the Wall. He had a clean bandanna in his hand. Jack started for him. When he neared him, Dave extended the bandanna. Jack took it, tied it around his neck, and said, "Thanks." He turned to the bartender. "Who has access to Korkeran's safe and bank accounts?"

Using his index finger, the bartender tapped his chest.

"Then I want you to settle up with Cooper and any other of your customers who are owed. Be fair, but be prepared for a few crooks trying to rip you off. I'll tell Cooper to see you, and I'll ride back through to check."

"I'm a fair man, Marshal. They'll get their due. What about the rest of the money?"

"Work with the sheriff. He has a good reputation, but just a piece of advice, stay away from the town marshal."

The bartender nodded. "He's a crook. He was deep in Roman's pocket. He'll do anything for a buck."

"Take care of Korkeran." He touched the brim of his hat in salute and followed Dave out the doors. Cooper was standing outside. As soon as Jack stepped through the doors, the farmer approached. "I'm mighty sorry, Marshal. I wasn't aimin' to get anyone killed."

"It had nothing to do with you, Cooper. A grudge was riding him from a long time back, and he thought now was a good time to settle it. You go on in, and the bartender will take care of your losses."

The farmer's eyes widened. "Really, Marshal? I figured with Korkeran dead, the money was lost."

"Just check inside. Have you seen the town marshal?"

"Yes, sir, he's with that bunch of fellas by the horse trough." He nodded to a trough across the alley in front of a dry-goods store, where seven or eight men were gathered talking. Jack caught a glimpse of a man trying to hide behind the others, McAllister. "Thanks, Cooper. Luck to you."

Cooper said, "Thank you, Marshal," to Jack's back as he strode toward the group, Dave at his side.

"You expect trouble, Marshal Sage?"

"Call me Jack, Dave, and no, I expect no trouble from that bunch. When they see us coming, in fact, I expect most of them will take off."

His forecast had been on the money. At their approach, four of the men scurried in different directions, leaving the town marshal and two others. The lawman stood his ground as Jack approached, but fear filled his eyes. Jack walked up and stood looking down on the man. Finally, the town marshal spoke.

"It's a real shame you had to kill Mr. Korkeran, Marshal Sage. Too bad it couldn't have been worked out."

Jack had no time for small talk and no patience for this thief disguised as a lawman. "Keep your mouth shut and listen, McAllister. I don't know how you managed to get yourself elected, either your constituents are blind or stupid, but I'm putting you on notice. Get rid of that badge, today. Take it down to the sheriff and drop it on his desk. If this town is so in need of a town marshal, they can call an emergency election, but your payoff days are over."

McAllister's face had turned bright red as Jack spoke. His eyes bugged out like a grasshopper's. "You can't talk to me like that. I'll tell the sheriff." Jack didn't have time to deal with this charlatan. He had killers to catch so he could get back to his family. He had just killed a man who was more man than this sniveling little officer of the law would ever be.

He slapped McAllister so hard it knocked him into the water trough.

The town marshal's two friends disappeared, and no one came forward to help the splashing man from the trough.

Spluttering and wheezing, his head shot out of the water. Jack grabbed him and yanked him bodily from the trough, turned him toward the sheriff's office, and gave him a hard shove. "Do what I tell you, McAllister, or when I come back through, I'll arrest you for graft and take you to Judge Bell's court."

The marshal's first few steps were stumbles until he steadied himself, then his speed picked up. Dave looked up at his mentor. "What am I supposed to learn from this?"

Jack's brows had been wrinkled and his lips tight while he dealt with McAllister. He glared at Dave, his expression remaining the same. "What not to do. Weren't we heading out to catch killers?"

"Yep, Jack, we were, and I'm ready to leave this place in my dust."

FOUR DAYS of hard riding had put the two marshals within sight of their goal. They camped near Teepee Creek, well hidden under a thick canopy of sycamore, red maple, sweetgum, and pecan trees. They had found several dried limbs of red maple, which provided them with a near smokeless fire, which they built while it was still daylight. The faint smoke drifted skyward through the canopy of trees. By the time it reached the open sky, it was hardly visible.

After making coffee, they put out the fire, drank their coffee, and moved a couple of hundred yards up the creek, where they found a good stand of grass for the horses and mules.

The trip had been hard on the men and animals, but each night they had managed to get a good night's rest. Tonight, they sat on a thick log and went over again what they had learned from the two killers who had lain in wait for them.

Dave clamped down on a piece of jerky and worked with it until he had torn off a sizeable bite. After chewing for a spell, he spoke in a low tone. "You think those two fellers were on the up and up with us? I mean, they were talking about gold. Who ever heard of gold in Oklahoma?"

Jack had dropped down to the ground so he could lean his back against the log. He nodded in the darkness. "Yeah, I think they were scared enough to spill their guts, and they appeared to believe every word they told us. You notice they said they hadn't seen the gold. Their leader, this Tate Morgan, had told them all about it. So it may be there, and it may not. But I know this kind of riffraff. They don't mind stealing a man's poke, but the only way they're going to work a gold mine is if the nuggets are lying on top of the ground, begging to be picked up."

"So you don't think they'll work a mine if they've found one?"

"Not a chance. Oh, there might be one or two in the bunch willing to put out some effort, but you've got to remember, one of the standard traits of thieves and lawbreakers is they're lazy. If there's any way they can get out of work, believe me, they'll try it. Now here's the second thing, you and I know this is Indian Territory. The army's here to keep the Indians on their reservations, but they are also here to keep the whites out. Just being out here, other than traveling across the territory, is against the law. Where—"

Down the creek, a chilling scream issued from the darkness. Jack looked in the direction of the sound. "What was that?"

Dave grinned. "You're testing me, right?"

Jack chuckled. "Maybe a little."

"A mountain lion. We call them panthers where I come from."

Jack nodded his agreement. "Yep, if it weren't the wrong time of year, I'd say he's out looking for a girlfriend."

The scream came several times, each time sounding farther away. Jack watched the mules and horses. All the horses' heads had jerked high at the first scream and stayed up until the last one.

Jack pulled a stem of bunchgrass, pointed it at the horses, and began chewing on the base. "Appears mountain lions aren't their favorite animals." He stood, walked to one of Stonewall's packs, and opened it. Dave, seeing what he was doing, joined him while Jack dug out enough cookies for all of the animals to have one, handed three to Dave, and kept three.

After closing the pack, he strolled, with Dave, to the horses and began speaking in a calm, soothing voice. "You want a cookie, Stonewall?" The mule had moved toward him when he started in their direction. He scratched the hardworking animal behind its ears while it crunched the cookie, and moved next to Pepper and then Thunder, giving each a cookie and patting them while talking reassuringly to each. He watched Dave doing the same thing. *I'm liking that boy,* he thought. *He's kind to his animals and doesn't have an ounce of backup in him.* He watched Dave with his buckskin. *He holds onto his temper a lot better than I did at his age.* Jack chuckled to himself. *Probably better than I do now.*

The night returned to its normal sounds, and the two men returned to their log. Dave dropped down on it, and Jack lowered himself to the same position he had been in before so he could relieve his back. It had been bothering him since he slapped McAllister. *I must've pulled something,* he thought. The two men sat silent, absorbing the sounds of the dark.

Dave broke the silence. "My pa always said the panther's screams sound like a woman screaming. I remember my sisters' screaming when they were playing, and they didn't much sound like a panther. They were too clear and high pitched."

Jack's mind went to a place he preferred it stay away from. He could hear the screams of war. The terrible guttural sounds of pain and death. "The screams he's talking about have nothing to do with play. Those screams are similar. Hopefully you'll never hear them except from a mountain lion."

They were both silent again. An armadillo crunched and rattled dry leaves nearby, searching for ants and grubs. Bullbats wheeled and twisted along the treeline, hunting for mosquitos and bugs, their short little chirps barely audible.

Jack yawned. "Reckon I'm gonna hit the sack." He pushed himself to his feet, his back feeling better, and moved to his saddle and bedroll. He loved having two mules on this trip. They made excellent guards. He and Dave could get a good night's sleep, and he was tired.

He could hear Dave rustling as he settled in.

"Good night, Jack."

"Night." The word had no more than left his mouth than Jack Sage was gently snoring.

HE OPENED his eyes to false dawn's faint light and lay still, listening. Dave's breathing was slow and steady. His were the only sounds of the morning. After listening for a few minutes, he was satisfied they had no company. He threw his blanket back, turned his boots upside down, and slapped each of them a couple of times before slipping them on. Grasping his gunbelt, he stood while at the same time swinging the belt around his waist. He fastened it, checked the loads of his revolvers, and dropped each back into its holster.

He bumped Dave on the ankle, and the deputy sat up, checking the surroundings. "Nothing happening," Jack said. "I thought we'd get an early start. We can hit the jerky when we're in the saddle. We'll have to hold off on coffee this morning."

"Sounds good." Dave began rolling his bedding. He hurried to the creek, and Jack could hear him drinking and washing his face. He strode to the horses and mules. They were busy cropping grass. "You fellas about ready for a drink?"

There were six of them, and he elected to take two at a time. Thirty minutes later, he had watered all of them and was staking them out again when Dave walked up. He had scooped some oats and fed each of the horses and mules. They devoured the oats. When they were fed, the two men began loading the pack saddles. Jack stopped to check the time, pulling his watch from his inside pocket. The hand-carved emerald exploding bomb stood out in the early morning light.

Jack gazed at it for only a moment and flipped it open. It was six o'clock sharp. Speaking low, he said, "We need to be on our way."

Dave nodded. "I'm ready." He held up a handful of jerky.

Jack had rolled his bedroll and stepped to Thunder. He patted the horse on the neck and then swung the saddle blanket onto the horse's back, smoothed it out, and followed it with his saddle. After fastening the cinches, he grasped the horn and the cantle, gave it a couple of good shakes, and moved to Stonewall. He had already fastened the frame, and the animal placidly munched grass while he secured the packs to the frame. When he had finished, he retained the lead rope, picked up Pepper's, and swung into the saddle.

Dave was right behind him. "We ready to hit the trail?"

Jack nodded. "You checked your weapons? We'll probably be needing them, maybe sooner than later."

Dave grinned. "First thing every morning. Never know who or what you might run into of a morning."

Jack bumped Thunder, pulled out a strip of jerky, and enjoyed the cooler air of the morning. *Good thinking, young fella,* he thought. *If I were a betting man, I'd wager we'll be smelling gun smoke before the morning's over.*

10

A fter leaving Teepee Creek, the two lawmen followed the meandering path of the North Fork of the Red River from where the two streams had joined. Though the river wandered in its journey, it provided excellent cover.

The mountain range wasn't tall like the Rockies, but it was as rugged as any section of the western mountains Jack had traveled. To their right, they had been paralleling the rugged boulders and jagged upthrusts for a good part of the morning.

At the edge of the pecan and elm trees that followed along the river, their search had taken them to a wide pasture covered with the bright yellow of tall sunflowers and the eye-catching red, yellow, and brown of the shorter, but thicker Indian blankets. The sun lit the flowers with a brilliant glow.

Jack was admiring nature's display when the aroma of coffee drifted through the trees. He pulled Thunder to a halt, and Dave, riding parallel, but at least thirty feet away, followed suit, remaining quiet and watching him. A loud laugh banged off the trees, then a curse and another laugh. Jack slid his Winchester from its scabbard, looped the lead ropes from Pepper and Stonewall around his saddle horn, and stepped, as softly as possible with the mass of pecan and elm leaves covering it, to the ground.

Dave followed his example. After he was dismounted, Jack flipped the reins over a stubby limb, pointed to a pecan tree ahead of them about twenty yards, and started for it. *It's a good thing we've got a stiff breeze,* Jack thought, *or whoever's enjoying their coffee could hear us in these dry leaves.* He continued to the tree, arriving at the same time as Dave.

The deputy whispered, "How do you want to handle them?"

Jack responded, his voice low, "Split up, but keep me in sight." Another laugh sounded. "Good, not a care in the world. We're about to fix that. If possible, stay hidden. Don't shoot unless you have to. The judge wants these fellas to swing." Jack paused. "After a fair trial, of course."

Dave nodded. "Of course."

"Let's go."

Both men stepped from behind the pecan tree with their 1873 Winchesters at the ready. Chambers loaded and hammers back, both were prepared for instant use. The wind, still cooperating, rattled limbs and fluttered leaves, making it difficult for them to hear their own footsteps in the crunchy leaves, but caution still dictated moving carefully through the woods. The sound of a dry twig snapping or a stumble might be loud enough to be heard in spite of the wind.

Jack watched his companion work his way toward the outlaws. *He's good,* Jack thought. *He places his heel down first, then gently lowers his foot, rolling it from the outer edge. The boy's been taught well.* He continued, following the same method Dave was using. He'd let his heel first touch the ground. Once it was solid, he'd slowly transfer his weight to the outside of his foot, feeling for debris like pecans, bark, or twigs. Once the outside of the foot was down, he settled the sole carefully to the leaf-strewn ground.

The movement was slow, tedious, and tiring. His knees were flexed whenever there was movement. Flexing gave him more control over his foot movement, making it possible to stop the foot in mid-stride should it feel something that might pop or snap. Slipping like this was time consuming, but charging ahead without utilizing this skill could garner a careless man a bullet or arrow from the individual being stalked or cause the hunter to frighten his game, thereby losing a chance for a shot.

Jack gradually drew nearer his quarry, moving from pecan tree to elm to the next pecan. Finally he neared enough to understand the conversation. He mentally shook his head. These two were idiots. Their voices were loud, interspersed with laughter, and it was obvious to anyone they were disregarding the possible dangers they could be attracting. Though, by now, just about all of the warring southern and eastern tribes had been moved onto reservations in the Indian Territory, it didn't mean they would pass up an opportunity to lift a couple of scalps or steal horses from two loudmouthed white men.

Drawing nearer, he eased behind a large pecan and, sneaking a careful look around the tree, saw there were only two in the party, and party it was. In Jack's quick glimpse, he saw one of the men pour something from a pocket flask into both of their cups. *These fellas deserve whatever happens to them,* he thought.

They both took sips, and the bigger one leaned his head back and let out a long, loud whoop.

The other man, big, but not as big as the one who had just yelled, leaned forward. "Shut it, Briscoe. Tate said there was Injuns around. I don't hanker to lose my hair."

"What's a matter, Jenkins, you yeller?"

The cautious man leaned farther forward, his right hand moving to his sixgun, and though his voice was softer, Jack could hear the threat in it. "Banks, I've killed men for less. You might want to take that back—fast."

The bigger man appeared to sober. "Aww, Clayton, I ain't meant nothing. That was the liquor talking."

Clayton Jenkins leaned back and removed his hand from his

revolver. "Good, but keep it down. If Tate happens to ride this way, he'll shoot both of us for drinking when we're supposed to be watching for lawmen."

Briscoe Banks let out a string of oaths. After which, he pronounced, "There ain't no lawmen coming into this country. First off, they wouldn't get past Wylie and Gordo, and second off, none of them marshals have the guts to come out here after we hanged those first two, and Tate sent along his note with their stinkin' bodies, and that'll scare the daylights out of them."

"Don't you bet on it. I know some of them fellers. They'll ride through hell to get to us, and you'd better believe it. What Tate did was sign our own death warrants."

Banks emptied his coffee and, this time, poured the cup full from his flask, offering the flask to Jenkins when he was finished. His partner shook his head.

"You'd best pour that back into your bottle. I'm not kidding you. If Tate comes along, he'll kill you for drinking on a sentry post. I seen him do it in the war."

For his answer Banks brought the cup to his lips and swigged half of it, then wiped his mouth with his dirty sleeve. "You're just too jumpy, Clayton. You need to relax."

Jack stepped out from behind the tree. "You should listen to your partner, Banks. He's got a lot better grip on reality than you do. You fellas best not reach for a gun, or I'll be forced to shoot you. My preference is to take you back to Fort Smith and let Judge Bell take care of you."

The more sober Jenkins threw his cup to the ground. "Dang it. I knew that was a bad idea. We're dead men. Tate sentenced us when he hanged those marshals."

"The two of you stand up nice and slow and keep your hands clear of your guns. Trust me when I tell you I don't want to kill you, but you try to shuck one of those shooters, I'll snuff your lights out."

The two men stood, Banks unable to keep from swaying.

"Look, Clayton, there ain't but one of him. He can only shoot once before one of us can get him while he's working that lever."

Jack, feeling the calm he always felt, moved the rifle to his left hand so he could draw with his right. "You boys can make your move anytime. I'm pretty sure I can take you both, but in case I can't, my partner can clean up what I leave. Dave, why don't you let these fellas see there's more than just me here."

Dave stepped from the woods. "Howdy, boys. You having a good day?"

Banks let out another string of oaths.

Jenkins turned on him. "Why don't you shut your nasty mouth, Briscoe. No one wants to hear that filth." Then moving deathly slow so he didn't attract a bullet, he unbuttoned his gunbelt and lowered it to the ground.

Jack nodded to Banks. "Do the same."

The drunk followed Jack's directions, letting his gunbelt fall to the dirt at his feet. Jack glanced at Dave and gave a sideways jerk of his head toward the weapons on the ground while at the same time speaking to the outlaws. "My partner's coming over to pick up your weapons. Then he's going to search you. The same thing I said earlier goes. Make a wrong move, and as much as I want to take you back to Fort Smith, I won't hesitate to put two hundred grains of lead in your belly."

Dave laid his rifle on the ground, eased close to the outlaws, and began to search them. He found a throwing knife at the back of Briscoe Banks's collar, and a derringer on the inside of his left boot. Jenkins had a Colt Pocket Pistol stuffed behind his waistband. After collecting all of the outlaws' weapons and their rifles, he moved to one side of the prisoners and brought his Winchester up again. "What now, boss?"

"You boys can sit back down." Jack watched them lower themselves to the ground. When they were down, he said to Dave, "Why don't you get our horses. On the way back, if you can find easy access to the river, water them. When you get back, get the irons out, just for the wrists, for now." He glanced at Jenkins. "How's the coffee?"

"Marshal, I make a fine cup of coffee. You're more than welcome to use my cup. It's the one with CJ scratched on it. You might rinse it out to get all the liquor out, but otherwise it's fine."

Dave disappeared into the woods, hurrying to the horses and leaving Jack alone with the prisoners. Jack laid his rifle down at his side, picked up a cup, turned it, and saw the CJ scratched on the side. He poured a little coffee in it, sloshed it around to rinse it, and poured it out.

"Get him!" Banks yelled, and jumped for Jack.

He had expected the drunk to make some kind of stupid move, and sure enough, he did just as Jack expected. He had held the cup in his left hand and reached for the pot with his right. When Banks yelled, he replaced the pot at the edge of the coals and, still in a crouch, spun to his left, drawing his right Smith & Wesson.

Jack had developed a real affection for the Smith & Wesson revolvers rechambered for the .44 Henry and further modified for him by his friend in Silver City. They weren't quite as heavy as the originals since the barrels had been cut down to four inches, and every ounce counted as far as speed was concerned, but they were still weighty enough to make a fine club.

Banks's leap carried him a little short of his goal, and his clutching hands grasped air when the butt of the Smith & Wesson struck the outlaw in his left temple. At the blow, the man stiffened momentarily, then dropped into the coals.

Using his boot, Jack shoved him out of the fire, then glanced at Jenkins, who hadn't moved. He holstered the revolver and picked up the pot. Motioning to Jenkins, he asked, "Want a cup?"

"No, thanks, Marshal, I've about had my fill of coffee this morning."

Jack poured his cup half-full, ensuring there was plenty left for Dave, and took a sip. It was hot and bitter. Not the way he normally liked it, preferably with a freight-car load of sugar and plenty of fresh cream, but it hit the spot. To Jenkins he said, "Mighty good coffee, mister. How'd you get mixed up with this bunch?"

Jenkins began to talk while Jack drank.

"You believe in fate, Marshal?"

"Can't say as I do. I've always believed a man makes his own bed."

"And lies in it. Yeah, I understand the thinkin', but I feel like this whole thing kinda slipped up on me. I was a young feller when the war started. My folks had moved to Missouri. They had a small farm. Pa was a good, hardworking man who didn't believe in the war and swore he'd never lift a hand against any man. That worked for us for a while, though we developed enemies on both sides by the time the war started. Then one day, I was off to town on the mule to get seed, and a bunch of fellers who was strong against slavery came by. Pa, he never believed in slavery, but he also didn't believe some high mucky-muck in Washington had the right to tell him what to do."

Jenkins stopped and looked up into the pecan tree Jack had stepped from behind. "Squirrels love these pecans, and there's nothing better than squirrel, biscuits, and gravy."

"Yeah," Jack said, "it can be mighty good." He waited while the younger man contemplated the thick branches spreading above him.

Finally, the outlaw looked down and began again. "He was plowing when these fellers rode by. One of 'em just up and shot him right between the eyes for no reason. They weren't arguing or fighting or nothing. He just shot him and rode on with those fellers laughing and congratulating him about how good a shot he was. I'll tell you something else he was, our neighbor. So when I got home and found out, I politely got Pa's shotgun and rode over to his house. He was in his barn, milking his cow. I walked in, told him to move away from the cow, and killed him right there. Then I finished milking the cow, set the milk on the porch, got back on my mule, and rode home. Right after that, I joined Quantrill's Raiders and rode with them for the rest of the war. Tate Morgan was a captain. I just rightly stayed with Captain Morgan when the war was over, and here I am."

Jack had heard quite a few similar border-state stories. An instance of violence against one neighbor drew others to respond, and if it happened enough, politicians would get involved, and before you knew it, you had a civil war. "Jenkins, that's a sad story, but you strike me as a man of decision, and, especially after the war, you could have decided, at any point, to step away, but you didn't."

"You're right, Marshal, I didn't, and I'll be paying for it before long."

Jenkins stopped talking, and the only sound was the low moan of the wind in the trees. Jack examined Banks's head. It had bled some. It seemed all head wounds bled more than other parts of the body, but Banks would occasionally snore, so Jack figured he was fine. If he had killed the man with the blow, Bell would be livid. He figured the worst the outlaw would have would be a headache, and he would've had that anyway from the rotgut he was drinking.

Finally, he heard the sound of horses moving toward them, and they were coming from the right direction. Cautious, Jack picked up his rifle and stepped to the side of a tree.

Moments later, Dave rode out leading the animals. "Sorry it took so long. It took a while to find a spot where I could get these fellas down to the water, and once we got there, they were thirsty." He glanced at Banks lying by the fire. "Any trouble?"

Jack shook his head. "Not to speak of."

"What's the plan?"

Jack threw it back at him. "What would you do?"

He thought about it for a minute or two. "We've got to get these fellers in a jail. We can't do anything with them hanging around. We could both pull out, but then if the gang gets jumpy and takes off, we'll have to spend time trailing them. I'd say one of us needs to take these two back to Fort Sill. I'm sure the army's got a stockade we can use. It's not that far, and whoever goes could be back in a couple of days, three at the most. The other needs to stay and keep an eye on that bunch up the canyon."

Jack grinned. "You just might make a marshal after all. You know which one of us is taking these fellas back?"

Dave frowned. "I can't say I'm happy about it, but I reckon I know."

"Good, you oughta get started as soon as possible. I'll hold the fort on this end until you get back, and then we'll take the rest of them." Jack stopped when Banks started moaning. "It looks like sleeping beauty is waking up."

Dave moved toward Jenkins. "We'd best get moving. The sooner I get out of here, the sooner I'll be back."

Jack held out his hand. "Hold up, Dave. I want to ask these fine gentlemen a few questions before you haul them off."

Jenkins shook his head. "Marshal, I reckon you have a job to do, but it don't matter what you do to me. I won't be tellin' anything on my friends. I've been ridin' with them fellers for nigh on fifteen years."

Jack turned hard gray eyes on the outlaw. "You don't have any idea what I'm about to do. I expect you'll be tellin' me everything I want to know."

The outlaw shook his head. "Reckon not, and that's the last I have to say."

Jack knew Clayton Jenkins's kind. Almost half the man's life had been spent with Morgan and the men in Morgan's gang. They had ridden together throughout the war, and Morgan had likely become a father figure to this man. Jack turned from Jenkins to face Banks, who had sat up and was holding his head, watching Jack warily.

"How are you feeling, Briscoe?"

"You could have killed me."

"You're right. I could have just shot you, but I wanted to save you for the judge. Where's the rest of your gang?"

The corners of Briscoe's mouth turned down, and his eyes narrowed. "I ain't talkin'."

Jack leaned forward just enough to reach the killer and threw a short right uppercut, catching Briscoe under the left side of his chin and knocking him over backwards.

The killer sprawled in the grass, then pulled himself back into a sitting position. After sitting up and rubbing his chin, he tried to glare at Jack, but his eyes were filled with pain and fear, and he wouldn't maintain eye contact.

11

J ack turned the cup up and drained the last bit of coffee, poured a little into it, rinsed it, and held the cup out. "Help yourself. It's not bad."

Dave took the cup and filled it a quarter full. "There's a bit left. You want it?"

"No, what's left is yours."

Dave grinned and emptied most of it into his cup, stopping when the dregs chased the coffee. "Thanks."

Jack eyed Banks, who refused to make eye contact. "Dave, after your coffee, why don't you take Jenkins for a walk. Banks and I need a little privacy."

The already bruised outlaw cut his eyes toward Jack, then looked away. "You're a lawman. You ain't supposed to be hurting a person you've arrested. It's against the law."

Jack showed Banks a humorless grin and thought, *This worthless excuse for a man is already afraid of me. I think the little trick I pulled with Gordo and Wylie might just work on him.* He motioned for Dave to move close and, holding his mouth close to the deputy's ear, whispered, "Don't come back until I yell for you."

Dave gave a short nod, finished his coffee, poured the grounds from the pot, and placed it and the cup away from the coals. He grasped Jenkins's arm and lifted. "Come on, we're going for a walk."

Jenkins tried to jerk his arm out of Dave's big hand but was unsuccessful.

"Settle down. I'm just trying to help you up." Dave turned loose of the man and stepped a safe distance away from him, then pointed toward the river. "Let's go."

Jenkins glanced at Banks. "Keep your mouth shut, Briscoe."

Indignant, Banks glowered at his partner. "You worry about yourself. They won't get nothing out of me." He shot Jack a quick peek. His eyes met Jack's hard gray stare and looked away.

Jack remained silent until the deputy and the outlaw disappeared behind the brush and trees. He knew he didn't have a lot of time, but as edgy as Banks was, he wanted to give the trick a try. He reached to his neck and slowly untied the knot in his bandanna, stopping to scratch at the scar around his neck. Then he jerked the bandanna free and wiped his forehead. The day was hot and getting hotter. When Banks saw the scar, he let out an audible gasp. His eyes were wide and locked on Jack's neck, and his mouth hung open.

"It's not pretty, is it, Banks?"

"My goodness gracious, how'd you come by that?"

Jack didn't have time to coddle this animal. "I was lucky. The varmints who did this didn't check the tree. The limb broke after a bit. It still hurt something fierce. This is what your neck is going to look like, except you won't be hanging from a limb. You'll be tied to a gallows, and it won't break."

The outlaw rubbed his neck and swallowed. "What if I tell you about the hideout? Will that keep me from hanging?"

Jack's tone softened. "Listen, Banks, I can't make you any promises. Judge Bell is a hard man, but I can promise you one thing. If you don't tell me, it's guaranteed you'll be getting a scar just like this one, only you won't be able to show it off to anyone."

Jack ran his hand around his neck, pulling his collar out of the way so the outlaw could get a good look.

"I don't have time to waste. If you're gonna tell me, make it now, or I'll call my deputy back, and the only thing between you and a noose will be a little time." Jack stood, returned the bandanna to his neck, and yanked the knot tight.

The answer came out in a whine. "Alright, Marshal. I'll tell you, but this cain't never get back to Tate, or I'm a dead man. I ain't kidding."

Jack squatted back down in front of the man. "I'm waiting, Banks. Go ahead."

Briscoe Banks went ahead, explaining in great detail about the camp and especially where Tate Morgan could be found. The explanation went on for several minutes, ending with, "He's a dangerous man. If he gets wind of me tellin' you anything, he'll kill me. He'll do it with his bare hands if he ain't got anything else."

Everything Banks told him matched exactly what Gordo and Wylie had said. "One last thing, how many are left with you and Jenkins gone?"

Banks's forehead wrinkled, and he counted on his fingers. After going through what appeared to be a torturous process, he held up six fingers and gave a single, affirmative nod. "That's it. There's six left. I'm sure of it."

It was Jack's turn to frown. Six was the same number Wylie Brown and Gordo Taylor had given him after they were captured. Either he wasn't getting the full story, or someone was lying. "How many do you have left without Wylie and Gordo?"

"We had four. That's why Tate hired a couple more fellas in Sherman. They brought us back up to six. They're the first new boys he's hired in a while. Tate don't like new blood. Says they're not as loyal."

"Gordo said you're prospecting for gold. Is that true?"

Banks grimaced. "Yeah, Tate has everyone taking shifts

digging in his mine. We ain't found a thing. He said a feller in Texas showed him a map where there was a big gold mine. The feller told him it was the only accurate map. All the others claimed the gold was in the Wichita Mountains, but he told Tate they was dead wrong. The boss believed him, so he shot the feller and took his map. He figures we're all gonna be rich. That's why he's trying to keep strangers out. He figured to throw a scare in the marshals, and that would give us more time. Cain't you see, Marshal, that's why we hanged those two and sent them back tied over their horses. We wouldn't have done it otherwise."

Jack shook his head. *This Tate Morgan must be crazy as a loon to think such a violent act would scare us off,* he thought. *If anything, it'll draw more marshals. They'll be looking for blood.* "One more question, Banks, where are you getting your supplies? You can't be riding down to Sherman, that's a long haul."

It was a hot May day, nearing summer, but up to now, though the man had been scared, he hadn't shown much sweat. Now, it popped out under his nose and eyes. He looked left and right, as if looking for an escape route.

Jack's arm shot out, and his big hand clamped around the killer's neck. He tightened. "Answer the question, and make it quick, Banks, or I swear you won't make it back to the noose."

His hands grasping Jack's thick wrist, Banks croaked like a frog, "Drovers."

Jack released the outlaw's throat and stood, disregarding the desperate coughing coming from the man. *Yep,* Jack thought, *of course, after they've sold their herds, they're loaded with money. I've seen this before.*

Jack stared down at the man. "From where?"

Banks squirmed on the log, coughed again, then tossed a furtive glance up at Jack. "Coming out of Kansas after selling their herds. Those trail bosses' saddlebags are usually jam-packed with money and a lot of times gold."

"And the people? What do you do with the trail bosses and cowhands after you get their money?"

Banks gathered courage from somewhere. He stared at Jack like, as a lawman, he had developed a bad case of stupid. "We do what has to be done. We kill 'em."

Jack felt cold, deep anger thinking about the innocent cowpunchers and trail bosses who had made a successful drive and were looking forward to getting back home to their loved ones, only to die at the hands of these butchers.

What had happened to the humanity of these men? How had they managed to survive for so long? He'd never heard of this Tate Morgan. Why hadn't this man and those who ran with him shown up on circulars or in newspapers? The war had been over for eleven years. Jack looked down at the man sitting on the log in front of him and felt a profound loathing. His stomach almost overpowered him. *I need out of this job. I'm tired of associating with the likes of these men. I've been doing it far too long. I want to be around happy, kind people.* He looked in the direction his partner and Jenkins had disappeared and, raising his voice, called, "Dave."

Within minutes, the deputy and Jenkins pushed out of the brush and trees, making their way toward him. Another thought came to him. "Why hasn't the army run you out of here?"

Banks, obviously relieved Jack was no longer accusing him, grinned. "'Cause as far as they're concerned, we ain't anywhere around."

Puzzled, Jack asked, "What does that mean?"

"Just what I said." Banks glanced toward Dave and Jenkins drawing near, and lowered his voice. "The captain ain't no fool. He pays off one of them soldier boy officers over there."

"With what?"

"The money we take from those ranchers. Like I said, most all of them are loaded with gold from selling all those cows. All we have to do is take it from 'em."

As Dave approached, he called, "You ready for us to take off?"

"Yep, but there's been a slight change of plans. I'm going with you. I need to talk to the commanding officer. After I'm finished, and we've gotten rid of these two, we'll head back and shut down this operation. If they should get nervous because their boys haven't returned and take off, we'll trail them. They won't get away." Jack motioned to the prisoners. "Let's get these two cuffed with their hands behind them, then get them in the saddle, and be on our way."

～

FORT SILL SPORTED no high walls, only a few buildings surrounding a large parade ground. They did have a road into the fort with guards posted. A Buffalo Soldier corporal pointed Jack toward a solid-looking building. "That's the stockade, Marshal. You can drop your prisoners there, but afterward, you'll need to check in with Colonel Mackenzie, our commanding officer."

"Thanks, Corporal. I'll do that." He touched his finger to the brim of his Stetson and, to warn the prisoners, since their hands were cuffed behind them, said, "Let's go."

Jack had the extra horses and mules on leads, and Dave led the two outlaws. Neither of the two killers was feeling very good today. Jack and Dave had gotten a good night's sleep with the mules on guard, and they had used Jack's method of securing the prisoners at night. After finding a good-sized tree for each prisoner, Jack had the man sit on the ground facing the tree. The prisoner stretched his legs on each side of the tree, and the leg irons were fastened around their ankles. Since the prisoners couldn't reach the leg irons because of the tree, there was no chance of them breaking loose.

Jack's entourage pulled up at the stockade. He swung down about the time the door opened, and a muscular sergeant stepped from the interior. "Morning, Sergeant, I'm Marshal Jack

Sage." He nodded at Dave. "This is Deputy Marshal Dave Cole. We've got a couple of prisoners to house in your stockade until the prisoner wagon can swing by to take them to Fort Smith for trial. They'll be tried for hanging two deputy marshals."

The sergeant opened the stockade door and yelled, "Jones, y'all get out here. We've got us a couple of customers."

A private stepped through the door. The man was much younger than Dave, but he was built exactly the same way, broad shoulders, thick neck, chest, and arms. They could have passed for twins except the private's skin was dark like the sergeant's. He spoke in a relaxed drawl. "Surely, Sergeant, I'll be glad to take care of those white boys."

Jack watched the shocked expressions on the faces of Banks and Jenkins. It was the first time he'd felt like laughing. Using his left index finger, he pushed his gray Stetson to the back of his head, leaned forward, and rested his forearm across the saddle horn. "Sergeant, you might keep a close eye on these two fellas. They're supposed to be mighty tough customers, seeing as they rode with Quantrill's Raiders."

The private maintained a straight face, but the sergeant gave Jack a wide smile. "Why, that's good to know, Marshal. We'll be mighty careful of these dangerous gentlemen." He grabbed Banks by his left arm and yanked him out of the saddle, releasing his arm when the outlaw tilted. He lost his balance and piled up in the dirt. Private Jones was more civil when he pulled Jenkins from the saddle. He held onto his arm until Jenkins had steadied himself on the ground.

The sergeant reached down, grabbed Banks by the upper arm, and yanked him to his feet. "C'mon, dangerous man. It's time for you to enjoy the hospitality of the Union Army."

"Sergeant," Jack said, "we're going to ride over to Colonel Mackenzie's office. I'll be needing those wrist irons before I leave."

"Yes, sir, I'll have them for you. You have a fine day."

"You too, Sergeant." Jack turned Thunder toward the colonel's office, and Dave followed. Reaching the hitching rails, he was glad there were two, each with a watering trough paralleling it on the opposite side of the rail. He was still leading Dave's extra horse and mule along with Pepper and Stonewall. That would put five on this rail, and three on the other, where Dave tied his mount and the two prisoners' horses. All of the animals had room to drink, which they did, greedily.

Jack stepped down from Thunder, looped his reins over the rail, and those of the other horses, before stepping onto the low porch of the regimental commander's office. He removed his hat, and, as best he could, beat the dust from his chaps. Dave followed his example. Jack couldn't tell if it did much good, but it was at least an attempt. He opened the door and stepped into the outer office, Dave right behind him.

A corporal looked up from the papers he was laboring over. Jack saw the man's eyes register the badge. "Marshal, how can we help you?"

"Corporal, we need to see Colonel Mackenzie. We just brought in two outlaws who, along with the rest of their gang, were involved in hanging two deputy marshals. They are currently in your stockade. I want to confirm with the colonel this will be alright, and also send a message to Judge Bell at Fort Smith to let him know we've captured two more of the outlaws."

The NCO rose from behind his desk. "If you'll wait here, sir, I'm sure the colonel will want to meet you."

The corporal knocked twice on the colonel's door and marched in, closing the door behind him. There were two other clerks in the outer office, and both were deeply absorbed in the forms they were filling out.

Moments after entering, the corporal opened the colonel's door and spoke. "Marshal Sage, Colonel Mackenzie will see you and Marshal Cole."

Jack stepped through the door, instantly recognizing the

officer from the newspaper pictures he remembered seeing in Washington during the war. If he remembered correctly, Mackenzie had received several awards and several wounds to go along with them. The memory was verified as the colonel stood slowly, trying to hide the discomfort he was feeling from old wounds.

"Marshal Sage, welcome." He stepped from behind his desk and extended his hand. "Rest assured, we are glad to hold your prisoners until the wagon comes for them. I received news of the marshals murdered in such a ghastly manner. I'm sure Judge Bell wants to mete out justice, but I could take care of the problem right here at Fort Sill."

Jack took the extended hand. "Thank you, Colonel Mackenzie, but you are right. Judge Bell is set on handling the outlaws in his court."

Mackenzie greeted Dave and waved his hand to the chairs in front of his desk. "Take a seat. If you came out of Fort Smith, I imagine you men are worn down. You're welcome to partake of our hospitality for a few days if, by chance, you'd like to rest up. You can stay with me. My quarters has several beds, and it would be much better than in the barracks."

Jack had removed his hat upon entry to the outer office, and Mackenzie noted the act as he stepped into his office.

Before Jack could acknowledge the offer, Mackenzie asked, "Marshal Sage, were you ever in the military?"

"Yes, sir, during the war."

Mackenzie's stare became intense as he examined Jack. "There was a Major Jack Sage, would you be him?"

Jack smiled. "I was a major."

The colonel leaned back in his chair. "If I remember correctly, prior to the war, you spent time in the French Foreign Legion."

Jack gave the colonel a slight nod. "You have me, Colonel. I was in the Legion for several years. If the war hadn't broken out, I might still be there."

The colonel leaned forward in interest. "I would love to hear what it was like in . . . ?"

"Algeria."

"Algeria," Colonel Mackenzie repeated. "It has a certain mystical ring to it."

"Colonel, I'll tell you this. The mystique wore off in no time. It was intensely hot, and most of the people hated us."

"Yes, I understand. A similar situation exists out here, but what else can I do for you, Major?"

Jack shook his head. "I left that title behind a long time ago. Jack or Sage will do fine, Colonel. I need to send a message to Judge Bell so he can direct the prisoner wagon here. Also there are six more outlaws, including Tate Morgan, the gang's leader. If you can spare three or four men, we can quickly remove them from your part of the country."

Mackenzie shook his head. "Jack, you can send all the messages you need, and, like I said, rest up as long as you like, but I can't spare a man. Our present assignment is to keep an eye on the tribes. In fact, Custer is up north in the Black Hills. Hopefully he'll have success. But I need all the men here and ready to ride at a moment's notice. I'm sure you understand."

Jack was disappointed, but he didn't show it. With four additional men, they could have cleaned up those outlaws quickly and efficiently, but with just the two of them, they would have to be very careful to keep from getting killed in their efforts to capture the outlaws. "Thanks, Colonel, I understand completely. If you wouldn't mind us spending the night and getting our animals taken care of, you'd help us a lot."

"Good." Mackenzie stood. "Join me and a few of my men for supper tonight. We'd enjoy it. See the corporal. He'll see to you, Marshal Cole, and your horses. For now, If you'll excuse me, I'm drowning in paperwork. You remember the army."

Jack stood. "I do indeed. Thank you for your hospitality. We'll definitely take you up on it, and see you at supper. I do have some information for you, but the evening will be soon enough."

Mackenzie paused, thought about Jack's statement, then sat. "Fine, we'll discuss it this evening." He waved in salute and was back into the stack of papers on his desk.

Jack motioned for Dave to follow him, and they exited the colonel's office, to be met by the corporal and a sergeant. The corporal spoke first. "Major Sage, you and Marshal Cole will be staying with the colonel tonight. Sergeant Early here will show you to the colonel's quarters, take your horses to the stables for you, and see to whatever supplies you may need. Food of course, but ammunition and whatever else will help."

"That's mighty generous, Corporal. Are you sure it's alright with the colonel?"

"Positive, sir. If you'll go with Sergeant Early, he'll take care of you."

"Thank you." Jack turned to the sergeant. "Shall we, Sergeant Early?"

"Yes, sir, Major. Follow me."

12

Jack lay behind a lightning-struck, partially burned pine that was lodged between two jagged boulders. His back rested against the flat side of one of the boulders. It had been a long, rough walk from where they had tied the horses, and his back was still giving him trouble from their ride from Fort Sill. The thought of Fort Sill brought a smile to his face. Sitting in the officers' mess with Mackenzie's complement of officers had brought back a load of pleasant memories. There had been many good times in the army. The friendships and camaraderie built in the bonding of war lasted forever. At least it had been pleasant for a time, until he told the colonel about what the prisoners had said about paying off an officer in his unit.

Jack went over again what had happened. None of it good except catching the thief. To all outward appearances, Colonel Mackenzie had appeared calm and reserved, but Jack could see the man was seething. He delayed supper, told the officers to have a drink and wait in the parlor, and with Jack, marched to the stockade. He had Banks yanked out of confinement and asked him two questions. First, if he was sure about an officer being paid to help them, and second, could he recognize the man? Banks answered yes to both.

With two large guards, one on each side of Banks, they marched back to his quarters. He burst into the parlor where his officer waited anxiously for their commander. It wouldn't have been necessary for Banks to identify the man, for when Banks stepped into the parlor, a lieutenant blanched. Banks pointed him out, and without a moment's hesitation, Mackenzie had the man marched, with Banks, to the stockade.

After searching the lieutenant's quarters, they found his stash of gold coins belonging to the many cattlemen who had been killed by Morgan. After his own officer's involvement, Jack thought Mackenzie might decide to send men with them, but he held to his decision. He needed them there to move out if need be.

Dave spoke up. "Jack, what's your plan?"

"Sorry, I was thinking about Colonel Mackenzie's thief."

"Yeah, that was tough, but at least they caught him. You think he'll get much punishment?"

"Oh yes. That young gentleman will probably spend a good portion of his remaining life in the new prison at Fort Leavenworth. It'll be a long time before he tastes freedom again."

The two men were silent as they both thought of the betrayal of the officer. Jack checked the location of the sun to prevent a reflection from the lenses, grasped the binoculars, brought them back up to his eyes, and studied the outlaws' den beneath them. There were two shacks, both built against the facing wall of the hill Jack and Dave were on, Flat Top Mountain. A creek ran from near the top of the mountain, down its side, to the bottom of Devil's Canyon and turned toward the mouth. Across the creek from the shacks, a corral had been built, and it held four horses and two mules. It concerned Jack that there weren't six horses in the corral.

Two men were digging and hauling their product to a

pathetic-looking cradle built to sift gold from the rock and debris. Several buckets of water sat near the cradle. The binoculars brought the men close enough to see their faces, and Jack could tell neither man was enjoying himself. They weren't overexerting themselves either. They spent more time leaning on their shovels than digging. Watching the two through the binoculars was almost funny. They'd fill the wheelbarrow, then argue about who was going to push it the twenty feet to the cradle. He handed the glasses to Dave. "You'll get a kick out of those two."

Dave watched for a few minutes and chuckled. "They're not getting much done. Hold on. Jack, I can't believe this. It looks like they're actually going to draw down on each other. What are we gonna do about it?"

"Nothing. We're too far to do anything without alerting everyone else. The judge said for us to try not to shoot any of them. He didn't say anything about them shooting each other."

Dave stiffened. "Wait, two men just came out of the office, and one is yelling at the two miners. He might be Morgan."

"Give me those."

Dave handed the binoculars to Jack. He readjusted them, bringing the action in clear, features sharp. Centering the one yelling at the two mining, he examined the man. His first thought was, *I don't know him. Somehow he's managed to keep his face off a circular for all these years.* Jack watched the interaction between the men. From the way the captured men had described him, this had to be Tate Morgan. He looked like he could kill either one of the two arguing men any second.

The other man who had accompanied Morgan from the shack said something to him. The second man was immediately waved off, but he wouldn't give up. He kept talking, and finally, Morgan began to calm down. He pointed at the two who had been arguing, said something, and turned back for the cabin. The man who had calmed him leaned toward the two men, spoke rapidly, and turned away, following Morgan back to the shack.

Jack watched them enter the shack and lowered the glasses. "Could you see the other man who came out of the shack with Morgan?"

Dave nodded. "I could. It looked like he was trying to calm Morgan down and save those two fellas' bacon."

"Yeah, that's exactly what he was doing. I'm thinking those two boys came close to meeting their maker. That fella Morgan appears to have quite a temper. He must be quick with a gun, because he looked like he was ready to take on those two at the same time. Of course, we don't know what was being said. One or both of those hard workers might be more than happy for the other one to die."

Dave looked back down the wall of the canyon. The two men had gone back to work, pouring a little of the rock into the cradle, then chasing it with a bucket of water. They still didn't appear very enthusiastic. "They don't look like men who have found gold or expect to."

Jack shook his head. "They sure don't, and I can guarantee you they aren't men who like to get familiar with hard work."

Dave tried again. "Have you come up with a plan?"

Jack stared down into the canyon, this time examining the canyon mouth and walls with the binoculars. At last he stopped, leaned back against the flat side of the boulder, and shook his head. "I haven't. I want to see if the two who are missing come back this afternoon. I wouldn't think Morgan would send them far, not with their numbers down to six."

Though he wasn't ready to tell Dave, Jack had a plan developing. Having the binoculars made a huge difference. Not only did they bring every crevice, bush, and tree almost into his lap, but they had allowed him to examine the slope of the creek, which flowed down the mountainside, past the cabins, and along the canyon bottom. With them, he had discovered the drop to the canyon floor was gradual enough to allow a horse to be ridden down it. Once at the bottom, and not more than thirty yards away, the corral sat across the creek and vulnerable to attack. It would be a straight shot across the creek to the corral, where the outlaws' overconfidence had caused the corral gate to be left unlocked, susceptible to attack. A minute or two would be all one man would need to empty the corral of the horses and herd them through and out of the canyon.

I can do this, he thought. *Dave can set up on the North Fork of the Red River and cover the mouth of the canyon. No one will be able to get out without having to climb one or the other of the canyon sides, and that will take time. If I can get the horses out of there without getting shot, we'll have them. No man is crazy enough to expect to survive in this country on foot. Any of these tribes finding a white man on foot will lift his hair before he knows what's happening.*

He let the binoculars hang loose around his neck and leaned against the rock. Getting the idea seemed to ease his backache. Dave was intently watching the two men work and fuss. Jack kicked the deputy's boot, and he looked up, his eyebrows raised in a question.

Jack removed his Stetson and wiped his hatband with the palm of his hand. "I've got an idea."

The deputy's face lit up. "I knew you'd come up with something. Tell me, I'm dying of curiosity."

Jack placed his hat on the back of his head and outlined the plan. When he was finished, he asked, "How good are you with that rifle?"

"Better than most, worse than some. If I'm on the edge of the Red, I can drill anything that moves out of that canyon. It'll be like shooting fish in a barrel."

Jack's voice was hard and clipped. "That's not your job unless they get past the mouth."

Dave, puzzled, looked at Jack. "It isn't?"

"No, what did the judge tell us about this bunch?"

"He said don't kill anyone if we don't have to."

"You think keeping them in the canyon is a have-to?"

"It is if they're going to escape."

"But they're on foot. Those are dead men on foot, and it won't take long for them to figure it out. They may already have. Think about the big picture. This is Indian Territory. If they get out of this canyon, they're dead men. Comanches, Kiowas, or Cheyenne are liable to come along anytime. When they spot these horseless white men, they'll kill them, and it won't be pleasant.

"Their only chance of survival is to go with us. It won't take them long to figure that out. When I come blasting out of that canyon behind their horses, all you have to do is stop them from doing the same thing afoot. Just slow them up so they have time to think about it. Keep them in the canyon while I'm rounding up those horses. When I get back, we'll make them a special deal—get left to the Indians, or drop their guns and take their chances in court. How does that sound?"

Dave thought about it for a couple of minutes and finally asked, "When and how do you plan on getting their horses away from them?"

"Good question. We still have a little hitch in the plan. If those other two outlaws don't show up, we'll not be able to execute, but if they do, I'll hit just at dawn. I figure to have enough light to make it down this little mountain along the creek and catch those fellers while they're at least half asleep. I want it to be light enough for you to be able to shoot, and by the way, I know I said keep them in the canyon, but if any do manage to get past the canyon mouth, drop them. We can't afford to have them out here trying to slip up on us. Can you do that?"

Dave thought for a second. "The judge will be awful mad."

"He's been mad at me before, and I survived."

The corners of Dave's eyes wrinkled with humor. "I seem to have heard about that. Seems it's happened more than once. In fact, one of the deputies said it happened every time you two got together."

Jack laughed. "Pretty much. We're like flint and steel, bring us together, and we strike sparks." Jack grew serious again. "I need an answer, Dave. Are you up to killing a man if you have to?"

Dave too was serious. "Yes, sir. I thought about that a bunch before I hired on as a marshal. I'm here to enforce the law. If I have to shoot someone to do it, I will."

"Good enough. One more question. Are you satisfied with the plan?"

"Yep."

Jack gave a firm nod. "Good. Now all we need is for the missing riders to show up."

The afternoon progressed, and the sun beat down on them like a hammer on an anvil. They managed to find a little shade, but it was miserable on Flat Top Mountain that afternoon. There was a small natural tank where they had left the horses and mules. At least the animals would have water, though they'd still be hot.

They had brought their canteens and jerky, anticipating a long stay at their observation post. They were right. The day gradually passed. Minutes felt like hours before the sun finally began to drop toward the horizon, still no returning riders.

Dave, resting against the rock face, had dozed off. Jack punched him lightly. The younger man's eyes popped open, but he didn't move. "What's up?"

"You'd better get ready. You'll want to get off this mountain before dark."

Dave stretched, crawled behind a boulder so he couldn't be seen from below, and stood. "Anything else?"

"Yeah. Unsaddle Pepper, leave the blanket and tack on the ground, and take him with you. Leave Thunder. Make sure he has enough rope to defend himself, should mister bear or mountain lion come along, and I should be set. Keep an eye out for those other two outlaws. Your job is to see them before they see you. Stay hidden. You'll know when I'm coming out. There'll be plenty of noise. Hopefully the morning will bring this chase to an end. Any questions?"

Dave thought for a second, then shook his head. He touched the brim of his hat in salute. "See you in the morning."

"Yep."

Jack watched the wide-shouldered young deputy, bent over, carefully moving away from the edge of the bluff until he was well clear and wouldn't be seen. He straightened and moved quickly toward the horses.

Putting Dave out of his mind, Jack glanced at the western horizon. It would be dark in an hour. The moon should be up around midnight, though only a sliver. Hopefully it would give him and Thunder enough light to see their way down the mountain. Breaking his horse's leg was the last thing Jack wanted to do.

He removed his hat for the last time today, lay down, brought the glasses to his eyes, and looked along the canyon toward the river. Several deer worked their way across the mouth of the canyon, undisturbed, each grabbing a mouthful of browse before its head popped up, searching. Jack shook his head in disgust. He'd rather see the deer bounding away in fear of the missing riders as they rode in. Light dwindled quickly, and the deer grew dim in the binoculars. About to remove them from his eyes, he caught sharp movement as one of the deer snapped its head up, followed by the others. They stared toward the river, then, white tails waving like flags, bounded up the opposite side of the canyon.

Jack didn't track them with the glasses, he remained focused on the mouth of the canyon, and at last, when he could barely make them out, two riders came into view, loping through the entrance to the head of the canyon. He breathed a sigh of relief and thought, *This just might work, and, hopefully, this time tomorrow we'll be planning our trip back to Fort Smith.*

He watched the two men ride along the bottom of the canyon until the remaining light had dimmed to where he could no longer see them through the binoculars. Lowering the glasses from his eyes, he could make out the outlines of the two mounted horses as they pulled up below. Light spilled across the yards in front of the two shacks when the doors were opened. Jack could see men stepping into the light. Two from the larger shack, and two from the smaller. He could just make out voices, but couldn't understand what was being said. The horses were led into the corrals, unsaddled, and fed. A trough was at the edge of the corral, located so any animal in the corral could reach it. The two horses that had just arrived drank deeply.

The men walked into the larger shack and were there for a while before coming out and moving to the smaller building. *So,* Jack thought, *the smaller shack is the bunkhouse or barracks, depending on how Morgan defines it, and the bigger one is the ranch house or officers' quarters.*

Jack rose from the log, put his Stetson back on, and leaned against what he was beginning to think of as his boulder, stretching his long legs to relieve the ache in the right. The old bullet wound didn't like being stationary for so long. Ignoring the ache, his mind went to the most important person in his life, Grace. *So what has your decision been, Grace? Have you visited the judge? Are we still married, or did you call it quits and have our marriage annulled?* Her tantalizing fragrance filled his mind. *It's funny,* he thought, *despite her beauty, the softness of her cheek, and those lovely green eyes, the one thing that brings her closest is how she smelled, the rose fragrance mixed with the aroma of fresh-baked bread.*

The moon wouldn't be up for hours, and the sun had been down for only one. Jack had been mulling over his plan. There was a problem, but he'd have to live with it. If the men in the bunkhouse heard him, they were the closest to the creek where it came down the mountain just before turning to run along the bottom of the canyon, he could be in trouble. If they could get out of the shack quick enough and stop him from opening the gate, the plan would be ruined, and he, very likely, would be dead.

He chuckled. *No plan I've ever come up with has been perfect. Why would I expect this one to be? Anyway, after the first engagement, the plan goes out the window. If I time it right, dawn will only be breaking.* He nodded and spoke softly to himself. "It'll work, Jack. It has to. You've got a wife to return to and persuade you're worth depending on."

He leaned his head against the boulder and closed his eyes. A couple of hours of sleep would do him good.

13

His eyes snapped open. His neck hurt, and he was as stiff as a cold corpse, but his back felt good. The moon had been up for at least two hours. Jack yanked his pocket watch from its pocket, slid well behind the boulder to shelter the flare of his match, and after pulling one from its waterproof wrapping, struck it on the butt of his Smith & Wesson. It flared, instantly destroying his night vision and illuminating his watch, two o'clock. He spit on his fingers and smothered the match, returning the mountain to thick darkness. He had slept for almost five hours. Fumbling in the faint light provided by the moon, he rose to his feet, grabbed his rifle and saddlebags, and started carefully toward Thunder.

Though he had a good distance to go and was in a hurry, he forced himself to step deliberately through the broken rocks, narrow draws, and shadowy scrub. The last thing he needed was a broken leg or ankle. He was running late because he had slept too long, and after he had warned Dave not to sleep. *A great teacher I am,* he thought.

It took him almost an hour to reach Thunder. The big gray stood stiff, ears forward and ready to fight as Jack neared. The wind was in Jack's face, so the devoted horse had no scent of his approaching master. All he knew was something was moving toward him. When Jack was close enough, he spoke softly. "Hey, boy, you ready to go to work?"

Jack could have sworn the horse smiled. The animal's muzzle and distended nostrils relaxed, and he started toward Jack. As soon as he was in reach, Jack grasped his bridle and rubbed his cheek, then his neck. He could feel the thick muscles relaxing. "Sorry, boy, I didn't mean to scare you, but we have a big morning ahead of us. I hope you're ready."

He quickly saddled the horse, tied his saddlebags, and slid his rifle into its scabbard. After checking to ensure the saddle was tight, he swung up and turned Thunder north, along the backbone of Flat Top Mountain. He had his route memorized, laid out like a map in his mind, and, unerringly, he guided his big gray horse to the head of the creek. Upon finding the spring, he let Thunder drink while he planned his descent and dash. Satisfied, he clucked, and Thunder started down the steep slope, following alongside the tiny creek.

Halfway down, Jack saw the first light of dawn break in the east. Only a glint now, but it would grow rapidly, and if there were any early risers in this bunch, they could put an end to him and his plan. He clucked at the big horse again, and Thunder picked up speed. The crunching rocks were now audible to Jack. He hoped the outlaws were sound sleepers. Then he reminded himself, *Hope isn't a plan, but I'll use it anyway.*

They moved nearer. Jack could see the outline of the shacks, and they weren't far away. In fact, the bunkhouse sat closer to the creek than it had looked. A thought dashed through his mind. *This is going to be close.* Thunder continued down the mountain. He waited. A little closer. Closer. Not yet. Now!

Jack leaned near Thunder's ear and said softly but clearly, "Go."

He felt the big horse gather himself and leap down the mountain slope. They landed in the creek where it made a right turn, and Jack was at the gate. He whipped the looped rope from the top of the gate post and swung the gate wide. Thunder dashed in, surprising the sleeping animals and forcing the horses and mules to race through the open gate.

As they leaped to freedom behind the escaping animals, the large shack's door burst open, and a man stood in the doorway, holding nothing! Jack let out a yell of triumph as Thunder carried him past the dumbfounded, empty-handed man in the doorway, and he recognized him. Tate Morgan. A second man almost bowled the first over as he burst from the shack behind him. He was holding a rifle, and Jack could see it snapping to his shoulder. He hugged Thunder and watched the man level down on him.

A tongue of flame leaped for him, and he felt the burn of the bullet slap him on his left side. He had his .44-caliber Smith & Wesson in hand and fired one, two, three rounds at the two men, scattering them, and he was past the ridge that blocked sight from the two buildings. He patted Thunder on the neck. "Good boy." He wasn't feeling faint, which he knew would happen if he were severely wounded. Maybe he had gotten lucky. Maybe it was just a graze. The horses started slowing, and Jack let out a yell, firing his revolver. He didn't want those horses slowing until they were well out of the canyon, where he could gather them.

They rode clear of the canyon mouth, and Tate Morgan's animals were down to a lope, and they were holding together. Jack thought, *I love it when a plan works.* He waited until the animals had slowed to a walk, and herded them across the Red, turning them back toward the mouth of Devil's Canyon. On his way, he heard a rifle crack, then two more shots, and the rifle fired again. *I've got to hurry,* he thought. *Dave could be in trouble.*

On the opposite side of the river and almost directly across from where he expected to find Dave, he crossed the horses again and called softly. He immediately received a response.

"I'm over here." Dave rose just enough where Jack could see him. Keeping the animals in the river bottom, Jack made his way to the deputy.

"How's it going?"

"I had to shoot one of them. I think he's dead. He's lying in the open, at the mouth of the canyon. The rest of them ran back into the canyon."

"How many did you see?"

"Only four. I think the others were behind them and decided to stay hidden. At least I hope that's what happened."

"Probably. Where are the horses tied?"

Dave pointed across the river. "I figured it would be safer if we kept them over there. They're well out of gunshot. Uh-oh, here comes another one trying to slip out. Hang on a second." He threw the rifle to his shoulder, it settled, and the crack echoed across the mouth of the canyon, sending a bullet sailing toward the adventurous spirit and striking at his feet.

Jack yelled, "This is United States Marshal Jack Sage. There's already one of you fellas dead. I'd suggest the rest of you throw down your weapons and come out with your hands high."

The man turned and ran, disappearing into the canyon.

Jack raised his voice again. "We're going to give you fellas more of a chance than you gave our two marshals. You come out with your hands up, and we'll take you back to Fort Smith for trial, or we can leave you out here without horses. We might even mention you to the first Comanche or Kiowa we meet. You think about it, but don't think too long. I'm itching to get back home."

Silence met Jack's offer. He had expected this type of initial response. They would have to talk about it, weigh the pros and cons, before making a decision.

"You're hit." Concern was evident on Dave's face.

Jack had forgotten about the bullet's sting. He pulled his shirt-tail from inside his trousers. As hot as it had been, he wasn't wearing his union suit, so he was able to see the wound when he lifted the shirt. About level with his belt line, it looked as if an auger had drilled along his skin for five inches, but nothing else. He breathed a sigh of relief. "I've always been lucky."

Dave opened the saddlebags he had laid next to him, and brought out a clean-looking undershirt. "This'll do." He ripped it in thirds, laid them on the leather bags, and poured water over one section. "This is gonna smart a bit."

Jack nodded.

Dave, with no hesitation, wiped along the wound, pressing into the damaged skin. Remnants of Jack's shirt were dragged from the wound and stuck to the bloody rag. Jack kept his eyes on the canyon mouth, laboring to ignore the pain. Occasionally, he scanned the sides of the canyon mouth where they turned into the next canyon. The outlaws hadn't had time to cross the mountains that made up the canyon, but he wouldn't take chances.

Dave rinsed the rag again. This time, after wiping the wound channel, the rag came clean with the exception of the blood. "It looks good, Jack, shallow, though the bullet churned the flesh a bit. I'll pack it with a dry section, and that should keep it until we get back to the fort. It'll be sore, but like you said, you're lucky."

Jack, still watching the canyon mouth, had seen no movement. "Thanks, Dave. I'm obliged."

Dave returned to his position. "You think they'll give up?"

Seeing Dave was on the alert again, Jack laid down his rifle and shoved his shirttail back inside his trousers. After Dave's efforts, the cleaned wound was throbbing like crazy. "If they're smart. They'll know it's a long way back to Fort Smith, and anything can happen. Also, trials are unpredictable. Each of them could be betting on getting off. They won't. Every man of them will hang. Of course, they could just be hardheaded enough to fight."

An hour went by, no movement, no response.

"How long do you think it would take for one of them to make it over Flat Top and circle around behind us?"

"How long did it take you to get here?"

Dave thought about it. "Reckon maybe two hours."

"And they still have to climb it first. Add another hour. I think the climb would take them at least two, but let's go with just one. You're still left with a total of three hours. We'll be long gone before they arrive."

"You're actually going to leave them out here without horses?"

Jack's forehead wrinkled, and his eyes tightened, trying to figure out what Dave was driving at. "Sure, if they don't come out soon. I'll give them a deadline. It won't be long, maybe thirty minutes or even fifteen. Once that's past, we're pulling out."

"With all this shooting, one tribe or another will be along here soon. You know what'll happen."

"I can't help that. What's your point, Dave? You want to sit here until they manage to get someone or several someones behind us and blow us to shreds? There's no point to waiting if they don't agree. We're just setting ourselves up."

Dave shook his head. "Marshal Sage, I just can't wrap my head around intentionally leaving men to be tortured by Indians, no matter how bad they are."

Jack was surprised by Dave's sudden concern for the outlaws. He had been well acquainted with both of the marshals who had been hanged at their hands. He stared at the opening of the canyon. The fluttering of cloth caught his eye. It was the back of the shirt belonging to the dead man Dave had sent to his maker. The boy wasn't hesitant about pulling the trigger when necessary, so why was this bothering him?

"You understand what would happen if we stayed and allowed them to get behind us? We talked about that."

"Yes, sir. I understand. I'm not saying I wouldn't go with you. I'm just telling you it bothers me. I've seen what happens to people when they get captured by Indians, especially Comanches."

Jack pursued the questioning while continuing to watch for the outlaws. "How old were you?"

The corners of Dave's mouth drew down in a frown. "Twelve, why?"

"Curious, that's all. When we're young, seeing something like that can leave a lasting impression."

Dave stopped watching the canyon and turned to Jack, his eyes narrowing in anger. "I ain't no coward, Marshal Sage, and I don't appreciate you saying I am. In fact, I don't take that from anyone, not even a marshal."

Jack frowned and continued to watch the canyon. "You listen to me close, Dave Cole. I never called you a coward. I was trying to figure out how you came to your thinking, but don't you go raring up at me. This is neither the time nor the place. You settle down and keep your eyes on that canyon while I talk."

People are interesting, Jack thought as he watched this burly young deputy strive to control himself. *They show anger in different ways. Dave's ears are so red they look like they'll start bleeding at any instant. There's no other tell other than his frown. Let's see if he can control himself.*

At Jack's command, Dave turned his head toward the canyon and resumed his watch, but his ears stayed beet red.

"Now, you listen close. When a man is young and sees such violence, it stays with him, making it harder to throw it off. Don't ask me why. It just does. It doesn't make him a coward, it's just the way it is. But if you're going to stay a lawman, you've got to push that sentimentality away so you can make your decisions logically, based on what you know. I'm not saying don't be mindful of the needs of your opponent, but don't let it put you in a position to lose your life. When you do that, you're giving control to the man or woman who's trying to kill you."

Jack watched Dave's ears begin to lose the deep red. He almost smiled as he thought, *You've got a tell, boy, and that's one I don't know if even you can change.*

Dave's head moved slowly in a nod. "You make sense, Marshal. I ain't never thought of it like that."

"You're young, Dave. It takes time to learn these things. Some you'll learn from the men who've been doing this for a long time. Others, you'll learn on your own, and they could be mistakes. Hopefully, none will ever be serious enough to get you or someone else killed. Shoot, boy, from what I've seen, you're about as lucky as I am."

A grin drifted across the young deputy's face. "You just got shot, Marshal. I hope I'm luckier than you."

Jack couldn't prevent a grin spreading across his scarred countenance. "I hope you are too, Dave. I surely do. Now are you ready to give these fellas an ultimatum?"

"Yes, sir."

Jack inhaled a deep breath, and when he spoke, his voice carried into the canyon. "Tate Morgan, listen close. You and your men can wait in that canyon all day if you like, but we're leaving in fifteen minutes. In fifteen minutes we're riding out of here with your mules, your horses, and your last chance to save yourselves from the Indians. You will be left afoot. Make up your mind."

Silence greeted Jack's announcement. He waited for ten minutes, then shouted one word. "Adios." He turned to Dave. "Let's go. They've had their chance. Fort Smith is calling us. We'll have four of them standing trial. He won't be happy, but the judge will at least have those in his court."

Jack was about to stand when Dave pointed toward the canyon. Less than seventy-five yards away, six men stood with hands held high. One of them called, "Don't leave us out here, Marshal. With all this shooting, our position is known. We'll be dead in less than a day without our horses. That ain't even human."

"Well now," Jack said, "isn't that a sight." He raised his voice. "You boys drop your guns, nice and careful like, or this here posse will ventilate you where you stand."

The outlaws dropped their weapons and quickly returned their hands high above their heads.

"I hadn't thought of that, Marshal Sage," Dave said. "I think those fellers think there's a big posse out here besides just you and me."

Jack laughed. "I believe you are correct, and we're going to continue that ruse until we get them cuffed in irons. Would you run to Stonewall and bring six cuffs back, then we'll go out there and fix those boys right up. Make plenty of noise while you're getting them. Leave me your rifle."

Dave frowned. "You've got yours, Marshal. What are you gonna do with mine?"

Jack grinned. "You'll see. Hurry."

Dave dropped over the bank and sounded like several men as he ran through the rocks of the dry portion of the riverbed. Meanwhile, Jack found a nice fork in one of the trees and rested Dave's rifle through it. He stepped past the first rifle and found another tree about the right size, with a perfect fork, and slid his rifle through it.

"Marshal," Morgan called, "what's going on? We don't like standing out in the open like this. If Indians come along, we'd be hurtin' mighty bad."

"Don't you worry yourself, Morgan. We'll protect you." He turned his head as if he were speaking to men with him. "Keep them covered, boys. If they get antsy, you know what to do."

Dave rushed back with the six cuffs, three over each shoulder. Reaching Jack, the marshal pulled three from his shoulder. "Alright, this is the hardest part. We need them to think they're covered by a posse so they don't make a move while we're locking them up. Otherwise, one of them might go for a gun, and that could set them all off. Just follow my lead, understand?"

"I sure do, Marshal. Don't you worry about me."

"Alright, leave your gun holstered. We wouldn't be worried about keeping them covered if we had a posse, but be ready." He handed the three chains and cuffs back to Dave. "It'll look better if I'm not carrying any. Are you alright with all of them? I know they're heavy."

Dave's lips spread wide, showing even white teeth. "They're not too heavy for me, Marshal."

Jack chuckled. "No, I reckon not. Let's go."

14

Jack felt a chill when he was close enough to recognize Morgan's number two man. He was the same outlaw from yesterday who had calmed Morgan and prevented him from killing one or both of the two men arguing over hauling rocks and debris to the cradle. Through his binoculars, it had looked like Number Two worked hard to calm Morgan, successfully. But nearing the two leaders, he recognized the most deadly of the two, and it wasn't Morgan. Where the other men were obviously concerned and agitated, even Morgan, Number Two was cold, expressionless. There was no frown or wrinkles of worry across his forehead. The man showed no emotion except for his eyes. They were an ice blue and active, moving over Jack and then Dave and back to Jack. Here was the man they had to fool. He went straight for him, ignoring Morgan.

He held out his hand to Dave, who lifted a set of cuffs from his shoulder. They weren't attractive contraptions, but they were simple and efficient. Two hinged iron bands joined at a raised reinforced bolt hole on each side, allowing a bolt to slide through and lock with a key. A chain from the bottom of each of the wristbands connected them, giving the prisoner enough length to move his hands but not by much. Dave dropped the set into Jack's big paw.

He stepped up to Number Two. "What's your name?"

The man examined Jack, finishing with eyes locked on his. "What's yours?"

Jack knew this was a war of wills, but he didn't have a lot of time to waste. They needed to get these men subdued before the outlaws became suspicious.

Jack let a faint smile crinkle the corner of his eyes. "Jack Sage. Now, I asked you a question."

Still holding Jack's gaze, the man nodded. "That you did, Jack Sage." When he said it, he had glanced at Jack's badge and smiled, a smile with no humor, no kindness.

Jack couldn't let the contempt pass. "Marshal Jack Sage."

"Ah, yes, United States Marshal Jack Sage."

Jack could feel the loathing of the man when he said United States.

"I'll not ask you again."

"Leon Stradling, United States Marshal Jack Sage."

"Turn around."

Stradling held Jack's gaze for another long moment, then turned. Jack latched first the right cuff and then the left and moved to Morgan. Dave was working quickly. He had already cuffed two of the men. Only three were left.

Stradling surveyed the treeline. "Your men are well disciplined. I haven't heard a peep or seen a movement from them, though I can see a couple of rifle barrels through the brush that haven't moved, not one iota. How many do you have, United States Marshal Jack Sage?"

Tate Morgan's head was turning from right to left as he gave the treeline along the river a close examination. He looked up at Jack when he moved in front of him. "You're a big one. I wish you had been one of those marshals we'd hanged. You would've made that rope pop."

Morgan had several visible scars on his face and neck. He wasn't afraid of a fight. "Turn around, Morgan."

"You planning on putting those things on me?"

"I'm not just planning. Turn around." He glanced at Dave. The deputy had spun his last man around, and Jack caught the quick movement of the man reaching for a hideout gun behind his waistband. Jack shouted, "Look out, Dave." His deputy, gripping the man's opposite arm behind his back, hadn't seen the man's movement and looked in Jack's direction.

Jack saw the tiny .44-caliber over and under derringer pop into view as the man brought it up toward Dave's left ear. Even as he drew, Jack knew he was going to be too late.

Everything became a blur of action. Stradling dove at Jack's legs while Morgan threw a thick right fist at his neck. One of the other outlaws Dave had cuffed kicked the deputy in the back of his leg at his knee, causing him to fall backward. Jack kicked at Stradling and dropped his head low, causing Morgan's blow to only graze his neck. He kept his target in view and continued his draw. He watched the derringer fire, and a spray of blood erupted from the muzzle of the derringer against Dave's head. Jack fired a moment before Morgan followed his right cross to Jack's neck with a left uppercut.

His bullet struck the outlaw in his right shoulder, spinning and knocking him to the ground. Seeing the derringer sail from the man's hand, he blocked the uppercut from Morgan with his forearm and swung the barrel of his Smith & Wesson into Morgan's temple, collapsing him to the ground next to Stradling, who was out cold from the kick to his head. The wounded outlaw lay on the ground, rolling, moaning, and holding his shoulder. The commotion finished as quickly as it had started, and in the quiet, Jack heard horses approaching. *Great,* he thought, *after this fiasco, I have to deal with Indians,* but the thought passed with the distinct sound of cavalry hardware and the clatter of an approaching wagon.

He double-checked Morgan and Stradling. Neither would be causing any problems for the next few minutes. He raced to Dave. Reaching him, Jack dropped to the ground and scooped the boy up in his arms. Blood covered the young deputy's head and shoulder. Jack, using his sleeve, wiped the blood from the head wound and breathed a sigh of relief. White skull was visible in the instant before blood gushed out again. The bullet hadn't penetrated his skull.

The cavalry rode up, followed by a prisoner wagon. They found an outlaw shot and moaning, two others collapsed on the ground, both bleeding from head wounds, several manacled, and Jack Sage holding his deputy in his arms, covered in blood, and roaring with laughter. The lieutenant looked at his sergeant, who shrugged and swung down to assist, followed by the officer.

When the lieutenant approached Jack, the lawman, still laughing so hard tears flowed down his cheeks, looked up and said, "He's lucky. He is as lucky as I am," and broke into laughter again.

TWO WEEKS later Jack Sage rode into Fort Smith, his deputy Dave Cole at his side. They led a prisoner wagon carrying eleven prisoners, the Tate Morgan gang plus two more they had picked up for one of the other marshals along the way.

Jack's feelings were mixed. He was ecstatic that Dave's head hadn't been blown off, which would've happened if one of the outlaws hadn't kicked his leg out from under him. That boy was really lucky.

But Jack also had an internal battle taking place between hope and dread. He hoped that Grace waited for him, but he dreaded the thought of her having their marriage annulled. Could it be possible she had waited? Or had she asked the judge to annul their wedding? Was he coming home to a wife and sons, or to an empty future?

Buck Walker stood on the boardwalk outside the jail when they pulled up. He strode out to meet the two marshals. Reaching Dave first, he slapped him on the leg. "I heard about you. I always said you had a hard head, and it's a good thing. Good to see you, boy."

Dave grinned down at the marshal. "Yeah, I'm like Jack, I'm lucky."

Buck shook his head. "I don't know if I'd call gettin' shot in the head lucky, but on the other hand . . . I guess it depends on which end you look at it from."

Dave's grin widened. "I'm feelin' mighty lucky, Marshal. If one of them outlaws hadn't kicked my leg out from under me, that slug would've spread my brains all over Indian Territory."

Buck grimaced, then laughed. "I'm thinkin' there wouldn't have been much to spread."

"How do, Buck," Jack said. "What that young fella is saying is gospel. Of course, a thick skull helps."

Buck nodded at the wagon. "Is that all of them?"

Jack was anxious to get to Ma Nelson's Bed and Eats and see Grace. "Yep, all except one who tried to shoot it out with us. He lost." Jack looked down the street. "I've got business. I'll see you later."

Buck held up a hand and shook his head. "Hang on, Jack. Judge Bell left word he wants to see you as soon as you get back."

"It'll have to wait."

"Jack, it's important, and you know the judge. When he says right now, he means right now."

"Let him talk to the kid, and you can tell him I quit, for real this time." He pulled the beat-up badge from his vest and tossed it toward Buck, who grabbed at it, fumbled it from one hand to the other, and finally hung on. Jack missed the show, for he had already clucked to Pepper, and with Thunder and Stonewall in tow, headed at a lope for Winthrop's Stables, which was right next door to Ma's. Chickens scattered, as well as people. An old bluetick hound raised his head at the commotion, in the June heat an unwelcome disturbance, then, deeming it below his interest, dropped his head back between his paws and was sound asleep.

Jack pulled Pepper to a stop in front of Pauly and his Winthrop's Stables. Pauly, hands on his hips, had watched Jack and his entourage approach. "Git off that horse and give him to me. I'll take care of him and the rest of your herd. It looks like they need it. You git on over to Ma's."

Jack, his heart pounding in both dread and anticipation, swung down and tossed the reins for Pepper and the two lead ropes to Pauly. He couldn't wait. He broke into a trot around the stable and toward Ma's. A long leap took him onto the boardwalk, and he swung the door wide, yanking his hat off and ducking as he plowed through, where he was attacked.

Wrapped in the fragrance of fresh bread and rose water, Grace's soft, sweet lips covered his rough chapped ones. Her arms encircled his neck, and she pulled him to her. At the same time, he felt two sets of smaller arms around his waist, his boys.

"Oh, Jack," Grace said, leaning back in his arms. "I am so glad you are back. We received reports you had been shot, and poor Davey. Is he alright? I love you, you big ox."

"I love you, too, Grace, and yes, Davey's great, excepting a fine scar." He looked into those green eyes pouring tears, which coursed down her soft white cheeks, and knew he was home. Anywhere she and the boys were would be home for him. He looked across the parlor to see Mary, her hands clasped in front of her, and tears running down her cheeks.

When she saw him looking, she mouthed, "Welcome home, Jack."

He smiled his gratitude. Then he looked again into Grace's eyes. "Grace, you have to tell me. Are we still married?"

She threw back her head, her thick black hair shimmering in the sunlight, and filled the room with a strong, happy laugh. "Of course we are. Do you think I would ever let you escape from me?" She held her hand with her wedding ring in front of him. "You'd better know you are mine forever, Marshal. You can't get away."

Jack crushed her to him again, feeling her warmth and vitality, knowing life couldn't get better than this. He released her and half knelt, wrapping his arms around his sons. "Who's ready to go to Texas?"

Together, Billy and Elijah yelled, "We are!"

He squeezed them until Billy stuck out a limp tongue and collapsed in his arms. "Argh, I'm squashed."

Everyone laughed at his theatrics, and Jack relaxed his hug.

The excitement ebbed, leaving happy people enjoying one another's company. Mary walked over to Jack. He stood, and Grace stepped back. Mary placed her hands on his wide shoulders. "It is so good to have you home. I hated to see you leave under such a cloud, but it is gone, never to return."

Jack looked at Grace as Mary made the announcement, and his wife smiled, nodding her head. He placed his arms around his mother-in-law and gave her a tender squeeze. "Mary, are you ready to go to Texas?"

She placed her wrinkled hand on his cheek. "Yes, son, I am ready to go anywhere, to be with you and my grandsons and my daughter."

Jack lifted her from the floor and spun around with her. "Then I guess that's settled. Is everyone packed?"

A resounding "Yes!" filled the room.

He had to admit, even with his sore leg and side, this had to be the happiest day he had experienced in a long time. He lowered Mary and turned to Grace. "Are you ready for your delayed honeymoon?"

She gave him a thoughtful smile. "Would you be terribly

upset if we put the honeymoon off to a later time. I'd like us to head to Texas as soon as we can."

"Music to my ears, but it's just on hold until later, then it might be to Paris. I'll talk to Pauly and see how soon the wagons can be ready."

Grace came back into his arms. "Oh, Jack, it is so good to have you home. When I'd heard you had been shot, I felt so guilty after the way we parted."

"There's nothing for you to feel guilty about. It was a sudden, difficult situation for both of us, and now it's over."

Buck strode through the still open door. "Jack, the judge is holding up court for you. He wants to see you now."

Jack lowered Grace gently to the floor and turned to his friend. "Buck, I told you I'm done with being a marshal. Did Dave tell the judge?"

"He did, and I gave him your badge. He's not angry, Jack. Trust me when I tell you it's important for you to see him. Come with me now. Get it done, and then you can go about your business."

Grace patted Jack's arm. "You go ahead. We'll be alright. Find out what the judge wants, and it will be over."

Jack knew a meeting with the judge never meant finality, rather, it meant a beginning, and he wanted no more beginnings that had to do with the judge or the law, but he gave in. "Alright. I'll be back shortly. Maybe you or Matthew could whip up something tasty. I'm almighty tired of jerky."

Grace's laughter sounded sweet to his ears. "I'll see if Matthew will let me in his kitchen. He is becoming quite the independent owner." Her soft lips touched his stubbled cheek. "Hurry. We'll have a nice hot bath ready for you when you return."

Buck stepped through the open door, and Jack followed. The two men, one a U.S. Marshal and the larger man a civilian, strode toward the courthouse. Reaching it, they entered and headed up the stairs. *For the last time, I hope,* Jack thought. Buck raised his hand to knock, and Jack pushed past him, shoving the door open. "He's expecting us."

The judge was behind his desk, in his robe, signing papers. At the opening of the door, his head jerked up, forehead wrinkled and lips drawn tight, but seeing the culprit who would enter his office without knocking was Jack, his face relaxed. A faint smile touched his usually tight grim lips. He rose to his feet, extending his hand. "Welcome home, Jack. You had us worried for a while."

Jack took the hand and gave it a cordial shake. "Thanks, Judge. I had me worried."

Judge Bell relaxed in his cushioned chair while Jack sat on the divan nearest the judge's desk. Buck remained standing.

"I can be on my way, Judge Bell."

"Nonsense." He looked at Jack, eyebrows raised in question. Jack gave a short nod. "Sit down, Buck. You can certainly be privy to anything I might say."

Buck dropped on the couch at the opposite end from Jack, who immediately got to the point. "You wanted to see me, Judge?"

Judge Bell opened his top center desk drawer and removed a badge. It was a scratched, worn, and bent badge. "What's this?"

Jack leaned forward on the divan, his face serious, and made a pretense of examining the object. "Well, I'd say that is a bent, beat-up old marshal's badge that needs to be retired." Having offered his opinion, he flopped back against the soft couch. It felt good against his back. Both Pepper and Thunder were smooth-riding horses, but out and back, he knew he'd ridden more than a thousand miles, and his back was letting him know it didn't appreciate the punishment.

Bell took the opportunity to balance the badge between his thumb and forefinger, and he too examined it. When he was finished, he shook his head. "I'm going to have to disagree with you, Jack. I'd say this badge has a few miles left in it."

Jack was tired of playing around. "Not with me, it doesn't. I'm done."

"Your letter from the president—"

"Is just a way to keep me tied to the law. It isn't something to be helpful to me. It's there so some judge I don't know from Adam can be contacted by the president to send me out chasing some no-account outlaw. I'm done with it. I'll be in Texas. The rangers take care of such situations down there. Anyway, they probably don't want me sticking my nose in their business."

"I disagree with you, Jack. I had a long talk with Major Wilson of the Texas Rangers, and he indicated a sincere desire to have you assist them."

Jack could feel himself getting angry. The judge always did this to him. "Judge, I'm going to say this once more. After that, if you even mention me and the law in the same sentence, I'm getting up and walking out that door. Is that clear enough for you?"

15

Jack could see the Judge was having a tough time controlling his temper. He watched him take a deep breath, let it out slowly, and then the man even managed a smile. "Jack, I have to give you a little piece of advice. Don't ever come up in front of me in my court. It might not go well for you."

Though Bell was smiling, Jack had the feeling he was completely serious. He thought, *Don't worry, Judge. A few more days, and you'll never see me again,* but said, "I understand what you mean, Judge. Now, you wanted to see me?"

Bell pulled the top drawer of his desk open again and dropped Jack's badge inside.

He had to admit, but only to himself, the metallic sound of the badge against the echoing bottom of the drawer sounded cold and lonely. He had worn that badge over a good portion of the west and had arrested and had to shoot a number of men because of the law it represented. He would miss the weight of it on his vest. He liked what it represented, but it was time for him to turn the page and begin a new chapter with Grace, the boys, and Mary.

"Jack, you and the law are not why I wanted to see you, although it could bear favorably on your situation. You have another problem. There's been two known gunfighters in town asking about you. Buck is having them watched. I believe they have been hired by Devin Slater. You remember, he wants your portion of the shipping company back east, and I suspect he has even found out about your gold mine. However, I would think there is nothing as important to him as killing the man who killed his twin brother."

Jack leaned forward to respond, but the judge held up his hand. "I understand his brother was out to kill you, and you acted only in self-defense, but do you really think that makes any difference to Slater?"

Jack shook his head and thought, *Will this ever stop? It seems like someone, somewhere is always out to kill me.* He rubbed a knuckle along his chapped lips. *If they keep it up long enough, at some point, they're just liable to be successful.* All levity or anger had left the room. Jack leaned forward again. "Do you have any suggestions, Judge?"

It was the judge's turn to lean back. He rested his elbows on the padded arms of his chair and steepled his fingers. Looking at the ceiling, he began slowly. "These two gunfighters are probably paid to do one thing, and that is kill you. Buck knows them, and they both have reputations of being men who meet their victims face-to-face. Of course, since they are good at what they do, up to this point they have always had the advantage. There is no paper on them other than alerts, no wanted posters. All of their fights have been fair, as far as the other man drawing first." The judge looked past Jack. "Buck?"

Buck had been watching the judge, but now he turned to Jack. "You've probably heard of them. They don't usually work together. The short one is from Texas. He goes by the name of Weston Boone, and it's rumored he's some kind of relation to Daniel Boone. He's supposed to be fast. Of course, they both have that reputation. The taller one is from Missouri. His name is Clive Reese. They usually work alone, but they showed up together here. They've been in town for almost a week. Haven't had any trouble from either of them. They either spend their time at the new Crystal Palace or the hotel.

"The one from Texas has been asking around about you. Both wear their gun low on their right side, and from what I hear, they're nice and polite to everyone." Buck looked at the judge. "That's about it."

Bell took over. "Jack, I'm going to make you a proposition."

Jack leaned back, crossed his arms, and couldn't help rolling his gray eyes.

The judge bristled. "Now you just wait, Jack Sage. I don't have anybody for you to chase or arrest. This is all about you. Listen to me for a change."

He and the judge had battled so many times, and the jurist had talked him into doing whatever he wanted, when he entered this office, Jack forgot the man was a friend, a hard, driven one, but nonetheless, a friend. He gave the judge a nod. "You're right, Judge. Go right ahead."

Surprised, Judge Bell became flustered. "Yes, well, as I was saying . . ." but only for a moment. He opened his desk drawer again and pulled out the bent and scratched badge, dropping it on his desk before he shoved the drawer closed and leaned forward. "Jack, it is in your best interest to continuing wearing this badge. Not only does it give you legitimate rights, but it also carries certain protections. When you wear this, you have the power of the United States government behind you. If it comes to you having to draw against either or both of those men, they will be drawing against the government. I, of course, expect you to function within the boundaries of the law, but the law should not abandon a man who has given so much. You deserve its protection. Please take it. Remain a marshal at least until you have settled down wherever you decide to go." He gave Jack a relaxed grin. "No strings attached."

Jack sat on the couch, looking at the badge he had carried since New Mexico and thinking about what had just been said. *The judge is right. That little piece of tin has a lot of weight behind it. It could help.* Jack had never been a man to mull over decisions. He made them and acted. He stood, reached across the judge's desk, picked up the old badge, and hung it back in place. "Thanks, Judge. What you said makes sense. Anyway, I don't want to be on the wrong side of your bench. Anything else?"

"No, Jack, I think that's it. Welcome back, and I've got to get back to court. Buck, you have anything?"

Buck shook his head. "No, Your Honor."

"Good, walk out with me."

Jack and Buck held back while the judge led the way from his office. Buck pulled the door closed behind them.

The judge paused before heading to the courtroom. "Good luck, Jack. Keep me posted." The two men shook hands again.

"I'll do it, Judge, thanks."

Jack and Buck headed down the stairs, and Judge Bell disappeared into his courtroom.

Before stepping outside, Jack paused at the door. "You know with these two in town, I'm probably going to have to shoot at least one of them and maybe both."

"It'd be a lot simpler if you could make it happen with plenty of witnesses."

Jack laughed. "That's what I'm interested in, Buck, making it easier on you. It's probably going to happen at the time of their choosing. I can't pick a fight with them, and, you said yourself, they have yet to break the law."

Buck pulled the door open and stepped outside into the hot afternoon sun. "Yet." He nodded to Jack and crossed the street to his office.

Jack watched him go, thinking how much Buck had matured

since he first met him. Buck made it across the street, and Jack realized he had been standing like a statue, watching and thinking. *I'm getting old,* he thought and headed down the boardwalk to Ma's. His stomach growled in anticipation, reminding him it had been weeks since he'd had a good meal. He picked up his pace. Passing the Crystal Palace, his feet, as if they were operating independently of his mind, took him through the swinging doors.

Immediately, he was assaulted with the banging of the piano. If for no other reason, the shrill notes of a piano would keep him out of most saloons. Jack had been born tone deaf, and the harsh sounds of any piano drove him crazy. However, the jarring assault of a saloon piano wasn't the only reason he preferred to remain clear of saloons.

The smells were equally bad. After all the years he had spent on the open sea, breathing fresh clean air, and then on the Algerian desert, except for the horrendous dust storms, the smell of a saloon was worse than any unkempt barnyard. The stench of stale beer, three-day-old vomit, sweat, overrunning spittoons, and cheap perfume assaulted the nose as much as the piano did the ears. His feet had betrayed him, turning him in here when he could be headed to Ma's for a delicious meal. He had to admit, he was curious to see if he could spot the gunfighters.

His eyes adjusted to the dim light, and he saw the Crystal Palace was laid out similar to every other saloon he had been in. To his right was the bar, which ran about thirty feet. Several railroad workers were scattered along its length. At the opposite end and to the right, a doorway opened into what must be the kitchen, for occasionally one of the scantily dressed women came out carrying a tray of stew or coffee or both. If the bartender walked straight away from the bar and past the kitchen opening, he'd run into an office door, which was closed. The office took a portion of the saloon, extending to the back wall. The remaining space was occupied with gaming and regular tables.

The bartender called, "Come on in, Marshal. What'll you have?"

Jack wasn't much on hard liquor. In just a few minutes, he was going to be eating with Grace and the boys. He didn't want the smell of liquor on his breath. "If you have a cool one, give me a sarsaparilla."

"Yes, sir, we've got just what you're looking for." He lifted the lid from a barrel, reached in, and pulled out a bottle of sarsaparilla, felt it, nodded, and unscrewed the cap, setting the bottle and cap in front of Jack. "You just brought that load of prisoners in, didn't you, Marshal?"

At the question, those nearest Jack quieted, listening.

"I came in with them. Several other marshals were also there."

One of the railroad men, deep of chest and thick of arm, looked down the bar at Jack. "That judge gonna hang them like he does everybody else?"

Jack lifted the sarsaparilla to his lips and let the cool, musky, wintergreen-tasting liquid run down his throat, ignoring the railroad man's comment. *It never fails,* he thought. *There's always one drunken loudmouth in the bunch. If I weren't on my way to see Grace and the boys, I might be tempted to teach this fella a lesson.* He took another swig. It had been a while since he'd had a sarsaparilla, and this one was mighty good.

"Hey!" the railroad man yelled. "You with the badge and girly drink. I'm talking to you."

Alright, fella, Jack thought, *you're about to get more of my attention than you want.* He picked up the cap and deliberately screwed it tight on the bottle, then turned to face the man who had yelled at him.

Jack waited while the railroad man picked up his shot glass and tossed it back, then said, "Mister, that's your last drink. You call it quits right now, walk out of here, and you'll get a free pass. I've just come in off a long trip, and I'm not looking for any additional paperwork. That's one of the things the judge is a stickler on, paperwork. Even when we bring in a sloppy drunk, we have to do the paperwork."

The man slowly swayed until he laid a hand on the bar. "Nobody throws me out of any place. Put your hands up, Marshal. I'm going to show you what a good railroad man can do against a marshal."

Jack slowly shook his head. "You don't want to try me, fella. I'm not kidding. I don't fight for fun. I know a lot of you railroad folks enjoy a chance to throw fists, but I don't. You mess with me, and number one, you're gonna get hurt. Number two, you're going to jail with those murderers I just brought in. You think about that. Do you want to be locked up with a bunch of murdering outlaws who would kill their mothers to get an extra dime?"

One of the other railroad men grabbed the man's arm. "Come on, Roscoe. You don't want to do this. That man's a United States Marshal. Let it go. He's offered you a free walk out of here."

The big man jerked his arm free and shoved his friend hard enough to cause him to lose his balance. The man backpedaled for a couple of steps before his body outran his feet, and he sprawled into a chair, causing it to tip over.

Roscoe turned back to Jack. "See what you caused. My friend there almost got hurt because of you. I'm gonna have to whip you now. I'm gonna have to whip you good."

Jack had had enough. He looked at the bartender and slid his sarsaparilla and a nickel across the bar. "Keep that cool for me, please. If anything gets broken, I'll take care of it when this is over."

The bartender shook his head. "Sorry, Marshal."

"Don't worry about it. By the way, would you have someone go for the doctor. This gentleman is going to need one."

Jack stepped away from the bar just as the big railroad man charged him. Though he'd had no desire to fight anyone when he stepped into the saloon, Roscoe had managed to get under Jack's skin. This drunk was going to make him have to explain what he was doing in the Crystal Palace while Grace and the boys waited for him. All he wanted to do was look around, and now this.

The big man had curled his arms out from his body like a big scoop so Jack couldn't get away, which was another wrong assumption on his part. Jack had no interest in running. He did have an interest in finishing this up quickly. He stepped outside the rushing man's right arm as he passed, wheeled, put a boot on the railroad man's rear, and shoved, hard.

The extra momentum drove the man off balance, and he continued face-first into the wall at the end of the bar, his big red nose leading the way. It smashed against the timbers, and blood poured from it. Roscoe shook his head, throwing blood everywhere, and wiped his sleeve across his now broken nose. After examining the blue sleeve of his shirt to find it was no longer blue, but blood red, he wheeled around. His eyes focused on Jack leaning against the bar, waiting. "I'll kill you for this."

Jack shook his head like he was in a lecture hall. "Roscoe, what you just said is not a smart thing to say to a United States Marshal. Are you done?"

Roscoe's friend yelled, "Call it quits, Roscoe, before you really get hurt."

But it appeared Roscoe the railroad man was dead set on hurting Jack. He held his bloody sleeve up for Jack and everyone else to see. "This is a new shirt, and you, Mr. Lawman, are gonna pay."

Jack had no desire to hurt this man. He'd had a few drinks too many, and now his pride was hurt, but Jack was tired. He put his hand on his right revolver. "Roscoe, I'm still going to give you an option. You can walk out that door, and I'll forget all about this. That's option one. Here's option two. If you come at me again, I'm going to take this .44-caliber Smith & Wesson from its holster and slap you so hard with it, you'll be knocked into next week. Do you understand me?"

Roscoe, blood coursing down his shirt, lowered his head and charged. This time, Jack stood his ground, and moments before Roscoe reached him, the Smith & Wesson appeared in his right hand. It slammed into the side of the man's head as Jack wheeled from his path. After the barrel and cylinder collided with Roscoe's head, he took three stumbling steps past Jack and sprawled on the floor, out like a light. Marshal Jack Sage dropped the revolver back into its holster and looked around.

The man who claimed to be Roscoe's friend made eye contact with him and held his palms up. There were two others who were with him doing the same thing.

Jack stepped to the bar and motioned the bartender over. "He didn't do any damage that I can see. It'll take some cleaning to get the blood off everything. Would five dollars cover it all?"

"Marshal, you don't owe me a thing. We'll have that cleaned in no time. Besides, he's a loudmouth, and it was a good show."

Jack pulled out a half eagle and a quarter dollar, shoving the half eagle across first. "That's for the cleaning, and I'll accept no argument. This quarter dollar is for five more sarsaparillas, and if you'd put them in a tow sack, I'll get them to Grace and the boys before they get hot."

The bartender slid the money into a pocket of his apron. "Thanks, Marshal. Give me just a second."

He grabbed a sack from under the bar, quickly counted out seven bottles of sarsaparilla, and handed the sack across to Jack, who nodded his thanks. As he was turning for the swinging doors, Buck and three deputies burst through and stood blinking in the dim light. Buck spotted Jack at the bar. His brow wrinkled in a questioning frown. "What's going on, Jack?"

"It's a long story, Buck. Let's just say this fella thought he was going to teach me a lesson. He needs to sleep it off behind bars. Keep him away from the really bad elements. You might hit him with a drunk and disorderly for the judge." He turned to the three men who were with Roscoe. "Why don't you boys take your friend to jail. When he sobers up, tell him I was feeling kindly today. If there's a next time, I might not be quite so generous."

The man who had tried to talk Roscoe out of assaulting Jack stepped forward. "I thank you, Marshal. He's not a bad man. He just gets this way sometimes when he's had too much to drink."

Jack toed Roscoe with his boot. "If that's the case, a smart man would stop drinking."

The friend nodded. "I'll tell him you said that, Marshal. I surely will." He turned to the others. "Come on, boys, let's get him out of here."

Buck had his hands on his hips, watching the proceedings.

Jack slapped him on the back. "Relax, Buck. It's all taken care of. Get Roscoe to the judge in the morning and tell him I recommend a couple of days of good old-fashioned hard labor, and I think this fella will be fine." The doc had shown up and was standing to the side, watching. "You might get the doc to look at Roscoe's nose. It looks like he mashed it pretty bad. See you." He grabbed the sack of sarsaparillas, nodded to the bartender, and started for the door.

A tall fella, with a Colt riding low on his right side, leaned against the bar. Jack's eyes swept over him as he was leaving. The man gave him a nod, which Jack returned, pushing through the swinging doors. Grace and the boys were waiting. He felt sure the sarsaparillas would go a long ways toward softening the questions.

16

Jack pushed the door open and, for the second time in one day, received a rush of greeting, except the boys each grabbed a hand and dragged him to the kitchen. Arriving, he found Dave Cole already there and digging in. The young deputy marshal looked up. He had a biscuit in one hand and a fried chicken leg in the other, both half eaten.

Dave nodded and pointed to his mouth, which was full and chewing.

Jack gave him a mock frown. "Thanks for waiting." His companion for so many weeks only nodded and kept on chewing.

Grace took the sack he was carrying and pushed him into another chair in front of a plate already filled with chicken, mashed potatoes covered with gravy, biscuits, and green beans. "I didn't think you would mind inviting Dave. Sit down and eat." The sack clinked as she held it up to look into it. "What's this, Jack?"

He had already picked up a biscuit, swiped it into the potatoes and gravy, and stuffed half of it in his mouth. He waved to Matthew, who was standing by the stove, and the new owner of

Ma's Bed and Eats waved back. "Welcome home, Jack. You cannot imagine how crazy your wife was while you were gone."

She gave Matthew an especially sweet smile and said, "Careful, I know where you live." Then she pulled a sarsaparilla from the sack. "Look what your pa brought you boys."

Elijah loved the drink. He was always trying to get Grace or Mary to buy them one when he and Billy accompanied them to the store. He leaped to her side, hand extended. "Thanks, Pa." She gave him the one she was holding, and pulled another from the sack, handing it to Billy. He yelled, "Thanks, Pa," grabbed the bottle, and shouted to Elijah, "Let's drink it on the porch."

The two boys dashed outside, slamming the door behind them.

Jack swallowed and grinned at his wife. "At least they're closing the door now."

She frowned at him. "Yes, each time I wait to hear glass falling after they slam the front door." Her frown softened. She held up another sarsaparilla. "Is one of these for me?"

Before shoving the remainder of his first biscuit into his mouth, he said, "For you, Mary, and Matthew."

She removed the top and handed it to Matthew.

"Thanks, Jack. I appreciate the thought. I really love these things." He turned it up and drained half of the bottle.

Dave had found a little space between bites. "Where's mine?"

Jack was about to take a bite of a chicken thigh when Dave asked his question. He stopped, eyed his deputy, and responded, "Honey, there's a couple of extras in that sack. Would you give one to the fella with the hollow leg?"

She pulled another out and slid it across to Dave.

He looked at it only for a second, spun the cap and, following Matthew's example, drained half the bottle, then took another bite of biscuit. "Sarsaparilla and biscuit are mighty good together. You ought to try it, Jack."

Jack swallowed a bite of chicken, "I just might," and smiled at Grace. "Honey, there's one in there that has a little out of it. Would you hand it to me?"

Before she could reach back into the sack, Billy dashed in. "Pa, there's a man out here asking for you."

"Tell him to come on in."

"I did, Pa, but he said it would be better if you came out there. He's about as tall as you."

Jack slid his chair back and in a hard voice asked, "Where's Elijah?"

Grace caught the change and leaped up, heading for the door.

"No! You stay here with Billy and Dave." He looked again at the boy.

Billy, concerned but not understanding the sudden change, said, "He's still outside, Pa, talking to the man. You know how talkative he is."

Dave was up, checking his revolver. "You think it's one of the gunfighters?"

"I do, but you stay in here where you can protect my family. I doubt he'll come in, but be ready, just in case." He looked at Grace. "Where's Mary?"

"She's at the dress shop, Jack, but she could be coming back anytime."

Seeing her lovely eyes wide with fear for Elijah and her mother, he reached out and slid his rough hand across her soft cheek. "Don't you worry. I'll make sure they're both safe. Now stay here with Dave, and I'll send Elijah in." He checked both revolvers were free and easy in their holsters, and began to turn for the door.

Grace flew to him and held him close. "Be careful. We just got you back."

"Don't you worry about me, but be sure to keep everyone inside." He gave a quick look at Dave, who nodded, then turned and strode from the kitchen, through the dining room, and out the parlor door. To his left, the tall man was sitting in one of the rockers next to Elijah, who was talking away about his upcoming move to Texas. When Jack stepped onto the boardwalk, the man glanced at Jack, nodded, and turned back to Elijah.

"I've got some business with your pa. It's been nice talkin' to you. Maybe I'll be seeing you in Texas." He shook hands with Elijah and stood, turning to Jack, who relaxed, seeing the Texas Ranger badge on the man's vest. "That's a fine boy you've got there, Marshal Sage." He extended his hand, and Jack took it. The stranger continued, "I'm Latigo Smith, Texas Ranger."

Jack held up his hand to halt the ranger from saying anything else, and glanced at Elijah. "Go inside, and tell your ma I'm out here talking to Mr. Latigo Smith of the Texas Rangers."

"Sure, Pa." Elijah jumped to his feet, dashed around the two lawmen, through the door, swinging it hard, and yelled, while he was running, "Ma, Pa's talking to Mr. Latigo Smith of the Texas Rangers, and he's as tall as Pa."

Jack jerked his hand up to catch the door just before it slammed, and Latigo shook his head. "I've got four of those, and they have yet to close a door softly. I'm surprised their ma hasn't already done 'em in." He pointed to the rockers. "You have a minute? Those rockers are a mighty comfortable invention."

"Sure." Jack moved to the rocker Elijah had been sitting in, and eased himself into it. It had been his experience a man his size dropping into a wooden rocker could produce kindling fast. The chair groaned but held together, and Jack relaxed, pushing with his heels to get it moving. "What can I do for you, Ranger?"

The door opened, and Grace appeared with a tray holding a coffee pot, two cups, spoons, sugar, and fresh cream. "Jack, I thought you and Ranger Smith might like a cup of coffee while you talk."

Both men rose to their feet. Jack, noting the relief in her face, smiled to her. "Ranger Smith, this is my wife, Grace Sage. Grace, I'd like you to meet Ranger Smith."

"I am so pleased to meet you, Mr. Smith." She looked at Jack, her relief obvious to him.

"Thank you, ma'am, it's my pleasure."

She motioned with her head. "Now sit down, please, and mix your coffee. If you like cream and sugar, don't be bashful. No one compares to my husband."

"Well, Mrs. Sage, when I get such an offer, I take advantage." He poured his cup three-quarters full of coffee, then spooned in two spoonfuls of sugar and added cream, almost bringing the coffee to the rim of the cup. After making a couple of careful stirs with his spoon, he laid it on the tray and took a sip. "Mmm. That's mighty good, Mrs. Sage. My wife makes the best coffee in the world, but I think you might have her beat, but please don't tell her I said that. You might meet her when you move to Texas."

"Please, call me Gracie, and I do hope to meet your lovely wife, but no word you've spoken shall pass my lips."

Latigo smiled. "Thank you, Gracie, and I'd be obliged if you and Marshal Sage would call me Latigo."

While the two had been talking, Jack mixed his coffee. He added one more spoon of sugar than Latigo had and finished filling the cup of hot coffee with cream, took a sip, and smiled broadly at his wife. "Honey, I haven't had a cup of coffee like that since I left, mighty delicious."

She dipped her head and graced him with a brilliant smile. "Thank you, kind sir. Now if you gentlemen will excuse me. I need to help with supper."

Both Jack and Latigo rose and started for the door to assist. "Sit down, you two. I know you have law business to discuss. I'm no invalid." She disappeared into the house, and the door closed gently behind her.

Jack took another sip of his coffee and pushed off again with his rocker. "By the way, call me Jack. Tell me what brings you to our door."

Latigo rocked a couple of times while he drank his coffee. At last, he cleared his throat and began. "I suspect you already know this, but a character from Texas, a hired killer, is in your town. His name is Weston Boone. Have you heard of him?"

Jack took a long sip of his coffee, contemplating the question. "Yep. I've heard of him, but I wouldn't know him if he were standing right here in front of us."

"What have you heard?"

"He's here to kill me, possibly with a Missouri gunfighter named Clive Reese. They're both on a contract from my half brother."

Latigo had just put the cup to his lips, but he brought it down and turned his head to stare at Jack. "You're well informed. This is the first time, as far as I know, that these two killers have teamed up. Do you know why your half brother wants you dead?"

Jack shrugged. "Money. My father was a sailor. Before he met my mother, he met this woman in Bermuda. The next day, he sailed away, leaving her with what would turn out to be twins. He never found out. Both my mother and father died when I was young. The woman hit on hard times and thought my father might be able to help her support her kids, but by then, as I mentioned, my father was dead. If she had contacted me, I would have made sure they were provided for. That's what my father would have done, but they contacted our attorney. He is very good for us, but not for others. He turned her down and never mentioned the incident to me." Jack went on with the explanation while they rocked and drank their coffee.

When he finished, Latigo shook his head. "So he sent his brother to kill you?"

"Yep, and the brother's luck wasn't as good as mine. Evidently I look a lot like his brother, and that caused him to hesitate, giving me a chance. If it hadn't been for his pause, I'd be six feet under instead of him, so now the living twin is after me for not only my money, but also for killing his twin brother."

Latigo continued to rock. Finally, he tilted the cup so he

could drain every drop. Once finished, he turned to Jack. "I always get told to mind my own business, but, as you might figure, I have an opinion on your situation. You've got to understand, the rangers checked you out pretty thoroughly after you saved all those young girls in Texas and California. The head honchos wanted to know more about you, so before I left on Boone's tail, they filled me in. Considering who you are, I suspect your brother is a lot like you, and you don't give up, so neither will he. Taking all that into consideration, I think your best bet is to go back to Virginia and kill him. I know it's a hard thing, but I feel sure it will be the only way you will ever be rid of him."

Latigo looked up and down the street as if he thought someone might be watching him. "I swear, Jack. That's the longest I've talked in a coon's age. It must've been your son. Seriously, that's the only way you're going to get this monkey off your back. You've got to make sure he's dead."

Jack sat silent, thinking. *Kill my brother, my own kin, but I've already killed one of them, and they are doing their best to kill me and take everything from my family. Maybe Latigo's right.*

Latigo had stopped rocking. "Jack, I've got one more thing. Since you did so well for the rangers, they sent me to make sure you are aware of the contract on your life. I have no warrant for Boone. We have nothing other than rumors, but this kid is supposed to be the fastest you've ever seen, and he is as cold as a fish. He has no family and cares about no one. One of the people he killed was a young farmer who, as told by his poor wife, never shot a handgun in his life. Boone goaded him into getting one and then killed him. Right in front of his wife and kids. Boone is worthless, but young and fast and smart. He'll call you out when you least expect him. You're the first lawman he's gone after, so you've got to stop him."

The ranger stood and extended his hand. "Good luck, Jack. I hope you kill this whole bunch, Weston Boone especially."

Jack took the man's hand. "Thanks, Latigo. Take care of yourself. I appreciate you bringing me this information."

Latigo nodded. "Remember what I said. Killing him may be your only chance. I think your brother will keep hiring killers until he finds the one who can do the job. You don't want to wait until then. You've got too nice a wife and sons. I'm heading back to the Crystal Palace. Who knows, I may get to see another show like you put on today. That was mighty entertaining, though I'd say you were pretty easy on him."

Jack watched the tall ranger stride back to the saloon. What a sorry job the ranger had been assigned. Follow and watch Weston Boone until the killer got himself killed. Jack reached for the latch to open the door.

"Howdy, Marshal Sage, it's nice to finally meet you." The voice came from the alleyway between the boarding house and the stable.

Jack turned his head to see a short, well-dressed cowhand, with a friendly enough face. And then the realization hit him, Weston Boone. He was young. In fact, Billy was taller than this kid and looked older. "Hello, Weston. You here to collect your money?"

The boy smiled. "Oh, no, sir, I always get paid up front, or I don't take the job. Most folks have confidence I'll do what I say."

Jack removed his hand from the latch and turned to face his opponent. "I understand you've never killed a lawman."

The baby-faced killer smiled. "As far as people know. I don't talk much about what I do."

Weston Boone stood in the dirt between the boardwalks, just past the corner of the boarding house, in the entrance to the alley. He was barely in sight of passersby. From his position, he could duck to his right and disappear down the alley. No one would be able to swear they saw him shoot Jack, if he was successful.

Jack could feel the old calm he was used to washing over him like a cool blanket. In minutes, maybe seconds, either he or the boy would be dead, for Jack had been told several times how fast the kid was. He couldn't take the chance of trying to place his shot in a non-killing area because doing that took time. He'd have to shoot by instinct, and that always meant a heart shot.

"You worried, Marshal?"

"Can't say as I am, Weston. I will say I hate to kill a young fella like you, but it looks like you're going to force my hand."

The boy grinned. "I heard you was fast, Marshal, but you're an old man. Reflexes slow as you get older. That's just a natural thing. I reckon you won't hardly get that shootin' iron out of its holster fore I drill you dead center."

Jack smiled at the killer. "I've gotten faster, Weston. I'm faster today than when I was your age. I can't explain it. I suspect that's what the Good Lord's done for me."

The boy's smile left his face. "Reckon you're gonna get to ask Him here mighty quick."

It was a hot day, and Jack figured the little bead of sweat that had just popped out below Weston's right eye was from the heat. "How many people have you killed, son?"

The killer's lips pursed, and his eyes narrowed to the point his yellow irises could barely be seen. "I ain't yore son, Sage. Don't you forget it." Then his frown softened, and his lips formed a wide smile, and his chest swelled in pride. "I've sent fourteen people to their maker. You'll make fifteen, old man."

Jack couldn't help but laugh, a harsh derisive laugh.

Weston Boone's frown leaped back to his face. "What's funny, old man?"

"Well, it's not really funny, *son,* I was thinking how wrong it was for a short, scrawny, lightweight like you to take the lives of so many good people."

The killer's face turned brick red. "You listen to me, Sage. They weren't all good people. Some of them deserved it, and I told you not to call me son."

Jack had accomplished his goal. He wanted the killer

emotional, his body filled with adrenaline. If he was faster than Jack, the anger just might make him miss. He definitely didn't want him to cool down. Now was the time to get him to draw. "How are you planning on killing me, son, talk me to death?"

Weston Boone, the baby-faced killer, looked as if his eyes would explode from his head. He yelled, "I'll kill you!" and went for his gun.

17

Jack was telling the young killer the truth, he had gotten faster. He was amazed at how fast he slicked the Smith & Wesson from its holster. He didn't think there was another man around who was faster, except Weston Boone.

The boy was lightning, but what surprised Jack was the kid's left hand had started moving almost as soon as his right. It wasn't until Boone had his Colt out of its holster Jack realized what he was doing. His mind yelled in relief. *He's going to fan his Colt.*

Fanning was the act of a novice. No gunfighter worth his salt would fan his weapon. Slamming the hammer back with the off hand moved the revolver away from its target. A man could shoot fast, but not accurately. At least none Jack had seen.

Weston Boone's Colt came level just a fraction of a second ahead of Jack's, and the boy slammed the hammer back in the fanning motion Jack had expected. Immediately he fired. Jack could plainly see, when the boy fired, the muzzle was pointing to his right. But the kid was quick. Jack's revolver leveled, and he fired as the kid fanned the hammer back on the Colt and was about to fire again.

Jack's weapon sent its two-hundred-grain slug an inch to the right of Boone's left pocket, tearing the boy's heart to ribbons. Jack had known men to keep firing after their heart was destroyed, but Weston Boone didn't have that kind of determination. His right hand relaxed, and the Colt thudded into the dirt.

The boy's legs collapsed, and he followed his weapon, crumpling into a heap, like he was doing an awkward bow.

Jack kept his weapon drawn and slowly approached the dead gunfighter. His ears rang like a thousand whistles were inside his head. From experience, he knew it would take a while for the ringing to subside. Firing under the boardwalk roof made the ringing even worse.

Reaching the boy, he placed his boot on one shoulder and pushed him back. The corpse flipped over on his back, his surprised yellow eyes open and already glazing over.

"Jack?"

The shock in his mother-in-law's voice spun him around. She was standing no more than five feet from where he stood, in the street, with blood flowing from her upper chest. He dashed to her as Dave yanked the door open from inside the boarding house, gun in hand.

Grace was right behind him. The first thing she saw was Jack holding a smoking revolver, and then her mother, wearing her favorite white blouse with lace around the high collar and cuffs, bright red blood spreading over the soft white cotton.

Mary stared down at the spreading stain. Surprised, she looked up at Jack. He dropped his weapon into the holster and grabbed her as her legs collapsed. "Jack?" she said again, fainting into his arms.

Jack yelled at Dave, "Get Doc Freeman. Quick!"

Dave took off in a hard run, arms pumping. Jack could hear him yelling, "Doc! Doc, come quick. Mary Nelson's been shot."

Jack wheeled into the house, past the parlor to the dining room. Grace leaped in front of him and jerked the tablecloth from the long dining table, dishes, saucers, and cups crashing to the floor.

"Hot water," Jack yelled, and she dashed into the kitchen. People started pushing into the house as Jack laid Mary on the table. He saw Buck. "Get them out of here, now, or I will. Where's the doc?"

Not waiting for an answer, he spun around and yanked Mary's blouse open as Grace came back into the dining room. She grabbed the boys and shoved them from the room. "Grandma's been shot, but she's going to be alright. For now stay out of the dining room."

Both boys' eyes filled with tears, but they turned and left the room.

Jack had seen the location of the wound. It was high, but it shouldn't be so high as to break the collarbone.

Matthew ran in with clean white dish towels. "Thanks," Jack said, keeping two and tossing the others onto one of the dining chairs. They began to slip to the floor, and Grace grabbed them. Jack lifted Mary enough to pull her arm from the sleeve and pushed it around her to the other side. While he held her, he took one of the folded towels and pressed it to the exit wound, then gently laid her back on the table.

Outside, he heard, "Get out of my way. Move, I tell you." He looked up to Grace and, relief flooding his voice, spoke the obvious. "Doc Freeman's here."

She gave him a curt nod, and the doctor stepped into the room. He saw Mary's frail body stretched out on the table and shook his head as he began to examine her. "I hoped it wasn't true. How could something like this happen?" He smelled the gunpowder on Jack and turned, glaring at him, then went to work on Mary. While he worked, he said, "Somebody tell me what happened."

Jack felt deep despair over the woman who had taken him in

and treated him like a son. "Gunfight, Doc. One of the gunfighters who were sent to kill me confronted me in front of the boarding house on the boardwalk."

The doc said, "What was he shooting? This is a big nasty hole, with pieces of timber in it."

"A forty-five Colt, but he missed me with his shot. It hit the front door post and glanced."

The doc shook his head again, "Gunfighters, they should all be hanged," and continued to work. Moments later he spoke up again. "I've got the bleeding stopped. I'll need to take her to my office."

Jack stepped up. "I can do it, Doc."

"Good. Keep those towels in place."

Jack scooped her up. To him, she felt as light as a feather. Grace placed a bath towel over her mother to protect her modesty, and the three of them headed out the door.

Doc Freeman glanced left at Boone's body when they stepped outside. "He's dead?"

Jack nodded.

"Good. How old was he?"

They were hurrying through the street to his office. Jack replied, "Don't know, Doc. Couldn't have been more than twenty."

Latigo had been following. He moved up beside them. "He was nineteen."

The doc looked at the man. "Who are you?"

"Texas Ranger. I was sent to keep track of the man Jack killed, and good riddance. That young feller has put ten people in their graves."

Jack glanced at the ranger. "He told me fourteen. He said I'd be number fifteen."

"I guess we're wrong about the count, and he's wrong about adding to it."

The doctor shook his head and began trotting, as Grace was doing, to keep up with Jack's long strides.

Having to break into a run to get there ahead of them, Doc Freeman took off. When they arrived, he stood at the open door, waiting and breathing hard. "Bring her in and put her on this table."

Jack laid Mary gently on the table and straightened. Doc Freeman immediately went to work while his wife ushered everyone except Grace from the room. "There's no sense in waiting. Dr. Freeman will let you know how she's doing as soon as he's done."

With a firm headshake, Jack indicated he was staying. "Ma'am, I'm not leaving until I know how Mary's doing."

Grace stepped from the room, came to him, and ran her arms around his neck. "Jack, you can't do anything here, but you can calm the boys. Why don't you go back, get cleaned up, and eat. You can talk to them. You know enough about bullet wounds to be able to give them your opinion. That's all they need right now. A little hope."

He buried his face in her thick black hair. "I'm sorry, honey. I'd give anything if it were me instead of your mother."

She kissed his rough cheek. "I saw that boy when we left with Mama. You couldn't do anything but what you did. I'm just glad you are alright."

"Grace," Doc Freeman called from the other room, "we're ready to get started, and we need your help."

She pulled back and gave him a reassuring kiss on the lips. "Don't you worry. Dr. Freeman is an excellent doctor. Now go. No telling what the boys might be thinking."

"You're right. I love you."

"I love you, too." She turned and pulled the door closed behind her.

Latigo had stepped to the end of the boardwalk and was

pretending a deep interest in a scissor-tail diving on a grasshopper. He heard the door close and turned to Jack, never to know whether the grasshopper survived or the scissor-tail had lunch. "Can you use company?"

"Sure, at least to the boarding house. I've got a couple of boys to fill in."

"I wouldn't worry. They seem like pretty levelheaded young fellas."

"They are, but we're talking about their grandmother."

The two men walked on in silence. Finally, Latigo said, "You going to tell me about it, or am I just going to have to make you a big hero when I'm filling out my report?"

Jack chuckled, realizing it was the first laugh he'd had since the gunfight. "Right after you left, I was about to go back inside, in fact I had my hand on the latch, and this kid says, 'Howdy, Marshal Sage.' I turned around, and there he stood, in the mouth of the alley."

Latigo nodded. "Yep, that's the kid. Had his escape planned. I'd bet if I walk down that alley, I'll find his horse tied and waiting, which I'll do after we're finished."

"Don't be surprised if Buck hasn't already grabbed it. He's pretty sharp.

"So we talk a little bit. That's something he should've learned after killing that many men. Get right down to business, but he seemed to like to hear himself talk."

"Yep, that's the story I've heard from all the folks who have seen him in action. They say he likes to make his victims sweat."

Jack nodded. "Pretty much how I figured him. He didn't like it when he saw I wasn't scared of him. In fact, when I called him son, he really got upset, so I called him that a few more times."

"Alright. I see what you were after. You wanted to get him mad, so maybe he might make a mistake."

"That was my goal. I'm pretty quick with a gun, if I do say so myself. In fact, as I've gotten older, I've gotten faster." Jack saw the skepticism written all over Latigo's face. "I know, that sounds stupid, but it's true. I can't explain how it's happened, but I'm sure glad it has."

Latigo's eyes were wide with surprise. "You outdrew him?"

Jack grinned at the ranger. "Shoot, no, I out-experienced him. He's a kid. He thought he knew it all. What he didn't know was the importance of staying calm. That cost him."

"Yeah, his life."

"Did you know he fanned his weapon?"

"No. You're kidding, right? No one ever said anything about him fanning."

"Did you ever talk to any gunfighters or lawmen who saw him in action?"

Latigo shook his head. "I don't know of any. Just townsfolk."

They were approaching the boarding house. Jack slowed his stride. "I'll tell you, Latigo. If he had remained calm, or if he hadn't fanned his weapon, he would've had me." Jack paused for a second. "And not Mary." He went on. "He got mad, and I saw his gun hand twist when his off hand slammed the hammer back. He pushed his muzzle to the right, clear as day. Lack of experience killed him, just as sure as the sun rises in the east, not me."

Latigo stopped at the front door of Ma's. "Jack, you've given me a lot of information for my report. If he's already gotten it, do you think Buck will let me take Weston Boone's horse and gear back to Texas? That goes a long way to convincing the head honchos of the truth of the report."

"I'm sure he will. Tell him I'd consider it a favor. You ever find yourself close to the Flying J, swing on by. We should be able to round up a cup of coffee and a meal for you."

"Much obliged."

Jack turned and strode into the house, his mind no longer on Latigo and his problems, but on two little boys who were afraid of losing their grandma.

Moving through the parlor, he stepped into the dining room and stopped. There was no indication Mary had lain on the table, blood running from her chest. The room was spotless. The table looked just like it had before Grace tossed all the dishes on the floor, breaking most of them. Matthew had done an excellent job of straightening and cleaning. Jack continued through the dining room to the kitchen, where Matthew and his new employee, Lannie Jean Porter, were busy at the stove. Billy and Elijah were at the table, snapping green beans. Everyone turned toward him at his entrance.

"Before the questions start, let me tell you what I know. Mary is in good hands with Doc Freeman and his wife." He looked at the boys. "Your ma is there with them, helping. There's no news yet from the doctor." He watched the boys' hopeful faces turn grim.

"But I've been around a lot of gunshot wounds. In fact, I've had a few, and as bullet wounds go, I think your grandma is very lucky. It's going to take some time for it to heal, but, from what I know, the bullet hit nothing major, no organs, no bones. Now, don't get me wrong, it is going to be pretty painful, but she should come through this with nothing worse than maybe a stiff shoulder."

Billy raised his hand like he was in school. At thirteen he was beginning to grow into manhood. His chest was thickening, and the hard work he did around the place was hardening him and building biceps, but today, he looked like a frightened little boy.

Jack moved to his side and placed his hand on Billy's shoulder. "Son, you don't have to raise your hand to me. Just say what you want to say."

His voice, too, was that of a little boy. "Pa, do you mean Grandma is going to be alright?"

Jack squeezed the boy's shoulder. "Billy, looking at her wound, with my experience with bullet wounds, I'd say yes. But she's going to be hurting, so she'll need all the help you can give her. Your ma, too. She's going to be concentrating on Mary, so she might miss something important to you. Remember, it's not because she doesn't love you, but because she is so concerned about her ma. Does that make sense?"

"Pa," Elijah asked, "when's Grandma coming home?"

"Now you've asked me a question I don't know. Only Doc Freeman can tell you that, and it may take a couple of days for him to make that determination, but I have confidence, as soon as he knows, he'll tell us." With a hand on each of the boys' shoulders, Jack squeezed them both. "Anything else?"

Billy shook his head, but Elijah looked up at Jack. "Was that fella who shot Grandma trying to kill you?"

"He sure was, Elijah. He missed and hit Grandma. I'm mighty sorry about that."

Billy spoke up. "Pa, I'm sorry Grandma got shot, but I wouldn't want you to get shot either."

Elijah joined in. "Me neither, Pa."

Jack knelt between them. They both spun around and threw their arms around his neck. He squeezed them tight and thought, *These two boys mean more to me than my own life. I couldn't stand the thought of them getting hurt.* They stayed in that position for several seconds, then each dislodged, and Jack stood. "Matthew, sorry about the dishes. You did a terrific job of cleaning everything. No one could ever tell Mary had been there."

Matthew and Lannie Jean had been steadily preparing supper. He looked over his shoulder to Jack. "Thank you. That was Lannie Jean's and the boys' efforts. I agree with you. They did a terrific job."

Jack patted the boys on the shoulders. "I'm impressed. The dining room looks spotless."

Lannie Jean turned around and smiled at Jack. "Oh, thank you, Marshal Sage. The boys worked so hard. We were able to do it very quickly."

"Impressive. Congratulations to all three of you. Now, boys, did you get that hot water in my room so I can get a bath? All your hard work cleaning the dining room won't make any difference if the folks smell me."

Billy wrinkled his nose, his humor returning. "I wondered what I was smelling."

Jack, in fake fierceness, said, "Careful, I may have to give you a bath."

Both of the boys started giggling, then Billy spoke up again. "Pa, the water isn't in your old room. It's in Ma's room, and she had us move all your stuff in there, too."

Trying to hide his touch of embarrassment, Jack only nodded and turned to go.

Elijah spoke. "Pa, that water might be cold by now. You want us to heat up some more?"

Jack saw Matthew's back stiffen and knew the owner had food to prepare. "Naw, boys, it'll be just fine. When I was in Wyoming territory, I used to wash up in waterfalls coming off ice. A little cool water won't bother me."

Jack felt uneasy going into Grace's room without her around, but his body needed to be cleaned. Opening her door, he was welcomed by the sweet smell of rose water. Her fragrance was over everything he touched, bringing her close to him, though she wasn't there. The tub was filled halfway, with two more buckets sitting full next to it. The water no longer steamed. It had been hours since he was supposed to have a bath. He noticed at one dresser, Grace had set a bucket of hot water next to the basin, along with shaving gear. On the bed, she had laid out clean clothes.

There was a light tap at the door. "Pa, if you'd give us your boots, we'll clean them up for you."

"Come on in here, boys."

They opened the door and looked around. "Come on, I need some help with these boots, and since when did you two get shy?"

Billy grinned. "It feels funny you being in Ma's room."

Jack laughed. "Yeah, it feels funny for me, too."

Elijah, eyes wide, said, "Really?"

Jack sat on the bench at the end of the bed and held a booted foot up. "Really, now get over here and help me get these things off."

18

_____

After finishing his bath and helping the boys haul the tepid water out and dump it, Jack helped Matthew and Lannie Jean in the kitchen. With Grace and Mary staying after they sold Ma's Bed and Eats, Matthew was retaining the majority of his customers. He was an excellent chef and had learned much from Mary and Grace, reciprocating with his New Orleans experience. Jack occasionally assisted with the serving. Surprisingly to him, he was good with the customers and never had one argue with him.

With the shooting having taken place just outside the house, they were packed for the evening meal. In fact, Matthew finally had to start turning people away. Everyone had questions for Jack when he came into the dining room, and he patiently answered those he could as truthfully and accurately as possible. Supper lasted much longer than usual, and everyone upon leaving told Matthew how delicious the meal had been. Three ladies gave Jack the eye, which he ignored, but Billy, having noticed a couple of them, became incensed and threatened to say something to them.

Jack managed to keep a straight face while he calmed his son and explained it meant nothing, and he wouldn't want to alienate Matthew's customers. Finally cooled down, Billy continued to refill water glasses, but it was Elijah who managed to spill water on all three of the women.

Later in the evening, as Jack was tucking the boys in bed, Grace returned. Jack admired his sweet wife. She had been working continuously to ensure her mother's comfort for all these hours, and though she was exhausted, her beauty glowed through her weariness.

After the boys were in bed, Jack swept her into his arms and carried her to their room. She was out on her feet. He helped her undress and guided her to bed. She slid under the single sheet and, in the flickering light of the candle, kissed him, running her fingers across his smooth cheeks.

"You shaved."

"How could I not after you prepared everything so well."

Her tired smile touched his heart like he never thought possible.

"Isn't it wonderful, Jack. Dr. Freeman says Mama will recover fully. Life is so good."

He pushed a stray curl back from her forehead. "It is with you here and Mary safe. Now get to sleep."

"Oh, Jack. You are so wonderful."

Her eyelids drifted down to cover those lovely eyes, and she was sound asleep.

Jack kissed her again on the forehead and stood. She turned on her side, and her long legs drew up like an infant's. He looked down on his wife and felt a tug at his heart like he hadn't felt in many years.

After blowing the lamp out on her side of the bed, he moved to the other and began to undress. He stood his boots, with his socks draped over the top, by the bedside table and unfastened his gunbelt. With the two revolvers and almost a box of ammunition in the loops on the belt, which he kept full all the time, it was a heavy load. Working diligently to hang the belt on the back of the straight-backed chair by his bed without making the least bit of noise, he smiled when he was successful.

Slipping one of the Smith & Wessons from its holster, Jack eased his big body onto the bed, careful not to wake her. Then he slipped the barrel of the revolver under his pillow, so the butt would be handy should he need it, and stretched his tired body, feeling the tension slip away.

As expected, his feet stuck out past the bottom of the bed, but it was something he was used to. He felt Grace's breathing, steady and soft, and realized how tired he was. His eyes closed, and the two newlyweds drifted off to sleep, to dream about their first night together.

JACK, due to his occupations over the years, was a light sleeper. The quiet, almost imperceptible sound of the door latch slipping invaded his subconscious, and his eyelids jerked open. There was no other sound in the boarding house except the occasional pop and creak of an old house. From the half-moon, faint light flooded the bedroom. He lay still, eyes and ears searching for invaders. His right hand slipped unerringly across his body to close on the butt of his revolver. There was no one in the room yet. He concentrated on the door, thinking, *Maybe it's one of the boys,* but he discarded the thought, because neither would be trying so hard to be quiet.

He waited.

Slowly, the door pushed open. Matthew's handyman was taking good care of his boarding house. The door swung smoothly, no squeaks. The assassin slipped into the room, stopped to assess which side of the bed to move to, and waited. A second man joined him. The first pointed to Jack's side of the bed and whispered something to his companion. Jack could make out the second man nod and take a step toward Grace. In their hands, long knives glinted in the moonlight.

When he first heard these two, he had suspected it was only one, and had hopes of capturing the assailant, but now, with two, his only thought was protecting Grace. So far, all of his movement had been under the sheet, but he wanted his weapon unencumbered when he engaged. As the assassins moved forward, he slowly brought the weapon from under the sheet. Both men halted.

Just what he wanted. In one motion, he lifted the revolver and shot the intruder angling for Grace in the forehead. The blast filled the boarding house and combined with Grace's earsplitting scream. Jack closed his eyes the instant he fired, and though the flash of the weapon registered through his eyelids, he still managed to retain some of his night vision. When he opened them, the first attacker, instead of racing for the door in an attempt to escape, charged him.

Jack had planned on also killing this man, but with him charging, maybe he could just wing him. He noted the way the man held the knife. This was to be no overhand stabbing. This man knew how to wield a blade. He held it low, planning to take Jack in the throat.

The stranger was almost on him when Jack fired. The bullet struck the man in the ball of the shoulder holding the knife. The blade fell, and Jack, using his left fist, slammed it into the assassin's jaw, knocking him against the bed, where he hit him over the head with his revolver. The man collapsed on the bed, and Jack kicked him off.

He waited, the revolver trained on the door until he was sure no others would be coming. Then he slipped the weapon into his left hand and wrapped his right arm around Grace, drawing her to him. "You're alright, honey. It's over." He could feel her warm body shaking like she'd been caught in a Wyoming snowstorm. "Take a deep breath. Try to relax."

"Ma, Pa? Are you alright?"

"Don't come in here, boys," Jack called. "We're fine. We'll be out in a second."

Lamps were lit in the hallway. Jack looked at his wife and could see she was pulling herself together. "You might want to get dressed. People will be in here soon."

She stared at Jack, eyes wide. "In here? In our bedroom?"

He nodded. "Yep. One of those fellas is dead, and the other is pretty banged up. Buck will be in here, along with Doc, deputies, and probably the judge."

Her lips narrowed as it dawned on her. "Jack . . ."

He nodded. "I know, but let's just get through this. Later, we'll have time to talk. Right now you probably want to get dressed."

Grace looked down at herself, then at Jack, and grabbed the sheet. She wrapped it around her nightgowned body and leaped out of bed.

"Be careful of the dead body." He checked the assassin on his side of the bed. He was out cold.

"Ma?"

Grace answered this time. "We'll be out in just a minute. Is Matthew out there?"

"I'm right here, Grace, with the boys. I've gotten the guests back in their rooms."

"Matthew, this is Jack." *That's stupid,* he thought and continued, "You'll be getting lawmen any second and probably gawkers. Let the law in, and keep the riffraff out."

"I'll do that, Jack." Footsteps headed toward the front door.

Jack finished getting dressed, jamming his feet into his boots. Swinging his gunbelt on, he smiled. As heavy as it was, the belt and the weight of his guns pulling against him felt comforting. He watched Grace.

She had just finished dressing. She grabbed a brush from her dresser and ran it through her long black hair. She had to step over the body of the dead man to reach her dresser. Grace began to put her hair up, but gave a hard sigh, dropping the brush and the handful of hair she was holding. Turning, she carefully stepped over the dead man again, placed both hands on her hips, and locked Jack in her gaze. "Can you tell me what is going on? A man tried to kill you yesterday and shot Mama, while these two just tried to kill us tonight. I'm not liking this, Jack, not at all. What if they had made a mistake and gone to the boys' room?"

"Honey, I said we'll talk about what's happening, but we don't have time right now. Do you have any rope or anything like it? I need to tie this fella up."

"He's not dead, too?"

Jack had turned his head, watching the assailant. At the tone, he turned and gave her a questioning look. "No, Grace, he's alive. I hope to get information out of him about who hired him, though I think I know."

"Who?"

"My half brother."

"Why do you think that?"

"Grace, the boys need you, and I just heard Buck come in."

"Oh, the boys." She rushed out of the room.

Jack stepped into the doorway so he could keep watch on the unconscious man and see what was happening in the hallway. Grace was herding the boys to the parlor. "Matthew, do you have any rope or anything like it that's about three feet long? I need to tie up one of these fine fellas."

Matthew nodded and rushed off, returning quickly with a piece of rope close to the length Jack had indicated. He handed it to Jack just as the front door opened.

"Hello?"

Jack called, "Back here, Buck." He then went to the man he'd hit, who was just now showing signs of life. He grabbed the man's two arms and yanked them behind him. The man's body convulsed with the movement, and he released a low moan. *Tough,* Jack thought. *I don't know if we'll get anything out of him.* He looped the rope around the man's wrists and tied them. He double-checked the knot and turned the man where he could see his face. It was a strong face, features set, determined, but unknown to Jack.

The assassin looked up at him. "You were lucky."

"No, you were stupid."

Buck walked in. "Won't you let a man get a little sleep? What's with you?" He walked to the dead body and examined the hole between the man's eyes. "In the dark?"

"Moonlight."

"Right." He left the dead man and approached the prisoner. "My gosh, Jack. Which did you do first, hit him with your fist, your sixgun, or shoot him? This must be one tough feller."

Jack couldn't help but laugh. "When you put it that way, it does look like a little bit of overkill, but you have to get the sequence right."

Buck shook his head. "You're gonna have to tell me about this. While the doc's looking at him, you can explain."

"How about if we take him to jail first? Then let Doc Freeman see him. This room has to be cleaned, and Grace is whipped. What time is it, anyway?"

"What, you don't have your fancy pocket watch?"

"Just tell me the time, Buck."

The marshal pulled out his beat-up watch, opened it, and snapped it shut. "Ten after four. Time to be getting up."

"Then what are you complaining about?"

Buck grimaced and grabbed the prisoner's good arm. "Come on, fella. You're going to jail."

The man had been silent until now. "What do you mean jail? This guy shot me. He should be going to jail, and I need a doctor. Why don't you take me to the doctor's office?"

Jack moved his face closer to the assassin's. "You'd best hope you make it to the jail." He saw a flicker of fear in the man's eyes. *Good,* he thought, *I might be able to get some answers from him.*

These strangers planned to kill Grace. He could feel his anger building, and he took a deep breath.

"You alright, Jack?"

"I'm fine, Buck. Let me say goodbye to the boys and Grace, and I'll be right with you."

Stepping into the parlor, Jack grabbed the would-be assassin's arm. This time he grabbed the one he had put a .44-caliber slug through the shoulder joint. The man, covered in blood, moaned, but didn't scream as Jack pulled him to face Grace.

With lips tight, Jack said, "She's my wife. She's the woman you were going to kill." He shoved the man toward Buck, who held his good arm. "Get him out of here, Buck. I'll be out in a second."

Turning back to his family, he saw three, wide-eyed, horrified faces. *Maybe that wasn't such a good idea,* he thought. "I'll be home as soon as I can. Boys, are you two alright?"

Both nodded their heads slowly. Grace glared at him. "Jack, how could you?"

He shook his head. "Sorry, I guess I'm a little upset."

"A little?"

"We'll talk when I get home."

"What are you going to do with that man?"

"Ask him a few questions. Don't you want to know who paid for this?"

She looked down and pulled the boys close to her, like a mother hen gathering her chicks under her wings. "I just want you home. Hurry."

He left to find Buck waiting with the prisoner on the boardwalk. The marshal examined Jack for a moment. "That was a little much, Jack, even for you. You scared the blazes out of those boys and your wife."

Jack could still feel the anger at these two men and his half brother for what they put his family through, but part of the anger was at himself. His family shouldn't have seen that side of him.

That was reserved for those who hurt others. Maybe now would be a good time for him to try to get rid of that side of himself, unless he might need it again. What if he needed it and didn't have it? He shook his head and walked with his friend to the jail.

Reaching the jail, Buck sent one of the deputies to fetch the undertaker. Since Jack had come to town, he'd been a boon for the undertaking business.

"Which cell?" Jack asked upon entering Buck's office.

"The one in the back corner. That oughta be perfect." After checking the jail, he said, "We don't have anybody to send for Doc Freeman."

"I'm sure he heard the shots," Jack called from the back cell. "He'll be here when he figures out he went to the wrong place."

Jack slammed the man against the wall and sat on the bottom bunk. "Maybe you'd like to tell me who hired you to kill me and my wife."

The man was weaving on his feet, but said nothing.

"I'm going to the doc's office," Buck called from the front. "He needs to see that fella."

"We'll be here."

The door slammed, and boots could be heard disappearing on the boardwalk.

Jack leaned toward the prisoner. "I'm going to ask you one more time. I can promise you, if you don't tell me, you won't enjoy the results." He paused, allowing his statement to sink in. After a few moments, he spoke. "Who hired you?"

The man said nothing.

"Alright, enough of this." Jack stood and placed his hand on the man's shattered shoulder. He watched the muscles bunch in the assassin's jaws.

"No? Mister, my family is at stake here. I'll do anything it takes to find out who hired you." His long fingers gripped the shoulder and slowly began to squeeze.

Sweat burst out across the assassin's forehead and upper lip. He tried to keep his eyes open, but reflex shut them.

Jack squeezed tighter.

The man let out a gasp, followed by, "Devin Slater."

Jack released his shoulder. Blood covered his right hand. "That's all I wanted to know." He helped the man sit on the lower bunk as the front door of the office opened.

Buck said, "Doc, the prisoner is in the back with Jack." The door into the jail opened, and the doctor and Buck walked down the aisle leading to the last cell. Buck swung the unlocked cell door open, and the doc walked in.

Dr. Freeman looked at Jack's bloody hand. "You might want to wash that before it gets all over your clothes."

"Good idea, Doc, thanks." Jack strode out of the cell to the front office, where there was a washbasin.

Buck followed. Reaching the basin, he picked up the bucket of water. "Hold out your hands."

Jack held his hands over the basin and, while Buck poured the water over them, rubbed his rough scarred hands together, washing away the blood. "Use the towel." Buck picked up the basin, opened the front door, and threw the water into the dark street.

A new and recognizable voice spoke up from the boardwalk. "Good thing I didn't come from that direction, or I'd be soaked."

Buck chuckled. "I woulda seen you, Judge. You looking to see the prisoner?"

"Actually, I'd like to talk to Jack."

Judge Bell stepped inside the office. "What've you been up to, Marshal Sage?"

19

Jack finished drying his hands and hung the towel on the peg. "You heard about Mary?"

Judge Bell dropped a hand on Jack's shoulder. "I heard she's going to survive. When did you see her last?"

"Yesterday evening. When Doc Freeman is done with the prisoner, I'll find out how she rested through the night."

"I hope well. So what is this I hear about you and Gracie being attacked this morning?"

"You're not going to believe it."

Listening, Buck walked to his desk and sat.

Jack moved to the coffee pot and lifted it, checking to see if there was any remaining.

"The boys just made a fresh pot," Buck said, lifting his nearly full cup.

Jack picked up a cup, offered it to the judge, who shook his head, filled the cup, and replaced the pot. He took a sip and began. "Less than an hour ago, two men slipped into our room and attempted to murder us. They were armed with knives. I managed to kill one and wound the other."

The judge, showing no surprise, nodded, and waited for Jack to continue.

Buck picked up the story. "The survivor is in the back with doc. He's got a busted face, head, and shoulder. The last is where Jack shot him."

Judge Bell responded by looking at Jack and asking, "Did you shoot him or hit him first?"

Jack took a deep breath. "Alright. The dead one was going for Grace. I killed him."

Buck jumped in. "Shot him between the eyes, in the dark."

Jack continued, "There was moonlight. Anyway, I swung on the other fella, who decided to attack me instead of leaving. I shot him in the shoulder. He was almost on top of me. I was still in bed, so I slugged him with my left fist. It knocked him onto the bed, and to be safe, I cracked him over the head with my revolver, then kicked him off the bed, and that's the whole story."

"You were lucky you woke up," the judge said.

Jack took another sip. It wasn't bad, considering there was no cream or sugar. "Judge, when you've lived my life over the last twenty years, you learn to sleep light. Waking up had nothing to do with luck. I heard them pull the door latch, and you should see the knives they were planning on using on both of us. It scared the daylights out of Grace. I don't know if she'll ever be able to get to sleep again."

The judge asked the question Jack knew was coming, but had hoped he wouldn't ask. "Did you find out who hired them?"

Jack nodded. "My brother."

Judge Bell shook his head. "I'm sorry, Jack. What are you planning on doing?"

Jack decided to be straight with the judge, at least as straight as possible. "I think I need to go back to Virginia and talk to him. I don't know what else to do."

Buck had set his coffee cup down and was leaning forward, listening to the two men.

The judge studied Jack for a few moments. Finally he spoke. "Jack, I think facing him, to get to the bottom of this, is an excellent idea. I'll have a warrant sworn out based on the prisoner's testimony. You can take it with you, but I'm sure you understand, it will depend on the judge you're dealing with there, but what about this Clive Reese? What will you do about him?"

"I don't see any answer other than taking him on. If I leave him here, I have no idea what he'll do. He might come after me, or he might go after my family. Reese has to be dealt with before I leave for Norfolk."

"Jack, are you planning on killing your brother?"

"I'm not. I'm planning on solving this problem with any solution necessary. If I can give him the remainder of the shipping company and get him off my back, I will."

Doc Freeman entered the office. "Buck, you need to lock that cell, but there's no rush. Your prisoner won't be going anywhere anytime soon. I gave him enough laudanum to make him sleep for the whole day. He's already out like a light." He nodded to the judge. "Quite an exciting night, Judge."

Buck left his desk and headed for the jail cell.

The judge nodded to Doc Freeman. "Too exciting. How's Mary?"

"She's sleeping. I managed to get the bullet wound cleaned out, but it was very painful, and she is getting up there in years. It was hard on her."

Jack had to know. "Will she live, Doc?"

"Oh, yes, Jack, but it's going to take several weeks of rest for her to heal properly. I'd suggest you consider postponing your departure for at least a month, preferably two. I know that's putting your travel in the latter part of the year, but I don't think she can survive the rough wagon ride until she is completely recovered."

"Thanks for saving her, Doc. I don't know what Grace and the boys would do if anything happened to her."

"Yes, well, she spoke very highly of you. I imagine you two have built a solid bond."

Yes, we have, Jack thought and laughed. "I think she puts up with me, Doc, and how's the prisoner?" From their expressions, Jack could tell that neither Doc Freeman nor Judge Bell fell for his little diversion, but the doctor answered his question.

"He will be healed enough for his hanging, I suppose, but it's a good thing he's not a cowhand. He'll never throw a rope with the damage you inflicted. That shoulder, once it heals, will barely move, if at all. There's still a possibility I may need to operate to get all the bone shards out."

The judge ignored Doc Freeman's last comment. "How soon will he be ready for trial?"

"Give him two weeks, and he'll be good to go."

Jack asked, "Did you get his name, Doc?"

"Nope. He never said a word. Jack, is everyone alright at your house?"

"Yeah, Doc, other than having the daylights scared out of them, everyone is fine."

"I can imagine that was a terrible way for Grace to awaken."

"Yeah, it was pretty bad."

The doctor headed for the door. Reaching it, he pulled it open and turned to Jack. "You should know, she was a big help with her mother. She's quite a woman."

"I'm a lucky man, Doc. For sure."

The doctor stepped outside, pulling the door closed behind him. Buck returned from locking the cell, and the judge told him what Doc Freeman had said about the prisoner, adding, "Figure on a trial in two weeks." Turning to Jack, he patted him on the shoulder. "Whatever you decide, I'll back you. Let me know when you're leaving. I have a few contacts in Norfolk. It might not hurt to have a few judges on your side."

Jack was stunned. Expecting a stern reprimand, he instead received empathy and support. All he could muster was, "Thanks,

Judge Bell," and watched the jurist follow Doc Freeman down the boardwalk. He looked at Buck. "Did I hear the judge right?"

"You're no more stunned than me. I've never seen that side of him. I like it better than the one I see all the time. Hopefully it will be showing up more."

Jack shook his head. "Don't bet on it." He tilted his cup, drained it, and poured water in it from the bucket. Using his fingers, he scrubbed the cup, stepped to the door, and tossed the contents out the door, setting the cup back where he found it. "I'm headed back to the boarding house. Grace and I have a long talk ahead of us."

Buck raised a hand in salute, and Jack stepped outside into the morning air. Daylight was breaking. A nearby mockingbird was competing with a rooster, and it sounded like the rooster was winning. A soft southern breeze flowed up the street, bringing a cooler morning for a change. *I hope Grace is alright,* Jack thought. *I've brought such misery to everyone since I've been back. Hopefully I can straighten it out.*

This time, when he opened the door into the boarding house, there was no rush of boys or wife to the door. Jack stepped inside, pushed the door closed behind him, and glanced into the parlor, empty.

The bullet wound in his side had started aching when he was dealing with the assassin in the jail. It seemed like it had happened so long ago, but he had just returned to Fort Smith yesterday. He straightened and then leaned to the left to see if he could relieve the ache.

An arm went around his waist. "Are you alright?"

He turned to see Grace staring up at him. Her concern was obvious in those lovely eyes. He bent and softly kissed her lips. Thankfully, she returned the kiss with dividends. He felt better already. "A bullet wound I got on this last trip. It's a lot better, but still achy." He changed the subject. "How are you and the boys doing?"

She pulled herself closer to him. "I think they're doing fine, at least Billy is. I'm a little concerned about Elijah. He seems to have slipped back to when he lost his folks. He's gotten very quiet."

"I'll see him in a few minutes, but first we need to talk." He slipped his arm around her, guiding her to the divan in the parlor. He allowed his wife to sit first, then while she held her skirt clear, dropped beside her. When she released it, the full, pale green skirt flowed over his left leg. She gathered it to her, the back of her right hand rubbing against the top of his thigh. It was like his leg had been hit with a bolt of lightning. Involuntarily, he took a deep breath, and she looked up at him, her voice soft and husky.

"You felt that."

The dress was the same green as her eyes. He had no idea how she had been able to take care of the boys, get dressed, do her hair, and look as exquisitely lovely as she did at this moment, after almost being murdered just a short time before. Her lips, full and inviting, beckoned to him, but he steeled himself. They had to talk. He had yet to take care of Reese, and he needed to talk to Elijah and get to Norfolk as soon as possible. He lowered his head and gave her what amounted to little more than a peck. "I'm sorry, but we have to talk."

He saw the disappointment and immediately followed up with, "I love you, Grace, but we really need to talk."

She took a deep breath and let out a long sigh. "You're right."

He could feel the warmth of her leg against him, but pulled away so he could turn and face her. "The men who tried to kill us were hired by Devin Slater, my half brother. I'm sure he hired the gunfighter who tried to kill me yesterday, and also Clive Reese."

She placed her hand on his wrist. "How do you know?"

"The one I took to jail admitted it. I haven't found out how much they were paid, but I will."

Her brow wrinkled in thought. After a moment she asked, "Why is the amount important?"

"I want to know how serious he is about killing us." He hated to include the family in Slater's desires, but it didn't take a lot of thinking to figure out he would want anyone out of the way who might inherit. So that would mean not only Grace, but the boys, and she needed to know the extent to which Slater would go.

She moved her hands to her lap and stared at the unlit fireplace.

She's thinking, Jack thought. *She's smart. It won't take long.*

Her head turned slowly back to Jack, and her eyes showed no fear, rather, they were hard like the emerald grenade on his watch. "He means to have you, me, and the boys murdered. Is that right, Jack?"

Jack's head moved in a slow nod of confirmation. "Yes. I don't think Reese is here for anyone other than me. According to Buck, he may be a gunfighter, but he draws the line at women and children. However, there are enough lowlife killers out there to supply Slater with exactly what he needs, and one of them is in Buck's jail right now."

This time, those green eyes were cold as they seemed to delve into Jack's psyche. "I know you. You must have a plan. I want to know what it is, and Jack, don't soft-pedal it to me. I want to know the stark truth. We're in this together, and I can handle it. This man is trying to kill my boys."

"First, I'm going to offer Reese a good deal. He may not take it, but I prefer paying him off to killing him. If it doesn't work, I'll kill him. Second, I'm getting on the train and going to Norfolk. The judge will give me a warrant for Slater based on the prisoner's statement, but I'll try to talk to him first. If he only wants the shipping business, then he can have it. If that doesn't work, I'll arrest him. It will depend on the presiding judge. Slater is running the company, and it's a big company. There's no telling whom he might be paying off. That part of the plan may not work."

Jack took another deep breath, attempting to sort everything for Grace. "But if he's not thrown in jail, and he wants payback for his brother, I'll offer him a duel. He considers himself good at duels, so he may go for it. If he does, I'll kill him. There are two more half brothers to Slater. I will make sure they have no desire to pursue us. If they do, then I'll challenge each to a duel. I don't want to, but if these men are set on stealing another's wealth, and willing to murder to accomplish their goal, then so be it."

Grace had sat silent while Jack gave her the truth of his plans. *She now knows to what lengths I'll go to protect this family,* Jack thought. *No other woman, not even Yasmina, has ever heard me speak this plainly. I hope I haven't misjudged her.*

He waited for what seemed like ages, though it must have been only a minute or two. Finally Grace put a hand around the back of his neck and pulled his face down. At first he wasn't sure what she was doing, then she moved her lips toward him and pressed them softly against his. He felt the love for this woman fill his heart. She released him and leaned her head back against the divan.

"Jack, what you just told me would shock most women, but I'm not like most women. I wish I could go with you and confront this animal myself. I can't imagine any person who would place more importance on their wealth than the lives of others. I only want one thing from you."

The left side of his mouth rose, giving her a lopsided smile. "For you, anything."

"Come back to us alive and well. Hopefully, you can accomplish your goals without having to harm anyone, but if you can't, do what you must to protect our boys."

"And you."

With that, her hand rose and caressed his cheek. "Thank you, but promise me you'll come back to us intact, healthy."

This time his grin widened to both sides, showing his white teeth. "Yes, ma'am, in one piece."

She shifted so she could extend both arms around his neck,

and pulled herself toward him. As their lips touched, Billy's voice came from the doorway into the hall. "Ma, people can see you."

Jack raised his head so he could see Billy. Elijah stood next to him. "What people would that be, son?"

"Us."

Laughing, the two adults separated, remembering, but putting their conversation behind them. Now it was time to deal with their boys.

"Come around here." He waved to them and directed them to the coffee table in front of the divan. He shoved it back far enough where they would have room to sit. "Have a seat, boys."

The two sat on the low table facing them. Jack asked, "So how are you boys feeling?"

Elijah looked at Billy and then Jack. "For real?"

"That's the only way we'd want it, son. Lay it out straight and true. We'll work on it from there."

Elijah looked down at his feet. "Pa, do you remember when those bad men killed my whole family and our friends?"

"I sure do, son. It was so gruesome, I don't think I'll ever forget it."

Elijah's head rose, and his dark brown eyes found Jack's. "Me neither. That's the reason I want to be a lawman like you. I want to bring those bad guys in and have the judge hang them so they won't hurt anybody else, just like you did."

The last thing Jack wanted was for Elijah to become a lawman. He knew the lifespan of men who carried a badge could be short, but by the time Elijah was old enough, maybe the west would grow up. He also knew that most kids changed their mind on what they wanted to do several times before they reached adulthood. "That's a mighty noble desire, son, but it's also dangerous."

"I'm going to be just like you, Pa, big and strong and fast with a gun, so nobody will ever hurt me."

Jack wanted to protect both Elijah and Billy from ever having to pull a gun in self-defense of themselves or others, but he knew each boy would have to live out his own life. Hopefully, neither of their destinies would include the pain and violence he had seen. "Hopefully, when you grow up, this country will be tamed, and they won't need men like me, but until you're old enough to protect yourself, you've got me and Ma and the other marshals. We'll all keep an eye on you. How does that sound?"

Elijah's grin spread across his face. "I like Marshal Dave, Pa. When you're not around, do you think he can keep an eye on us?" He turned to look at Billy, who nodded his head enthusiastically.

"Yeah, Pa. I like Marshal Dave, too. He's fun, and he saved your life all those times while you was gone into the Indian Territory."

Jack leaned forward and patted them both on the knee. "I bet I can arrange that, if you think Mr. Matthew won't mind feeding him. You know he eats a lot."

Both boys' faces grew serious, and Billy said, "He does, Pa, but that's to keep him big and strong like you."

Jack glanced at Grace, who was smiling at him. "That's right, boys. We sure want to keep him big and strong. Now, I've got something I need to tell you. I'm going to be leaving for a few days, but the marshals will be looking after you, so you won't have anything to worry about."

Elijah's eyebrows rose. "Marshal Dave?"

Jack winked at him. "You bet. I'll make sure Marshal Dave is here."

"Good," Elijah said, "can we go now?"

"Not before you give your ma and me a big hug to make us feel better."

The boys leaped off the table and took turns giving each of them a hug before they dashed out the back door. Moments later the slamming door announced their departure.

Grace's smile disappeared. "You think they're safe?"

"Yeah, for now. You can't keep those two penned up inside, or they'll drive everyone crazy."

She dropped both hands to her knees, then stood. "You're right. I'm going to the Freemans' to see what I can do for Mama. When are you leaving?"

Jack stood along with her. "As soon as I can get the Clive Reese situation resolved."

"Stop by before you go."

"I'll do that. Tell Mary I'll see her before I leave."

She stretched on tiptoe and kissed him on the cheek, turned, and headed for the door. Jack watched for a moment, then started for the bedroom. He was planning on taking only his saddlebags and needed to pack some clean clothes.

He had just stepped through the parlor doorway, into the hall, and taken two steps when he heard the front door open, and Grace gasped, "Oh."

Jack spun to see a tall man, his Colt low on his right side, the holster tied to his leg, standing in the doorway, his hat in his gun hand. "Sorry to startle you, ma'am. I'm looking for Marshal Jack Sage. Tell him it's Clive Reese."

20

R eese, Jack thought, *and Grace is between us.*

Reese's eyes met Jack's over Grace's head. He raised both hands, his gun hand holding the hat. "I ain't lookin' for no trouble, Marshal. I just want to talk."

Jack strode to the door. "Grace, step out of the doorway."

Reese shook his head. "It ain't necessary, Marshal. I won't be starting a thing. I just want to talk to you."

Grace moved to the side, giving both Reese and Jack a clear line of fire. "Reese, just so neither of us makes a mistake, I'd like for you to hand your Colt to Mrs. Sage. When you leave, we may return it."

Clive Reese was an older man, as gunfighters go. He looked to be about Jack's age. At Jack's remark about returning his weapon, the man gave him a cool smirk. He switched his hat to his left hand and lifted the Colt from the holster with his thumb and forefinger, handing it to Grace. "Ma'am, I'd be much obliged if you'd be mighty careful with that. It's the only companion I've ever had who never let me down, and I'd like it back before I leave."

Grace took the weapon, thumbed the hammer back, but kept

her finger outside the trigger guard, and held the muzzle on Reese's belly. Then she slowly moved toward Jack until she was close enough to hand him the Colt.

He took it, pointed the muzzle at the floor, and lowered the hammer. "Come on in, Reese. We've got some talking to do."

Grace, her eyes on Reese, walked back to the doorway. "Jack, I'll be at Doc Freeman's."

"Thanks, honey. I'll see you there."

Grace pulled the front door closed, and Jack pointed to the wingback across the coffee table from him.

Reese lowered himself into the chair and cleared his throat. "I was hired by Devin Slater to kill you."

Jack said nothing.

"Both Weston Boone and I were hired by the same man. Boone told me. That boy talked a lot. He begged me to let him try you first. The kid always figured he was the fastest man alive."

Jack broke his silence. "Do you think that way?"

The gunfighter relaxed into the chair. "Marshal, there's always someone around who's faster. Take the kid. He was faster than you, but you outsmarted him. You got him mad. He didn't have the experience to recognize what you were doing. Though, I'll give you this. You are fast. Between you and me, it'd be a tough call. You could be a little faster than I am."

"You saw the gunfight?"

Reese nodded. "Watched it from across the street. The kid had you, but then he fanned his weapon. What a stupid trick. I ain't seen any gunhand who's been around a while fanning a handgun. How about you?"

Jack shook his head. "Nope. That was a juvenile move. I can't believe no one ever took the time to show him the difference. Of course, I'm glad they didn't."

Reese glanced at his Colt, then looked back at Jack. "He wasn't a bad kid."

Jack snorted. "You think not? He killed at least fourteen men, some of them with families. I'd say he was very bad. Now what can I do for you? I'm busy."

Reese examined Jack. "I'm leaving."

Jack said nothing.

"Do you understand me? I'm not going to kill you."

"Reese, since I heard you were after me, I pretty well believed you weren't going to kill me. In fact, your casket was going to be more expensive because of your height."

"Yeah, I've been told that before. I just wanted you to know so your family won't have to worry about me coming around when you're gone."

Jack watched the killer. "Why would I be gone?"

"Because you're going after Slater. That's what I'd do. Hiring me and Boone and those two knifers you caught last night. That's not my style, Marshal. I don't harm women and children."

"No, you just kill the breadwinner of the house, so the rest of the family starves to death."

Reese stared outside. "Reckon you're right. That gets to be a load to carry. I figure if a person wants someone dead, he ought to have the gumption to do it himself, so I'm giving up this line of work. I've saved a little money over the years and bought me a little farm back in Missouri. I always liked growing things. You got me thinking real serious about it. If it ain't too late for a feller like you to settle down, I reckon it ain't too late for me."

"How can I trust what you say?"

"You've got my gun. You can do with me any way you please."

The man is right, Jack thought. "Then our business is done?"

Reese nodded. "Yep. There's way too many marshals in this town for my comfort. Reckon I'll pull out right now. You gonna keep my Colt?"

Jack examined the weapon. Reese's Colt Peacemaker was a fine weapon. He had tried one like it when he first saw one in '74, but it took too long to load. With his Smith & Wesson, he could press the latch, break the weapon open, and eject all six of the empty cases at one time. The Colt required you clear each cylinder one at a time, but he had to admit, it fit a man's hand well. He opened the loading gate. Turning the cylinder, he dropped all of the cartridges onto the table, scooped them up in one hand, then handed the revolver and the cartridges back to Reese, who was eyeing the cartridges.

"I lived this long by being a cautious man."

Reese nodded and took the cartridges. He dropped them into his vest pocket, then taking his Colt, he slipped it into his holster and stood. Jack rose at the same time. Reese eyed Jack's weapons. "I almost went with the Smith & Wesson. It was just a little heavy for me."

Jack said nothing.

"Alright, Marshal. I'll be moseying along. Guess I'll always wonder which one of us was the fastest."

Jack motioned the gunfighter to the door. "Better to wonder than to be under six feet of dirt, Reese, because I would've killed you."

Reese opened the door and stepped outside. "You just might have. I did see you draw against the kid."

"Ride, Reese. Don't let the sun set on you in Fort Smith. This is not a friendly town for you. Go grow something on your farm, maybe kids. It's not too late."

Jack watched Reese walk toward Pauly's stables. He still stood on the boardwalk when the gunfighter rode out of Winthrop's Stable's on his pinto and headed north. The man never glanced his way. Buck stood on the other side of the street, leaning against the hitching rail and watching the gunfighter ride by. A little farther along, watching from the same side of the street, Deputy Marshal Dave Cole watched the pinto lope past him.

It's nice to have friends, Jack thought, then headed to the bank. *I may be needing a little extra cash for this trip.*

SIX DAYS LATER, Jack halted in front of an office in Norfolk, Virginia, near the wharf. A large brass placard was fastened to the wall adjacent to the entrance. The placard drew the eye of every passing citizen. Engraved in bold lettering, it proclaimed the excellence of Attorney Layton T. Miller, who resided behind the wall. Jack smiled and had to agree. Mr. Miller had been his father's and his uncle's attorney as long as Jack could remember. He had never steered those men wrong, nor him. But Jack, stepping through the doorway, wondered if this was a problem Mr. Miller could not solve.

The elderly male secretary looked up from the document he was working on. His face went from studious to surprised to happy. He leaped from his chair and rushed forward, grasping Jack's hand in both of his, and pumped like he was trying to get water from an old well. "Mr. Sage, it is so good to see you. Congratulations on your recent marriage." He leaned forward, lowering his voice. "It is a blessing you are here. Mr. Miller has been keeping long hours in an effort to keep Devin Slater from ruining your family's company, and I am so sorry about the deaths of your dear aunts and uncle." He pursed his lips, cocked his head to his left, and continued, his voice even lower. "They all happened too close together. I fear that D. Slater is the responsible party, but there seems to be no evidence."

Miller's baritone voice called from his office, "Nathan, who might you be entertaining?"

Nathan was the only lawyer's secretary Jack knew who got away with calling his boss by his first name, and it never seemed to bother Mr. Miller at all. "Layton, you will never believe who just walked in our door. Why, it is—"

"Jack Sage perhaps?"

With fake frustration, Nathan shook his head. "Can you tell me, Jack, how does he do that? I don't know, and he's been doing it for the past fifty years. Come, I know you didn't travel all the way to our fine town just to listen to me prattle on."

Jack smiled at Nathan and followed the ancient, gray-haired man into Miller's office. He allowed Jack to pass inside and said, as he was closing the door, "I'll make a new pot of coffee, Layton, and have it right in."

"Thank you, Nathan." Layton T. Miller was in his element either in court or in an office, especially his. He stepped around his desk and grasped Jack's hand in the same warm manner used by Nathan, though he only shook it three times. "Jack, my boy, it is good to see you again so soon, for you are certainly needed here if we are going to save the company your father and uncle built."

He grasped a large padded leather chair and moved it slightly to indicate where he wanted Jack to sit, then stepped around his massive desk to his equally padded chair. "Sit, Jack, though if you'd like to stand, please do. I know you've been sitting for how many days, six?"

Jack eased himself into the padded leather. "Right again, Mr. Miller. I think you keep Nathan busy trying to figure out how you do that."

Jack's comment elicited a chuckle from the older man, but it was short lived. "I'm glad to see you are still alive. I feel certain Slater had your uncle and aunts murdered."

Jack told him about the gunfighters and the two men who slipped into their bedroom.

Layton T. Miller was a master at remaining calm in the face of conflict, but the story Jack told about their bedroom had the old man livid. "We need to do something soon about him, before he sells everything."

"And kills everyone. That's the reason I'm back. I want to confront him. I'll even offer the company to him, anything to keep my family safe."

The attorney shook his head. "But, Jack, I'm sure he already knows about your gold mine and your ranch. He's going to want those. The man is eaten up with greed. I've been talking to several of your captains. Slater is trying to contract contraband. So far, it hasn't been allowed aboard the ships, but it's just a matter of time."

Jack had managed to change on the train. He no longer wore his regular garb, but was dressed in a dark frock coat with a cream-colored vest over his white shirt. His badge was in his vest pocket. He had also changed to a pair of dark wool trousers. Unfortunately, the now wrinkled coat and trousers had been rolled in the saddlebags, with his gunbelt and holsters, with the exception of one revolver. It wouldn't do to walk around with his two-gun rig in Norfolk. The local gendarme would probably throw him in jail.

Miller had stopped talking and was looking Jack over. "That frock coat and pants look terrible. Where were they, in your saddlebags?"

Jack shrugged. "Matter of fact."

"You're staying with me. I'll send Nathan over to pick out several of your suits, and he'll have them cleaned and ironed. You can't be seen by anyone who counts looking like that. I assume you have a weapon."

Jack pulled away the left side of his coat, exposing the butt of his Smith & Wesson protruding from his waistband.

Miller nodded his approval. "Good. Stay ready. When he finds out you're in town, he'll send out a couple of his thugs." He opened a drawer of his desk, removed a set of keys, and handed them to Jack. "Go straight there. Don't do anything else until you change. Mrs. Adams still works for me. If you have to go out, have her press something, even what you're wearing will do. I'll be home later."

Jack stood. "Thanks, Mr. Miller. I owe you."

The attorney waved his hand. "Not at all. Your folks took care of me for a long time. Just be careful."

Jack started for the door and stopped, turning back to the

attorney, who already had his head down, working on another document. "One more thing."

Miller looked up. "Yes?"

"Start thinking about who we could sell everything to. It doesn't have to be the same person, but, now with my aunts and uncles gone, there are several residences that need to be disposed of, and also the company. I'm going to be staying out west, and while I'm here, I'd like for you to find someone who would take good care of our employees. It doesn't have to be the best price, just the best person."

"What about—"

Jack shook his head. "Don't worry about him. If this shakes out like I expect it to, he will no longer be in the picture."

Miller stood at his desk and pointed a finger at Jack. "He is an excellent duelist, and it is against the law."

Jack smiled. "But I have an excellent lawyer." He turned, opened the door, and pulled it closed after walking through, calling, "See you later, Nathan," as he passed.

The old man beamed at him, as if seeing the little boy running ahead of his father, set on escaping to the outside. "You take care of yourself, Jack, and be careful."

"Nathan," boomed from inside the office. Jack smiled to the man, opened the door, and stepped into the smells he had been so used to in his younger years. The marsh smell drifted up from the bay. It was a sweet, not unpleasant smell, made up of shellfish, fish, exposed mud when the tide was out, and barnacled ships lashed to the nearby piers. Because most of his business originated with the sea trade, Miller had insisted on having his office near the people he helped.

Jack thought, *I'll miss Norfolk. I had a few wonderful years here. I'll never forget Papa taking me out in the rowboat, and we would fish for redfish and trout, catching the occasional drum and flounder. We would dress them when we returned, and Mama would cook them.* Just the thought of the fresh fish cooking caused his mouth to start watering, and he realized he hadn't eaten since breakfast this morning. Toward the wharf, there were several eating places providing fresh seafood. He threw his saddlebags over his left shoulder and headed in their direction.

The wharf area was humming with arrivals. Fresh catches were selling at their stands. The smell of fresh-caught fish added to the aroma of the marsh. Jack took a deep breath. Almost like being home.

The enticing aroma of fish frying, potatoes cooking, and fresh bread baking drew Jack to a small eating place with no more than six tables. Stepping inside, he spotted the only table available. It was perfect. He strode to it, pulled out a chair, and swung the saddlebags across the back. He sat gently on the chair and leaned back, locking the saddlebags safely between his muscular back and the chair. It creaked, but remained standing. Jack relaxed, removed his hat, and hung it on the corner of the chair next to him just as a big, burly man, sleeves rolled up to expose hairy forearms and thick rounded biceps, marched in leading two other men, smaller but equally rough looking.

They looked around, noting all the tables were full except Jack's, and strode in his direction. He looked up at the obvious leader of the group and said, "Just right, three more chairs available. Help yourself."

The big man eyed Jack, who, since he was sitting with a wrinkled frock coat on, had much of his height and bulk hidden. "Move along, matey. It's three hungry sailors you're holding up."

I don't need this, Jack thought and said, "Look, gents, feel free to have a seat. We can all enjoy our meal without any problems."

"Have a seat, Mr. City Boy says. He don't know he's dealin' with Jonny McCormick and his buds. City boy, we don't plan on sharing with the likes of you. Now up it is with you, and be on your way before Jonny McCormick has to thump you a wee bit."

Jack looked around and saw who he figured was the owner. The man shrugged, indicating he wanted no part of the altercation. Jack stood, picked up his saddlebags, and handed them to the owner, along with his hat. "If you'd hang on to these, I'd be obliged."

The man took Jack's things, but his mouth was pulled down in concern. "If you just let them have the table, mister, it might be easier. There'll be another table available any minute."

Jack said, "Good suggestion." He turned to the bully and, in his best brogue, said, "And were you hearing what the proprietor was a-saying, Jonny me boy? It seems a table be yours in a just half a moment."

McCormick's face had been showing a wide smile with the knowledge he was running over another citizen, but when Jack made fun of his accent, his eyes narrowed, lips pursed, and big hands clenched into fists. His brogue disappeared. "You just made yourself a big mistake, mister," and he drew back his right to smash Jack square in the face.

21

Jack shook his head. "You're the one who made a mistake," and released a short straight punch, his fist shooting out like a piston, driving Jonny's nose flat against his face. Blood flew all over his companions, who turned and raced for the door. Jonny had the presence of mind to keep his roundhouse punch moving. Jack jerked his head to the side, allowing the blow to slip past his chin. The force of the swing spun Jonny completely around. When the opposite side of the big man's head came around, Jack threw a hard left, striking the man dead center on his left temple. His hands dropped to his sides, and he stared out the door, the direction he had come from, perhaps thinking it would've been better to stay outside. After a few moments Jonny fell across a chair, shattering it, and continued to crash against the plank floor.

Jack waited for the man to get up, but when he didn't, he grabbed him by the collar and dragged him outside, dropping him clear of the door. He watched the man for a moment to make sure he was breathing, then went back inside and retrieved his hat and saddlebags. "How much for the chair?"

"Couple bucks."

Jack reached into his vest pocket, pulled out a quarter eagle, and held it out to the man. "Will that cover it?"

The owner nodded. "The chair and the meal. Have a seat. We've got some fresh redfish today. Would fried fish, potatoes, coleslaw, and the best homemade bread on this wharf work for you?"

"Sounds mighty good. Bring it on."

Jack hung his saddlebags on the back of his chair, and his hat on the chair next to him, and again lowered himself slowly onto his chair.

Within minutes, the owner was back with one plate loaded with steaming redfish and another with potatoes and coleslaw accompanied by a quarter loaf of bread. "How does that look to you?"

"Great. I'd be obliged if I could get a sarsaparilla to go with it."

"Yes, sir. Coming right up."

Within moments the man was back with Jack's drink. It had been a year since he had tasted redfish, and eating it here with the smells and sounds of the harbor around him brought a feeling of relaxed contentment. Between bites, he watched Jonny push himself to his feet and stagger away. His coleslaw and potatoes were almost gone, and he was working on his last slab of redfish when Jonny staggered back, led by a policeman.

What's with that guy? he thought. He looked at his fists, his left one was still red, and the right had a little bit of skin missing from the middle finger's knuckle. Jack continued eating right up to when the police officer poked him with his baton. Irritated, Jack looked up into the eyes of an almost duplicate copy of Jonny. Except the officer was shorter, not so wide, and a little older. The man motioned him to stand up, so Jack stood.

"What can I do for you, Officer?"

"You can tell me why you broke my brother's nose."

"I'm sure you know your brother pretty well, so you probably have a good idea as to how it started. However, I'll save us both some time. I'm a United States Marshal, and your brother attempted to assault me. Rather than arresting and throwing him in a federal lockup, I elected to show him a little consideration and delivered the punishment directly."

Jack could see the police officer was deeply disturbed with the situation. He wanted retribution for his brother, but he didn't want things to progress to the federal level, which they already had with his brother taking a swing at a U.S. Marshal.

"Could I see your badge, Marshal?"

"Sure." Jack reached inside his coat to his vest pocket. In the process, the butt of the Smith & Wesson was visible to those on his right side.

A citizen at the next table said in a conversational tone to his friend, "Did you see his gun?"

The police officer heard gun and went for his. Jack immediately raised both hands. "Officer, I am a federal marshal. Of course I have a gun. I'm going to show it to you." He grasped the lapel of his suit coat with his thumb and forefinger and gently pulled it back, exposing the revolver. "Now either you or I can reach into the top pocket of my vest and retrieve my badge."

The officer jerked the barrel of his Pocket Colt twice toward the vest pocket.

Jack nodded, slowly pulled his badge from his vest pocket, and extended it to the officer, who took it, looked it over, then looked at his brother like he'd like to punch him. Instead he slid his Colt back into its holster, "It's sorry I am, Marshal, for disturbing your meal," and returned the badge to Jack.

Jack dropped it into his pocket. "Think nothing of it. I would suggest you corral your brother. The way things went, I imagine this isn't the first time. One of these days, he'll run into someone who will leave his body in an alley. It'd be best if he learned from you now, than someone who doesn't care about him later."

"Aye, it's words of wisdom you're speaking." He turned to his brother. "Apologize to the marshal, Jonny."

Jonny snapped back, "Like h—"

The officer threw a short punch that landed dead center on the already broken nose, causing his brother to grab his face with both hands. "Our darlin' mother would be hurt to hear you speaking like that, Jonny boy. Now before we go, apologize to the marshal."

Blood ran beneath Jonny's palms where he was holding what Jack knew had to be a throbbing nose. "It's right sorry I am, Marshal."

Jack didn't miss the glare he received from Jonny even as he was voicing an apology. He gave a short nod and said to the officer, "Good luck to you."

"Thank you, sir." He grabbed Jonny and shoved the bleeding man through the door.

They are not messing up a fine meal, Jack thought and sat back down to his remaining potatoes and coleslaw.

The proprietor came from behind the short counter with another plate full of fish. "With my gratitude, Marshal. Jonny is always messing with the customers along here. What you did should slow him down for a while."

Jack inhaled the aroma of the freshly fried fish. "Obliged." He quickly finished his meal while he planned his approach to Devin Slater.

STANDING at the door of the office both his dad and uncle had occupied brought memories and a touch of sadness. The man inside there now did not belong and never had. Did he deserve a stipend from the company? Of course. His mother had deserved it. Much of the problem, as it existed today, could probably be laid at Layton T. Miller's door, but he was doing his job as he saw fit.

Actually, Jack thought, *the fault is mine. If I had been running the company like I should have, instead of gallivanting all over the country, this wouldn't be happening.* But Jack knew that laboring over past mistakes never did any good. Go forward and try to make a difference. Unfortunately, things had progressed too far. People had been hurt. Laws had been broken.

He shoved the door open and stepped into his past, but it was different. The people were different. Mrs. Davis, who had worked as receptionist since Jack's father had died, was gone, and in her place was a young and curvy blonde. She examined him from the top of his hat to the soles of his boots, and there was a lot to examine. With boots and hat on, Jack stood a little over six feet and eight inches. Today, thanks to Nathan, his suit was freshly cleaned and pressed, but the receptionist wore a somewhat stunned look, continuing to stare at him.

"Good morning, sir." There was a pause between statement and question. "How can I help you?"

"I'm here to see Mr. Slater."

Under her intense gaze, Jack began to wonder if he had missed a spot shaving. He unconsciously reached up and rubbed his chin.

"I'm sorry, sir, which Mr. Slater would that be?"

That's good information, Jack thought. More than one of the brothers was working here, or at least had an office here. "How many Slaters are there?"

She gave Jack a tentative smile. "At least three. There's Mr. Dante Slater, Mr. Dustin Slater, and Mr. Devin Slater."

Jack couldn't figure out what was going on with the young woman. "I want to see the boss man. Which would you recommend?"

Again the smile. "Why, Mr. Devin Slater, of course. Whom should I announce, sir?"

He gave her what he thought was his best smile and said, "United States Marshal Jack Sage."

Her smile dropped. Her face puzzled. A slight quiver was in her voice. "I don't believe Mr. Devin Slater is currently in, Marshal Sage."

"In case he is, tell him his brother is here to see him."

Her eyes widened, and her smile returned. The confusion she had previously displayed disappeared. "Of course, by all means."

She pushed back from her desk and walked briskly toward the corner office that looked out over the bay, his father's and uncle's office. She stepped inside, closing the door behind her.

Jack reached under his suit coat and made sure his Smith & Wesson would be an easy draw. Satisfied, he smoothed his coat but left it unbuttoned. This was the moment he had been looking forward to, confronting Slater.

He thought of the two killers who had slipped into their bedroom, the one he'd killed heading for Grace to stab her to death and drain her life's blood from her body. He was ready. All of his training centered on this one meeting. It was difficult to wait. He wanted to burst into a run, crash through Slater's door, and smash him into oblivion for what he had caused Grace, her mother, and the boys, but he stood motionless, waiting for his opportunity.

The young woman stepped from the room and started toward him. She waved and smiled another dazzling smile. "Mr. Slater is anxious to see you."

"Thank you," Jack said, thinking, *Not nearly as anxious as I am to see him. Be ready, Jack. Prepare for anything.* He remembered the walk. It had never been this long. Even as a little boy, anticipating seeing his papa, it had been shorter. It seemed to take forever, and then he was there, walking through the door he had been through so many times before, seeing his father at the big desk. He stopped.

The other man, Slater? He was in the process of standing, but he stopped, partially out of his chair, and hands on his desk, frozen, staring, as was Jack.

This was why Derek Slater had paused in his draw against him. It was like Jack was looking in a mirror at himself except the other man was slimmer, not as thick in the chest, neck, and arms, almost skinny, out of proportion.

Slater recovered first. He continued to push off the desktop until reaching his full height. Once erect, he spoke. "If I weren't seeing it for myself, I would never believe it."

"Nor I. I might even say you killed your brother. Possibly not knowingly, but just sending him after me almost guaranteed his death. He had me cold if he had pulled the trigger. But I had a newspaper between me and him. When I dropped it, he was stunned and hesitated." He could see the anguish of the other twin as Devin Slater played the meeting through his imagination. No matter how many times he went over it, it would always end the same, with his brother dead, and Jack Sage standing here, alive, telling him how and why it happened. Slater continued to stare. "You look more like me than my twin brother."

Jack said, "Yes." He continued, "You should have contacted me when Mr. Miller turned your mother down. I would have made it good. If our father had been alive, he would have also made it good. He would have invited you and your brother into our lives, sorry he had missed the time with you. He was a good man, a good father."

Slater's face turned into a horrible grimace. "Liar! Miller was acting on your orders. He did what you wanted. You're just saying that now because you're going to lose everything just like we did. It's your turn now, brother. You'll find out what it's like to lose everything."

Jack watched the bitter man before him and realized that could have been him. If he had turned against the world after losing Yasmina and their child, he would have become this man.

What was the difference? He didn't have time to think about that right now, but it was something he would consider in the future, in depth. "I came here to make a deal with you to give you this company in exchange for leaving my family alone, but after meeting you, I can see there is no way your word means anything."

Jack stepped forward and withdrew the warrant from his inside coat pocket and tossed it on Slater's desk. "Therefore, Devin Slater, as a United States Marshal, that is a warrant for your arrest for conspiracy to murder Marshal Jack Sage and his wife, Grace Kathryn Sage, and the wounding of Mary Nelson. This warrant authorizes me to take you back to the federal juris-diction in which this crime occurred, Fort Smith, Arkansas, and turn you over to the federal court of that location."

Slater's eyes bugged out like a frightened squirrel. "You can't do that. I have friends in high places. I'll have your job for this. I already have your company, and soon I'll have your gold mine and your ranch. It will all be mine, and you'll have nothing, just like we had when Mama died." His voice rose to a yell.

"Nothing." Veins distended on Slater's neck and forehead. The skin over his forehead quivered. He gasped for air and yelled again, "You hear me. Nothing."

Jack had closed the door after he had recovered from seeing Slater. After the man screamed, he heard footsteps racing down the hallway toward the door. He moved farther to the side of the man's desk so he could keep watch on Slater and the door. Two men burst into the office. They saw Devin Slater standing at his desk, his eyes wide in madness.

Jack spoke in a level voice. "I am a United States Marshal."

At his first words, they both moved their focus from Slater to Jack and stared. Jack said, "Nod your heads if you are Dustin and Dante Slater."

Still obviously numb from what they were seeing, the two men nodded their heads.

"Good, I want you to listen closely to me. You need to understand. I am a United States Marshal. I have a warrant for Devin Slater and only for Devin Slater, but I have a suggestion for you both. The U.S. government will investigate your company. During the investigation, we might find information that will incriminate others, but, for now, no warrant exists for either of you. Take a moment, and think about what decision will be in your best interest."

The two brothers looked at Devin, who still stood staring into space, then at each other.

One of them asked, "We are free to go?"

Jack nodded his head.

The two men turned and raced out of the office.

Jack stepped to the side of his brother and grasped the man's bicep. He was surprised at how thin it was.

"Time to go, Devin. Your game of revenge is over. You strike me as a meticulous man. I am certain we will find further evidence of your involvement in the murders of my aunts and uncle. Come along peacefully. It's time you face judgment for the pain you have caused others. I'm truly sorry for the pain your family suffered, but it did not warrant what you have done."

Devin Slater had stood frozen since he yelled at Jack. Blood dripped from his fists where his fingernails dug into his flesh, but he seemed to be oblivious to the pain. All he could do was stare at Jack, who had yet to draw his weapon.

Jack guided his brother toward the door. Walking out of the office he knew so well, he ran into a man who had worked in the mailroom when he had last been here. He sent him to Layton Miller's office to tell him to get over here as quickly as he could and take control of all documents in the building.

He would visit the federal court and provide them with the warrant he carried, and have his brother confined in the jail until they could leave for Fort Smith.

His goal was to turn everything over to Miller and sell the

company to an appropriate buyer. His family had put their lives into building a stable company for themselves and their employees. Only a buyer who could convince Miller their goals meshed would be accepted.

He hailed a hansom cab, thrust Slater into it, and said, "Federal Court Building." It would be a long day.

22

Jack woke to sunlight filling the room. His right hand tingled from lack of circulation, and he started to move his arm, but there was a weight on it. He turned his head to see his beautiful black-haired vision. Grace lay in the crook of his arm. Black hair cascaded across his arm and the pillow, framing her face. Brilliant green eyes glistened in the early morning light, softly gazing at him. Her full lips were spread in a loving smile.

"I thought you'd never wake up."

"Why would I when I'm with such a beauty as you?"

An eyebrow raised, one corner of her wide mouth rose a little higher in what he had learned was her teasing grin. "There might be something of greater interest than sleep."

He slid closer, feeling the warmth of her. "What did you have in mind?"

The door burst open, and two excited boys raced across the room and leaped on each side of the bed. Billy yelled, "It's time to go."

Elijah joined in. "Pauly has the wagons out front." He stopped to look at his ma and pa, his brow creasing with a couple of wrinkles. "Wait, you're still in bed. What are you doing in bed?"

Grace glanced up at Jack and said, pointedly, "Nothing. Now you two get out of here while we get dressed. We'll be on our way soon enough. Go help your grandma."

Immediately the two of them slid from the bed and dashed out of the room.

Grace raised her voice. "Close the door."

Jack was about to remind them not to slam the door, when, bam, the door slammed. They both winced, then Jack turned back to his lovely wife. "Unfortunately, whatever you had planned is going to have to wait."

She pulled his head down to hers and pressed her warm lips to his. Jack said a silent prayer of gratitude and enjoyed the thrill that went through him. Suddenly, she pulled away, threw the covers off, and like her sons, leaped out of bed.

"Come on, Jack. You've got a family to herd to Texas. Get out of that bed."

He marveled at the beauty getting dressed in front of him, and thanked the Man above for this great reward. It had been a long time coming, but was sweeter for the wait. Jack swung his long legs from under the cover, stood, and stretched. "I keep waiting for someone to send a message from the judge that there's an outlaw on the loose and only I can catch him."

Grace had slipped on the clothes she had laid out the night before and was busy buttoning her blouse. Her head snapped up. "Wash your mouth out with soap, Jack Sage. We don't need any messages from Judge Bell. All we need is to get those wagons rolling."

"You're right. Do you think Mary is up to this?"

"Absolutely. It may have taken two months, but in the last two weeks she has gotten as strong as a horse. I don't think she'll have any problems, even if we need her to drive a team now and then."

Grace grew serious. "Jack, I'm so sorry about your brother and your company. How are you doing?"

"I'm fine, honey. Devin settled down quite a bit on our trip back. We had a chance to talk. No matter how much I tried to explain, he would never believe me. I feel bad about his hanging, but I think the judge did the right thing. He was a bitter man. I hope he's seeing the error of his ways, on the other side."

After pulling his trousers up, he sat on the edge of the bed to shake out his boots. When he was comfortable there was no stinging or biting critter in his boots, he slid them on, pulled them farther up, stood, and stomped. Satisfied, he lifted his gunbelt and swung it around his waist.

Grace finished her last button and grabbed her bonnet before gazing around the empty room. Tears filled her eyes. Jack saw them coming and moved to her, putting his strong arm around her shoulders. She sniffed. "I'm sorry. I swore I wouldn't do this, but so much has happened here."

He squeezed her tight. "You'll be making new memories in Texas. Maybe more than you even know."

She smiled up at him. "I know. Thank you, Jack."

He grinned at her. "Before we get to Texas, you won't be thanking me. I'm just hoping you're not cursing me."

A quick frown covered her face. "Jack, you know I'd never do that."

He laughed. "I hope so. This'll be an adventure, but it won't all be fun, I can guarantee that."

She poked him in the chest with her forefinger. "Listen, mister. I've traveled by covered wagon before. How do you think we got here?"

He grabbed her around the waist. "You ready?"

"I am, but you didn't answer my question. Are you sorry about your company?"

He released her and thought for a moment. "No, honey, I don't think I am. According to Mr. Miller, the man who bought it is a good man. I never met him. I heard about him and never anything bad. No, I think the employees are happy, and we made quite a bit of money in the sale, as if we needed it the way the mine is doing."

She came to him again. "We must be going, but you have to know we are some of the most fortunate people on this earth."

"Yep, that we are. Let's get out of here before the boys drive off in the wagons."

They opened the door and walked through the parlor. Jack, his forehead wrinkled with concern, said, "It sure sounds noisy out there," and opened the front door.

The street was packed with people, and they were cheering and clapping. Jack smiled down at his wife. "That's real nice, Grace. These folks are here to see you and Mary off."

Her smile was wide. "Jack, sometimes you can be so thickheaded. Most of these folks are here for you. It was you who returned their money to the bank. It was you who killed the serial killer who was murdering marshals, and it was you who stopped the Clagg brothers. Not to mention all the help you've been to everyone."

He looked down at Grace like she was crazy. Folks wouldn't cross the street for him. He'd done nothing. He looked out across the faces, and they were all looking at him. He realized what she had just said was true, and shook his head in disbelief.

Mary was sitting next to Casey Carter, the bank teller who had given up his job and the bank owner's daughter, to drive one of Jack's wagons to Texas. She was watching Jack and clapping. Tears filled her eyes.

It must be hard for her to leave all this behind, Jack thought. He looked back to check the second wagon. Elijah sat on the driver's seat, waiting for Grace. He hadn't believed his wife could drive a four-horse team until she demonstrated her ability with a team Pauly had put together. *She is truly an impressive woman,* he thought. *Impressive and determined.* Tied to the back of the second wagon was a cow with a calf alongside. Grace had wanted a cow so that they would have milk on the trip. He had been against it until she had argued he could have cream in his coffee. He laughed and shook his head. Who in this world would bring cattle to Texas? Bronco was going to have a ball with this.

Pauly, at the corral with Dave Cole, waved to Jack. He lifted a hand in return. It was time to hit the road. People were gathered around, everyone talking at the same time. He leaned down to Grace. "We've got to be going."

He walked her to the wagon and lifted her to the seat. Laughing, she settled in next to Elijah, who was so excited he was bouncing on the wagon seat. Jack turned to untie Smokey, who seemed to be as excited about hitting the trail as Elijah and almost knocked the judge down.

The judge never apologized about hanging anyone, but he took Jack's hand and said, "I'm sorry about your brother. It had to be done, but it didn't make it any easier for you."

Jack, surprised, validated what the judge had said. "It was the right thing. He caused the death of so many people, and after spending almost a week with him on the train, I could find no remorse in him for anything he had done. I hope Pa understands."

"He does, Jack. Don't you worry about that." The judge cleared his throat. "Harumph, well, I guess I won't be assigning you any more missions, but you did good with all I gave you. If there is ever anything I can help you with, let me know."

Both men felt awkward. The judge patted Jack on the shoulder. "Good luck." He first walked to Grace's wagon, spoke to her, and then to Mary. Mary gave him a hug.

Jack watched the judge walk back to the courthouse alone. *Probably already thinking about his next trial or outlaw who needs to be brought back for justice.* He untied Smokey and swung into the saddle. It felt good to be riding his devoted grulla. Matthew Marcel, the current owner of Ma Nelson's Bed and Eats, stood on the boardwalk in front of his establishment. Jack raised a finger to the brim of his Stetson in salute. Marcel waved in return.

Jack rode to the corral. "Alright, Dave, this is your last chance to stay and work for Judge Bell."

"No, sir, Jack. I have a hankering for Texas. Plus, with the wages you pay, how could I turn you down?"

Pauly laughed and crossed the corral to open the gate. Once it was open, he stepped up to Jack and extended his hand. "It's been a pleasure knowing you, Jack. Good luck in Texas."

"Thanks, Pauly. Any friend of mules is a friend of mine. You'll always be welcome at the Flying J."

Jack wheeled Smokey around, riding slowly through the crowd, nodding and speaking to those who called to him. Reaching the first wagon, he made eye contact with Casey. "Move 'em out."

Casey waved and popped the reins. The four mules stepped out together, and the wagon rolled forward into the street. A cheer was lifted again.

Jack watched Grace closely, but she handled the mules like she was born to drive. She gave him a wide grin as her wagon rolled by. Elijah was jumping up and down and waving something fierce. Jack couldn't help but wave back, which only seemed to energize the boy more.

The crowd was settling down when a voice in the crowd yelled, "You going after that Indian Territory gold, Marshal?"

Jack couldn't believe that rumor was still going around. The bunch he had brought in with Dave Cole had been prospecting like madmen, but never found a flake of gold.

He yelled back, "Those fellas I brought back found absolutely nothing. The only thing a man will find in those hills is a Comanche knife to rip off his scalp."

There was no rejoinder to that, and the crowd quieted down.

Billy rode up on his new buckskin. "How long before we get there, Pa?"

Jack laughed. They hadn't even gotten out of town, and one of the boys was asking how long it would be. "I'll tell you, son. I expect in about six weeks, maybe less, we will be rolling into the yard of the Flying J. How does that sound to you?"

"It sounds great, Pa."

"Good, now why don't you ride back and give Dave a hand. I'm sure he'll appreciate it."

Billy raised a finger to his hat in acknowledgment. "See you in a while, Pa." He spun the buckskin around and loped back to Dave.

Jack watched his son for a minute longer, then glanced over at Grace, who was watching him. She gave him a bright smile and winked as she drove the team by.

He laughed at the promise in those beautiful green eyes and thought, *Can life get any better?*

～

**Find out if life gets better or worse for Jack Sage and his family. You can ride along with him on his new adventure, *by clicking the title below.*
Book 9:
*Home Beneath the Star***

AUTHOR'S NOTE

I hope you've enjoyed reading *Honor of the Star*, the eighth book in the Jack Sage Western Series.

If you have any comments, what you like or what you don't, please let me know. You can email me at: Don@DonaldLRobertson.com, or fill in the contact form on my website.

www.DonaldLRobertson.com

I'm looking forward to hearing from you.

Reviews on Amazon are also appreciated.

I look forward to sharing Book 9 of the Jack Sage Western Series, *Home Beneath the Star*, with you in the near future.

Also, if you enjoyed the Logan Mountain Man series, the most recent adventure of Floyd Logan is out. You can find *Burden of a Mountain Man*, book four in the Mountain Man series, on Amazon.

Have a terrific day.

BOOKS
A Jack Sage Western Series
STRANGER WITH A STAR
WITHOUT THE STAR
RETURN OF THE STAR
THE HANGING STAR
FIVE WOMEN AND THE STAR
THE LOYAL STAR
JUSTICE OF THE STAR
HONOR OF THE STAR
HOME BENEATH THE STAR

Logan Mountain Man Series
(Prequel to Logan Family Series)
SOUL OF A MOUNTAIN MAN
TRIALS OF A MOUNTAIN MAN
METTLE OF A MOUNTAIN MAN
BURDEN OF A MOUNTAIN MAN

Logan Family Series
LOGAN'S WORD
THE SAVAGE VALLEY
CALLUM'S MISSION
FORGOTTEN SEASON
TROUBLED SEASON
TORTURED SEASON

Clay Barlow - Texas Ranger Justice Series
FORTY-FOUR CALIBER JUSTICE
LAW AND JUSTICE
LONESOME JUSTICE

NOVELLAS AND SHORT STORIES

RUSTLERS IN THE SAGE

BECAUSE OF A DOG

THE OLD RANGER